Fighting Addiction

This is a work of fiction. Names, characters, places, and incidents either are the product of the author's imagination or are used fictitiously. Any resemblance to actual events, locales, organizations, or persons, living or dead, is entirely coincidental and beyond the intent of either the author or the publisher.

Fighting Addiction
TOP SHELF
An imprint of Torquere Press Publishers
PO Box 2545
Round Rock, TX 78680
Copyright ©2012 by BA Tortuga
Cover illustration by BSClay
Published with permission
ISBN: 978-1-61040-379-5

www.torquerepress.com

**If you enjoyed Fighting Addiction,
you might enjoy these BA Tortuga titles:**

Just Like Cats and Dogs

Living in Fast Forward

Old Town New

Racing the Moon

Rain and Whiskey

Fighting Addiction

Fighting Addiction
by BA Tortuga

romance for the rest of us
www.torquerepress.com

Fighting Addiction

Dedicated to Stephanie, for understanding little books and Texans, but not to Miguel, because he was no technical help at all. Love y'all, this much.

BA

Author's Note:
I have to thank my research assistant, Jessica, for all her help, for dealing with hysterical emails in the middle of the night, and for looking up things guaranteed to make the FBI start a file on her. Don't ever leave me.

Also, a snuggle to my niece, A., who introduced me to one of the songs that will always be Markus and Sebastian and will always make me cry.

Fighting Addiction

Prologue

Y ou have eight weeks, Mr. Michaels, then we'll take our situation to the authorities." Icy blue eyes stared at him from across the table, and Jack felt like pissing his pants.

Eight weeks.

Eight weeks to pay back money that he'd been slowly siphoning from Sebastian Longchamps' accounts for years.

Years.

The first time it had been simple, really. He'd gambled on the Cowboys versus Redskins game and it had gone badly, and suddenly he found himself short. Seb always had said yes, had covered his slip ups and there was no reason to believe that the man would say no that time. None at all.

But Seb had been in the middle of a huge Asian tour, had been out of pocket and Jack had slipped out five thousand to cover the bet.

He'd taken two thousand the next month, then only eight hundred after that. It had started to add up—twelve thousand here, fifty-five hundred there—but it hadn't gotten uncontrollable until it had gotten easy. Now he was almost six million dollars in and... Shit, it wasn't easy anymore. Not at all.

Tad Jonston, Seb's account manager at the label, had retired two months ago, and this guy, well this guy wasn't part of the old boy network.

"How am I supposed to do that in eight weeks?"

"I don't particularly care. I advised Mr. Lyons to have you arrested immediately. Due to his longtime friendship with you, he decided to give you time. I suppose he hopes you own a pistol."

Jesus. Jack's mouth felt like it was full of quick dry cement. Simon Lyons had been with the label since the seventies, and he was a senior vice president now. He and Jack had been friends forever. Jack took a deep breath, faking it like he'd been doing with loan sharks since his early twenties. "If I make an earnest attempt to replace the money in that time, we can negotiate an extension, right?"

Those pale-pale eyes never wavered, that patrician upper lip curling a little. "I suppose that's within the scope of Mr. Lyons' offer. Shall we say at least thirty-five percent?"

Christ. Sweat beaded at his right temple and ran down his face. It felt a lot like a tear. His mind was racing, though, thinking of ways to get more money flowing into the machine, money he didn't have to share with the label. Money he could rob from Peter to pay Paul.

"Deal," he agreed, holding out a hand to the man, who raised a brow.

"I'll let Mr. Lyons know." The guy turned on one well-shod heel and left.

Jack stared after him, a plan forming in his mind already. That was what was wrong with this business. No one wore cowboy boots or shook hands on a deal.

He was just damned lucky that old Simon Lyons had a fondness for him, and that the old man believed what the artist didn't know wouldn't hurt them.

Now he just had to get something going in eight weeks. Good thing he knew all of Sebastian Longchamps' secrets. And just the carrot to dangle in front of Seb's face to keep everyone off balance long enough to get his shit together. No pistol required.

Chapter One

The phone woke him up early, maybe seven-thirty, and Markus Kane rolled over, giving the sleek, black thing a baleful glare. He was half-retired, right? That earned him the right to sleep in when he wasn't on the road.

Sighing, he grabbed it, looking at the display. Unknown number, huh? Well, good. He could vent his spleen against some random wrong number.

"Hello?"

"Candy? That you, man? It's Sebastian. Seb."

He blinked. Seb? Sebastian Longchamps? Had to be the only person who called him Candy. What did the crazy little Cajun want?

"What the hell is up, man? I haven't heard from you in--" Had it been years? If it had, it made him a pretty shitty friend. They'd toured together for three years back in the early days.

"Eight years. Well, we shared a stage in Vegas two years ago, but that doesn't count. How the hell are you?"

"Good." It was the truth. He felt better then he had in years, and he was in fighting trim. "What are you up to?"

"Working. Got a business proposition for you, actually."

Huh. What the fuck did the current Entertainer of the Year and the biggest fucking tour draw in country music want with semi-retired him? Maybe Seb needed someone to ghost write some songs. That was still one of Markus' strong suits, no matter what genre.

He heard splashing, laughing in the background, right before Seb snarled. "Y'all hush. Bev! I told you to clear everyone out!"

He could hear a murmured apology, and Seb cleared his throat. "Sorry."

"No worries." Looked like that temper was still in place. "What is this thing you're asking, buddy?"

"I'm thinking of an EP, five, six songs, a tour. You and me, old friends on the road."

If he hadn't already been lying down, he'd have fallen on his ass in shock. What the hell? Him? Riding on Seb's wagon? Hadn't they decided years ago that couldn't happen again? Oh, he wanted to jump right at it, but he had to think, not react.

"Why?"

"I saw the spread you did in *Southern Music*. You look great, not puffy anymore. And the last album had some kick ass cuts. You're back into the music, off the whole 'I'm a rock star' lifestyle thing." Brutal and honest and lacking anything that could distantly be considered a filter, that was Seb. Hell, that was one of the reasons they had parted ways as much as they had.

"Thanks." If he followed protocol, he would have to call his people and see what they thought and go through Legal for the contracts and all. Thing was, Markus was from Texas. He liked to do music his way. "When would I have to be in the studio?"

"Eight weeks, give or take? I'm in... New Zealand?

Somewhere. I'll be back in the States by mid-January, can be in the studio February."

That would give him plenty of time to get the rest of his team on it and write some songs. They would have to do some writing time together, come up with an anthem.

He pondered on it a while, long enough for Seb to speak again. "So, give it some thought, talk to Tawny. If you're into it, have them nudge Jack and he'll set shit up. If you're not, we'll all pretend that I never called. I got to run, man. I have an appointment with a scuba tank."

"Hey." Whoa. God, he wasn't even awake yet. "Hold up. Can I call this number?"

"Absolutely, man. Hell, you get a wild hair, fly out. Water's fucking fabulous."

"Yeah?" He could so do that. "Give me someone's number so I can set it up." Seb had one foot out the door. Markus knew that distracted voice well.

"I'll text you Bev's number. Beverly Chacon. She's my right hand; she'll get you what you need. You come, you bring a guitar."

"Will do, buddy."

The line went dead, but sure enough, he got a text five seconds later. He stared at the phone, completely floored. A little tickled.

Okay, a lot.

This kind of tour could be an enormous shot in the arm for a semi-retired fool like him.

Markus grinned, dialing not Seb's assistant, but his longtime manager, Tawny. She was a sharp old broad. She'd get it all fixed up.

"Hello? Markus, what's wrong?" Tawny sounded like hell. He'd forgotten it wasn't quite eight in the morning.

Markus settled his butt more firmly on the bed, digging in for the negotiations. This would take some talking.

Him and Seb, they had history, and it wasn't all sparkly spotlight shit.

"Hey, Tawny. You ain't gonna believe who called..."

Chapter Two

Ninety-four. Ninety-five. Ninety-six. Ninety-seven. Sebastian moved in time with the metronome app on his phone. Three more pushups and then it was back to crunches.

Music filled the room as he worked, sweat pouring off him as he moved. Candy's plane had come in yesterday at some point, the man and his entourage supposedly in one of the huge condos close by, maybe even next door; Bev hadn't been clear.

The man would call after sleeping off the jet lag. Candy, which he always teased Markus about thanks to the last name Kane, was worse about the jet lag than anyone Sebastian knew. He didn't get his beauty sleep, the beautiful fucker got downright grumpy.

Grinning, Sebastian rolled to his back. He couldn't wait to hear that slow Texas twang.

Two hundred crunches into his set of three hundred, Bev knocked, perfectly coiffed, her platinum blonde hair up in a tight bun-deal, eyes like chips of ice behind her horn-rimmed glasses. It was unnatural how she was always put together. They were in the middle of Southern

Hemisphere summer, living on the beach, and she was in a fucking pantsuit and clacking heels. "I have your protein shake, boss."

"Thanks, doll. What's on for today?" He couldn't function without her, evil woman.

Two ten. Two eleven. Two twelve.

"Pretty much you meeting with Mr. Kane. He's ready when you've showered." Her nose wrinkled and he was incredibly fucking tempted to throw a sweaty towel at her.

"Cool. What time is it?" Like he didn't know.

"Eight-forty. You have twenty minutes."

"Cool." He could handle that. Ten more minutes of work, ten to clean up. That was perfect. He liked a schedule.

"Don't forget to drink your shake."

"I won't." They kept him going, nasty, thick things. Bev was obsessed with them. "Offer Kane some coffee and make sure, if you feed him pastries, they're gone before I..."

"Get in there. Yeah, boss. I know. You don't like the smell of food before noon. He's already eaten, and he's bright-eyed and chipper." She paused, grinning a little. "Nothing like what I read about in *Country News*. He's not a puffy has-been. The man is stacked to the ceiling. I mean, Jesus, boss."

"No?" He chuckled. Like he hadn't seen his share of that body—top to bottom. "He's gone the rehab route. Looks good, too. Got his shit together. Booze fucks with you, makes you veiny and fat."

Two fifty four. Two fifty five. Two fifty six.

"Yeah, yeah. Whatever it is, it's working. Eighteen minutes, hardbody. Don't forget your shake." She slid out the door, leaving him to finish up.

"Nag."

He busted out his last thirty crunches and jumped in the shower, the water pouring off his newly-waxed body in beads. He let himself enjoy the only five or so minutes he had to himself most of the day that he did absolutely nothing, his mind buzzing with words and music.

Then he dried off, got dressed, and headed off to see Candy for the first time in an amazing amount of years.

Markus wiped his hands on his jeans. The place was an island paradise, and he felt seriously overdressed, but this was a business meeting first, right? He'd chosen jeans, boots, and a white shirt, no starch. That was his concession to the tropical location.

Later, when he was sure he and Seb could still see eye to eye on anything, he'd bust out the board shorts and flip flops.

Jesus, why was he suddenly so fucking nervous? This was Seb. There wasn't much Markus hadn't known about the man, once upon a time. From the way Seb whistled in his sleep to the way those muscled shoulders looked when the hot little son of a bitch was on his knees sucking cock.

Oh. Bad image.

No remembering that, not in these jeans.

Seb came in the door, the tiny bald fucker wearing a pair of gauzy pants that hung so low Markus could see the hipbones holding them up, an LSU T-shirt, and a pair of dark sunglasses on. "Candy! Damn, man!"

"Hey, Seb!" He shook the man's hand, not sure if anything else was appropriate.

"You look great, dude. Happy, healthy. You get some sleep?" Seb tugged him in, gave him a solid man hug, hand slapping his back.

"I did." Seb smelled like coconut and musk. God, that was yummy.

"Excellent." Seb stepped back, grinned. "So fucking glad you showed. Have a seat. Did Bev take care of you?"

"She's been great." Hell, he'd had everything he could ever want. Seb's assistant had even taken the wet bar out completely, just leaving juices and sparkling water. The woman was inhumanly efficient.

"She's a champ." Seb settled in a chair across from him, muscles rippling under the thin T-shirt. "So, Jack says you have demands. Demand away."

Markus blinked, trying to remember what all he'd wanted to talk on. "Well, Tawny has dealt with all the advertising equality and all that bullshit."

Seb waved one hand. "If the suits had a problem with that shit, we wouldn't be here. I know that. I'm not looking to fuck you over, man. I just want to make some music and some money."

"I know that." He rolled his eyes. Blunt little fuck. "I also know you're a control freak. We write the EP together. We do at least one duet. And I can't tell your boys what to do on tour and all, but I need to know there won't be booze backstage or on my buses."

There. That was the hard part, right out in the open.

"Works for me. I don't drink, and my boys are family men now. They may have a beer on their bus, but that's their issue." Seb stretched. "Your people are taking care of your buses; mine mine. I want my boys to play on the recording, at least on half the songs."

"Sure." Half of Markus' band had actually retired last year. He'd made them a pretty good living over the years. "I want Kyle on fiddle, but other than that I'm easy."

"Kyle still with you? Even after rehab? I'm impressed."

"Dude, Kyle is on Weight Watchers. He's way more scary on sugar detox than I was on withdrawal." It could be hell to get old. Markus knew from experience.

"Oh, man. I mean, I get it. I know what I eat. I'm

careful." Shit, careful. There wasn't an ounce of fat on Seb, that Markus could see. It was a good look, but he had to admit it was a little unnerving.

"You know me. I get off the sauce and I can eat a lot." He could still devour the Waffle House as long as he hit the gym.

"Rock on." One near white eyebrow lifted, rising above Seb's dark glasses. "So, you want to do a couple of rocking cuts, one ballad, one cover and something... patriotic?"

"Something summertime, maybe?" He could think of a thousand song choices that wouldn't offend anyone... Yeah. Something they could base a tour on.

"You know me, I'm a sun baby." Yeah, Seb'd made a career on being the wild child—hang gliding, snowboarding, motorcycles, airplanes. Anything and everything. Extreme sports events vied for the man to do shows like rodeos begged for Markus.

"Good." What else was there? He knew he'd had a list.

"So, studio in February, first release in April, tour starts in May?"

"Yeah. Yeah, that works. I've got some award shows in May, so we'll have to schedule it."

"Sure. Tawny and Jack will run with that. Who's your assistant?"

"Uh. Tawny has one." He didn't have a PA anymore.

"Dude. How do you function?"

"I got my laptop. My phone. Tawny is superhuman." His ears felt hot. He wasn't as busy as he'd been once, either.

"I'm impressed. I'm not smart enough to keep all that shit straight."

He surprised himself by wanting to growl. "You do fine."

Seb chuckled, bare feet curling up under his legs. "So. I'm yours until noon. Wanna write?"

"Hell, yes. I got my guitar." He pulled off one boot, then the other. The business meeting was over.

"Fucking A!" He got this grin—wide and wild and pleased. "I'll grab the pens and paper."

Markus found that he had the same goofy grin on his lips, too. They had always connected best over music. Wherever they were.

Seb came back with two bottles of water, a pad of paper, and a guitar case. "Let's do it."

"Start with the stadium rocker?"

"Uh-huh. I was thinking something about fireworks and flames?" Seb plopped down beside him, pulled out the ancient six-string. God, how many memories did he have about that man and that Gibson? Shit.

"Old flames, maybe. America loves an old love story come back to life." He popped his acoustic out of the case. It wasn't old, but he loved it and it was custom.

"Oh, man. *Fireworks and Old Flames.* I fucking love the hook." The words were scribbled down in Seb's weird, backassward script.

"Yeah." He keyed up the first chord, already having a good idea where they were going. Man, he hadn't been this fired up to write in months.

Hell, maybe Seb would be good for him, like a B12 shot or one of those juice fasts.

Either way, Markus figured it wouldn't be boring, and that was a shot in the arm to his semi-retired life.

"It's fifteen 'til nine, Seb." Bev had one of the damned protein shakes in her hand. "Mr. Kane is at the pool and says to meet him out there."

Sebastian looked at the treadmill. Nine miles. Not bad. "Did you tell him I'd be there?"

"He has his guitar, boss. That's working, right?"

No. That was breathing, but whatever.

"Yeah. Get my stuff for me. I'll be out there after my shower."

She gave him a nod. "You got it."

He did five minutes cool down, eyes on the TV, which was playing ESPN, just like normal, the talking heads yammering about football, saying nothing at all for hours and hours. He approved.

The water in the shower was hot, the pressure beating down on him. He drank his shake when he got out, the pineapple masking the flavor of canned coconut protein goo. He loved that. The pineapple, not the goo.

Shorts, gimme cap, sunglasses. Supplements. Time to work.

Time to go admire Candy's bod and the way the man's eyes wrinkled at the corners when he smiled. Candy had always had great smile lines, but a few months out of the spotlight had done wonders for Markus' skin. Sebastian stopped on the way into the pool area, staring through the big window at the carved-from-oak son of a bitch sprawled out on a lounge chair, wearing a white pair of board shorts and nothing else. The man needed a haircut, too, the typical cowboy buzz cut and shave given over to shaggy and stubbly and fine. Oh, yeah. Candy looked good in the sunlight, chest and belly bare and ripped, covered with a mat of deep, chocolate brown hair. Nice.

Sebastian thumped his cock, which was altogether too interested in old trouble, and headed out into the private pool area, loving how the sun was already beating down. "Hey, man. Morning."

It was adorable, how Markus thought he was an early riser now, instead of the truth wherein his happy ass crashed in the afternoon.

"Hey." Markus waved the hand not holding some kind of juice. "Man, they have the best fruit here. I had breakfast before I came in, though. Bev told me how you don't do food in the morning."

"Nope." Calories. He had an image to protect. "The pineapple's good."

"It is." Markus looked him over, the faintest grin pulling the corners of that well-shaped mouth, and for a moment he remembered all the things that mouth could do.

Remembered long, late nights fucking like bunnies in the back of a bus, in hotel rooms, limos.

It was the limo that had done them in, though. One blow job, one fucker with a camera, and then it was payoffs and damage control and he'd lost the best friend he'd ever had. Shame, too. There'd been moments in the last few years where he could have used a friend like Markus.

Candy cleared his throat. "You okay, ba—man?"

"Absolutely. Just woolgathering." He grabbed his guitar. "Worked on the chorus for *Denim Heaven* some last night."

"Yeah? We were going the wrong direction, I think. Let's hear it."

He had to admit, this was way more fun than it was work. The EP was going to end up with them sharing the writing credits on every song. He'd dropped the key and cleaned up some of the lyrics, making them a little slinkier, a lot hotter. Markus could pull it off, too. Maybe Sebastian couldn't; he was more... bouncy.

Still, it would work.

Markus licked his lips at the end, nodded, gave him that wicked, near-demonic grin. "I like it."

Oh. He liked that, too. Christ, he needed to focus.

"Yeah? Excellent. You'll work it like no one else."

"Thanks." Candy stretched, wiggling his toes. "This is the life, buddy."

"You know it. I spend every winter here." He'd purchased the entire block of condos, after all. A guy needed investments, at least that was what Bev said.

"Cool." Grimacing, Markus shook his head. "I put a hot tub in at my place, but I wasn't real bright about it. It's on the wrong side of the house for winter use."

"Damn. That sucks. Too windy?"

"Too much shade. Great in the summer, though."

He chuckled. "When you don't need a hot tub."

"Not right now, no. We will when we're needing a little tour break."

"You don't have one on your bus?" He winked. He didn't either, but he did have a decent tub.

"Nope." Those long toes poked his leg. "Hedonist."

"You know it." He hooted, leaned back toward the sun.

"You still want that ballad?"

"Yep. Girls love those, and they sell."

"We might have to watch some chick flicks." Markus strummed a little ching-a-ling. "I haven't had much romance."

"That's a fucking shame." He blinked, ducked his chin. "Sorry, man. Uh... Love gone wrong? New love? Booty call?"

"Booty call is very in." He couldn't look at Candy at all, not with the way the man's voice had gone gravelly.

"Yeah. Yeah. Old lovers needing to get it on?" Seb knew his cheeks were burning. He could so get it on with that long, muscled hardbody.

"That works. I think people can relate."

When he did finally glance up, those dark eyes were pointed down toward the guitar and Candy's face was bright red.

"Yeah. Yeah." He chuckled softly. "We got something to build on, for the song, I mean."

"We do." Now he got a sideways glance. "I mean, we ought to know, as old as we are."

"Positively ancient, you and me." Asshole.

"Yep. You're a year older."

Oh, that deserved something. Ice water to the chest maybe. Sebastian took a drink of his water, then went for it, squirting the hairy bastard smack between the nipples.

"Fuck! You little shit." In a flash, Markus had gently tossed the guitar aside and was hunting his ass.

He backed up, brandishing the water bottle, this time getting Candy in the crotch.

"Jesus."

He could almost see things shrivel. Taking time to gloat was a mistake, though. He ended up in the pool, Candy pulling a wrestling move on him. Like TV wrestling.

He floated up to the surface, treading water, sputtering and laughing. "Caveman!"

Markus yodeled. "You know it."

He flattened his hand and sent a huge wave from the pool, right at the big gorilla. The big gorilla who was now soaked.

"Yeehaw." Markus did a cannonball, sending water right into his face.

He dove deep, pinching Markus' ass as he moved underneath, swimming hard. The man was a fine swimmer, pacing him pretty good considering the head start he had. They reached the side of the pool at the same time, bodies slamming together.

His abs rolled, his hips bucking in a dance move older than music. For a long moment Markus rocked back against him, and that hard cock made itself known. Then Candy pulled away, pushing up out of the pool.

Sebastian took a couple of laps, cursing himself for all

sorts of a fool. They weren't starting this shit again. Not at all. They couldn't afford to. Oh, he could pay people off with even more money than before, but it had damned near killed him to lose Candy the first time. He wasn't as strong as he used to be. Sometimes he thought that it would only take one more earthquake for his internal framework to come crashing down. God was a shitty contractor, taking the lowest bidder.

That would make a decent lyric, really.

He pulled himself up out of the pool, drying his sunglasses off before putting them back on.

"Sorry." Markus gave him a crooked grin, the look apologetic. "You know me and a challenge."

"Not a problem." He grabbed a towel, wrapped it around his waist and tucked it in, then went to get his guitar and his phone. He punched Bev's link. "Bev. Coffee, huh? You want anything, Candy?"

"More juice would be great." Markus toweled off, too, water glinting in his chest hair.

"More juice for the giant fuzzball gorilla, too."

"You got it, boss."

"Thanks, lady."

"Are you saying I need a wax?" Settling back in his chair, Markus grinned. "I thought I could wait for the tour, at least."

"It's a thing, the fuzz." He'd waxed for the first time ten years ago and never looked back. He wasn't sure he could get fuzzy anymore. "How much gray's in it now?" He chuckled at himself, tickled.

"Shit. A ton." That got Markus laughing, too, the sound like sandpaper on barn wood.

"Well, there you go." He waxed so there was zero evidence. Maybe the eye lines told a story, but there was always Botox if that got bad, right?

"You got nothin'. You wear those sunglasses to hide the wrinkles?"

26

"Yep." That and the fact that his pupils were the size of small third-world countries and the light hurt like a dozen pick-axe wielding garden gnomes.

"I'm beginning to wonder if you got eyes, man. I kinda miss them."

He chuckled, hoping to hell he didn't blush. "They haven't changed—still the color of stagnant water."

"Oh, stop it. Hundreds of thousands of screaming fans think you're the hottest thing going."

He flexed and grinned, making his abs roll. The fans loved that. His grin faded when Markus just stared, tongue touching that pretty lower lip.

"If I don't go, man, I'm going to do something we'll both regret later." His cock was hard as steel and he didn't bother to hide it as he stood, grabbed his guitar.

"Yeah." Markus nodded before hopping back into the pool. "I'll just swim it off. Later, buddy."

"Later." He headed back to his condo at a trot. It was eleven. He could write for an hour, jack off like a madman, and then crash.

Dream a little.

Something.

Fuck.

Chapter Three

Markus was damned surprised at how hard it was to see Sebastian.

They spent three hours a day or so writing. The rest of the time Seb just wasn't around, which was crazy. What on earth did the man have to do in New Zealand on his off time? There were a constant flow of surfers, cowboys, skateboarders—but they made an appearance for the press and left, Bev gently showing them the door. Seb went out once that he'd seen—swimming with fucking sharks, the press all over it, and then hid.

Markus never saw the man eat. Never saw him sleep. Bev was pretty damned secretive when Markus asked her about it. He thought about sneaking into Seb's condo, but the security was better than he'd ever had, even in the height of his *Bull in the China Shop* days.

He grinned a little. Man, that album had gone platinum with a bullet...

Sobering, he pondered how he could get in to see Seb. Three days it had been since that silliness at the pool, and now the man was avoiding their writing sessions.

They could sit inside. With the air on high. In clothes.

He saw Bev's shiny, unnaturally blonde hair as she headed over to Seb's front door at eight-forty a.m. sharp, a glass of something in one hand, key in the other.

Time to stalk.

Markus slid in behind her, grabbing the door before it could close. "Hey."

"Mr. Kane! Good morning." She offered him a careful smile. "Can I help you?"

He heard weights clinking, heard the talking heads on ESPN. The place he could see was all white—walls, furniture, carpet—real people didn't live in here. Seb, the Bayou baby who'd painted their first studio apartment bright purple and yellow and had covered every inch of the ceiling with Mardi Gras beads, that man didn't live here. No way.

"Yeah. I need a place to work out. The pool is great, and body weight is okay, but I'm going to get soft." There. See what she did with that.

"I. Okay. Okay, can you wait here for a second?" She headed to a closed door, tapped it. "Hey. It's eight- forty-five. I have your breakfast. Mr. Kane is here and he'd like to work out."

"It's almost nine."

"I know. What do you want me to do?"

"Hey. Seb?" Markus didn't go to the door. Just called out.

Seb's bald head popped out, drenched with sweat, beet red. "Hey, Candy. Come on in."

Bev's eyes went comically wide, obviously surprised. Go him.

"Thanks, man. I need the weights." Damn, this was a nice set up. The room was all windows and TVs on two sides, then all the weights and machines and cardio shit a guy could need. Impressive.

"Yeah. I get it." Seb was in the tiniest set of workout

shorts on earth, muscles bulging. "I'm almost done with the bar. You can use the rest." Seb went over to Bev, talked quickly and took the glass of goo. She disappeared for half a second and then she brought a pair of those damned dark glasses.

Markus shook his head, not sure what the hell he'd done to deserve the barrier. Still, he got to look a minute.

Seb turned the lights up as soon as the glasses were on. "There you go. I have to finish my set. How you been?"

"Good. I'm good." He couldn't help but drool a little.

"Rock on. I been working on the ballad." The bar was picked up, and those amazing pecs started clenching. Jesus.

His mouth felt like quick-dry paint, and he licked his lips. "Any luck?"

"Some. I'll need to put my head with yours." Up. Down. Up. Down. The sweaty work-out shorts slipped down, the top of a black tattoo peeking out.

"Okay." Christ, was that his voice? He cleared his throat, trying to remember how to work out.

He grabbed the thirty pounders, looking everywhere but Seb. The man really did have an entire gym—treadmill, stairs, weights, ab machines. Damn. There were dry erase boards—keeping track of weight, workouts, inches, everything. That was a level of obsession even he couldn't claim. Oh, Markus knew his stats okay. He just knew how to keep panic about getting out of shape at bay.

It wasn't like Seb was fucking puffy or anything, right? The man was a fucking Greek god.

Cajun god.

Whatever.

He breathed deep a moment, taking in the amazing smell of Seb's body. Musk. Mint. Pineapple.

Seb worked hard, sweating, panting before stumbling over to the table, gulping the shake down with a cupful of tablets.

"So, what's all that?" He tried to go for casual, starting up the treadmill to warm up.

"Hmm? Protein shake. Want one? I can call Bev back." Seb went over to the dry erase board, started recording.

"No. I had breakfast, thanks." He cranked it up a little and started jogging.

"I'm going to get my shower. You mind?" The words on the board were a little shaky. The man must've been working out a while.

"Nope." No, he could concentrate on his workout better if Seb wasn't there, especially now that he knew the man would let him in, would see him when they weren't working.

"Cool." Seb headed off, and soon he heard water, then singing, the man just wailing on a bluesy version of *Golddigger*.

He chuckled, reminding himself that he needed to bring his little iPod next time he came over to work out. Which would probably definitely be when Seb did.

He looked at the dry erase board, shook his head. Apparently Mr. Stud Hardbody worked out every day. Damn.

Seb came out of the shower, freshly shaved and gleaming, towel around his waist, those glasses back on.

Good thing Markus was off the treadmill or he would have fallen. He lifted the free weights, grinning. "Looking good, man."

"Thanks. I work at it." He could feel Seb's eyes on him. "You got it going on. You haven't looked that tight in five years."

"Yeah. Amazing what happens when I get off the juice." He was pretty prosaic about it. Puffy went away when he stopped drinking.

"Good for you, man. There's a shitload of calories in that stuff."

"Do you ever eat?" All he'd ever seen Seb consume was shakes and pineapple.

"Nope."

Well, okay then. That was definite.

"Why not, man?" He changed out to thirty-five pound weights. Those would challenge his biceps.

"The shakes keep me going just fine. Keep me lean."

"Your teeth will fall out. People are made to chew."

"Bullshit." Seb chuckled for him, shook his head.

"Well, what about fiber?" His doctor was huge on fiber for a "man his age". Asshole.

"It's in the shake. No worries. I look good." Good, but skinny. And solitary. Fucking monastic. Seb had always had a shitload of friends, no matter where he was. Here, though, there hadn't been a soul that actually connected with the man.

The tip of his tongue begged to ask what had happened, but that was stupid, wasn't it? Markus knew it was a fucked up night in the back of a limo, a bunch of pictures and the threat that the band might starve. He knew because he'd been through it, too. Everyone reacted differently. He'd been on the cover of every magazine, out with beautiful women, out with groups of manly men. Total media coverage. Seb had become the workhorse of the tour circuit—hell, the man's last tour had been what? Thirty-five fucking weeks long?

Markus had drowned his sorrows for years; Sebastian had just ruthlessly pushed his out with work and exercise.

When he looked up, Seb was gone. Just like a fucking dream come morning. Sighing, he set the weights down and went back to the treadmill for an interval.

Beverly came knocking about half an hour later, a tray of juice and water for him, along with a huge, greasy doughnut. "Seb says it's a peace offering and that you're welcome to the workout room, whenever you need it."

"Look at that." God, how did Seb even know about his daily doughnut allowance? "Thanks."

"You're welcome. He'll be in the music room for another..." She checked her watch. "Two hours and eighteen minutes."

"Thanks. I'll grab a shower and get in there and get to work." He winked, giving her a thumbs up.

She grinned at him, winked. "Have fun, man."

"Thanks."

Actually, writing with Seb was the most fun he'd had in years. He looked forward to it every day.

He'd have to make it a quick shower.

Seb wrapped up the radio interview at six and then headed back to the condo for a hard-core writing session, possibly a few laps in the pool. He felt itchy, after dealing with Mad Mike and the screaming girls in the ready room.

Really, Markus should have done the interview. He was off work. The man who didn't have a schedule should have to do shit like that instead of jet-skiing. Anonymously, since no one knew Markus was even there.

Asshole.

He headed in, growling at Bev, who stood there with a shake. Not now. "Taking a shower now. Leave me alone."

"You need the protein, Seb." Her mouth set in that stubborn way he'd come to know, which meant it would be easier not to fight her. Still, maybe he could have a little fight, work out some of this muscle-deep itch and burn from strangers messing with him, talking to him. Touching him.

"I just want a fucking shower." He loved her dearly, but he didn't want the fucking shake.

"Seb, please." Her lip quivered now, and he knew it

was damned sexist, but it wasn't fair for girls to pull the tear card. One day he was going to fire her for it. Not that he really would.

"You're a butthead." He took the drink, drinking deep. "You got my pills, lady?"

"Yeah." She handed them over. He took them all in order, red, yellow, the orange vitamins.

Bev took the glass back, nodding. "Markus wants a jam session tonight. Not writing, just seeing how you sing together."

"Okay. Okay, sure." He worked 'til midnight, then he needed his down time. "Tonight like now or tonight like when I usually rehearse?"

"I think he means sometime around eight."

"Ah. Okay. I'll be there." He nodded, rubbed his head. "Need my shower."

The pills were starting to work on the headache.

"You okay?"

He nodded, waving her away. Interviews sucked.

He had to scrub all the hands off him.

Markus waited for Seb, but the man hadn't appeared yet. He had two guitars and he had a rhythm guy he trusted to sit in and give them a little something. Now he just needed a jam session.

Seb showed up at eight on the dot, in sweats, sunglasses, and with a giant bottle of water. "Hey, y'all."

"Hey. This is Abe. I've known him a bit. This is Sebastian."

"Mr. Sebastian." Abe stood, shook Seb's hand. "Pleased."

"Ditto. What's on the playlist, Candy?" Seb's voice was tight, like the man had just swallowed a bad pecan.

"I thought we'd start with *Fireworks and Old Flames.* See if we really got that bridge figured."

"Works for me." Seb settled down on a stool and picked off the opening riff. Jesus, the man had become a picker. A real fucking picker.

Made Markus feel lazy. Still, he could sing, and he knew it, so he came in with the first verse. Seb let him take the verse and the first round of the chorus, then that bluesy voice started fucking seducing the second verse.

Oh, hell, yeah. This would rock the stadiums.

They hit the bridge, working it together, Seb's voice sliding under his, rich and low, pushing him. The man still knew him too damned well, knew how competitive he was. He pushed it, breathing deep, working up from his diaphragm.

They came to an end, looking at each other, grinning like fools.

"Goddamn." Seb hooted, bare feet stomping. "Fucking A, man!"

"Shit, yes." They still had it. He couldn't wait to get a band in and get in the studio.

Seb nodded, just beaming. "We need to book studio time back home, man."

"Read my mind, buddy." He was glad Abe was there, or he'd be hugging on that fine body. "Wanna do one of your old ones? *Ride the Sun*, maybe?"

Abe grinned away, looking like nothing more than a big, tanned orangutan. "Love that song."

Seb snorted. "Me too. In E. Let's go. Keep up, Candy."

"I got this." He'd sung this in the shower a million times.

They started off, singing hard, Seb letting him have the lead for a little while before stealing it back.

God, this was fun. Truly fucking fun. He wished his guys were here. Markus sobered a little, fingers fumbling.

Yeah. His fiddle player Kyle would be the only one to come...

Seb stopped, looked over. "You cool?"

"Huh? Yeah. Yeah, just hoping I jive with your band."

The man's lips tightened, the look knowing. "Yeah. You got your holes filled? I hurt for you, when I heard."

"I do. They won't do in the studio, though. Too raw." Most people used studio musicians, but he knew Seb was like him. They recorded with their own bands.

"Well then, we'll rehearse with the Horsemen until you're happy. I want this to be good, man, for all of us."

"Cool." Markus grinned over at Abe. "You're welcome to sit in once we get dates. You're a good match."

"Get off the grass! You got it, mate. I'm yours."

"Good deal. Yeah?" He supposed he should have asked Seb first.

Seb chuckled. "Well, there you go."

He winked at Seb, relaxing back into the music. "Where were we?"

"We were being painfully talented. How about your *Hunting and Wishing*?"

"Sure. I like that one." He'd closed his show with it for damned near two years.

"Me too." Seb grinned wide, winked at Abe. "I wrote it, after all."

He looked over. That was a matter of opinion. "You helped. I did the good parts."

"I had the hook and the second verse. That won you a Grammy, that verse."

"Yeah, yeah. Let's see if you remember it."

Abe was watching them like they were playing tennis.

"Are you still capable of singing it in A?" The opening riff sounded.

"I sure hope so." He'd actually gained some range back since he'd quit drinking.

"Me too." He got another of those smiles and they were off, singing hard, the harmonies like rusty gates at first, then going clear.

They sang three more before anyone even broke for water, then three more after that. They were gonna be solid gold. Possibly platinum.

God, wouldn't that work for him? His foot tapped, his hand slapping the guitar in time with the final verse.

They headed into a cover of *Luckenbach, Texas* that had Abe rolling. The yodeling at the end was impromptu and made them all cackle like a bunch of crows.

Seb was laughing, head thrown back, throat working. His belly clenched, the need to kiss Seb's smiling mouth almost more than he could bear. This was why he'd brought along another picker.

"Okay, mates. I need to get home. You call if you need to jam again?" Abe stood, shook his hand, Seb's.

"You know it, man. Thanks for sitting in." Sebastian was gracious, which he really appreciated.

They helped Abe pack his stuff up, load up, then, suddenly, they were alone.

"Thanks, Seb. I needed to know I still had it in me, I think."

"Anytime, man. That was fucking great."

"It was. I wasn't sure I'd still mesh. Now I just need to work on stamina, huh? Stage shows." It had been awhile.

"You'll do fine. I'm the one that gets breathless there."

"You do?" That had never been Seb's problem, but who knew what had gone on for the past eight years?

"It's a lot of running." Seb's lips quirked. "Sucks getting old."

"I never did bounce as much as you." He watched those lips, his heart picking up its beat. "You look fucking amazing."

"Thank you." Seb tilted his head, looking like a puppy

that had heard a whistle. "I think I'm going to go jack off about a dozen times before my balls explode. I want you like I want my next fucking breath."

Christ. Markus' cock went from interested to "oh, my God now" in about two seconds. It hurt his belly, it happened so fast. He blinked. "Ain't nobody here but you and me."

Seb moaned, took a step toward him, those lips parted. He loved how they'd looked wrapped around his cock, sucking like Seb's life depended on it. Markus moved, too, meeting the man halfway, wondering if Seb still kissed like the very devil. Seb pushed up, lips crashing against his, one hard hand behind his head as that tongue pushed in to taste him. Fuck. Fuck, yes. That hard body was like a fucking flame, slammed up against him.

Moaning, he grabbed Seb's tight little ass and lifted, pulling that fine body against his even more, kissing back. He had eight years of pent up need to get out.

Seb cried out, the sound pure music, and one leg wrapped around his hip so they could grind together. His breath came in short bursts, his hips rocking. His lips felt burned from the strength of their kisses.

"Markus." Seb arched, humping against him. "Please."

"God." He brought one hand around and shoved it down the front of Seb's sweats, looking for that hot cock. His fingers wrapped around it, heavy and fat and so fucking hot, and he stroked, base to tip. The touch liked to set him on fire, and he damn near tugged Seb's dick off when a knock came to the door.

"Seb? Honey? I have your pills and your shake."

"No." The single word was broken, raw.

"I'm going to kill her." Markus rested his forehead against Seb's.

"Uh-huh."

"Boss? Boss? You have to eat. You've only had four

hundred and twenty calories today."

"Oh, for fuck's sake." Seb pulled away from him, stalking toward the door. "Leave me the fuck alone!"

"No. No, you work out three hours, you have to have this."

Markus stepped away from the view of the door, trying to be unobtrusive. Jesus, he hoped he hadn't pulled Seb's pants down too far.

"God damn it, Bev!" It was like Seb had just totally lost his shit, the door slamming open, trembling on its hinges. "What do I fucking tell you about fucking bothering me when I'm working?"

"It's not midnight. I have three minutes, you *asshole*! And you want to collapse again, fine, but you're not doing it on my watch!" One hand pushed the shake over. "DRINK IT!"

Markus shook his head, trying to clear it. There was something seriously messed up here. Something he didn't have a handle on yet.

Seb drank the shake, then threw the glass, the thing shattering against the wall. "Happy, you fucking harpy psycho? Give me my pills, you bitch."

"Stop being a drama llama, you spoiled brat. I'm going to hide your guitar and not let you jam if you keep throwing temper tantrums."

Markus was fairly sure Seb was going to have an aneurysm. That was just a little scary, that whole throbbing vein in Seb's neck. Seb took the pills, though, and slammed the door shut as hard as he'd opened it.

"Sorry." A thin sheen of sweat was covering Seb. "I'm sorry."

"Hey. It's okay." A bottle of water sat nearby, and Markus cracked it open. "For your pills."

"Thanks." Seb took the bottle, drained it. "Guess I killed the mood, huh?"

"Getting interrupted did that." The ache was still there, still unfulfilled, but the fact was it wasn't safe for them to be together as long as Seb was still a star.

"Yeah." Seb took a deep breath, then just turned around and walked out, the line of the man's shoulders pure defeat.

Shit. Markus stood there, torn between going after the man and going back to his shower. It would be smarter to choose the later.

Bev came in with a broom and a rag, blinking as she saw him. "Hey, Mr. Kane. I'm sorry. Really. I didn't mean for you to have to see that."

"It's fine. He was just hungry, I think." Markus' stomach growled, proving his point. "Does this happen often?"

"Only daily." She chuckled and started cleaning up. "No, that's unfair. He's a perfect angel, if his schedule isn't tripped up. There was an interview; that means a fight."

"What sets him off there? The waste of time?" Markus hated dealing with the press, but he was good at it.

"You're friends, yeah? He wasn't always this... OCD?" She blinked up at him, obviously confused.

"Honey, we haven't talked in eight years. When I knew him he ate food and let loose with the boys at least three nights a week. His trainer had to browbeat him." Okay, both of them.

"Well, that's not the man I work for. I try to get two thousand calories a day in him. Most days I manage fifteen hundred. His days are all scheduled to the minute. It works for him."

"It does, huh?" That sounded like hell. "Well, I guess I'm glad you came when you did. We kept jamming, he woulda got all off schedule."

"I had three minutes. He would have called a halt."

Yeah, Markus didn't think so. Not the way they'd been cooking with oil. That was gonna go until it ended. Damn it. "I guess he's in bed now, huh?"

She shrugged. "I know he rehearses from three to six, works out from six to nine."

Good Lord. "When does he sleep?"

"Noon to three p.m."

That was three hours. Three. People went crazy from that shit. As in raving loony. They'd have to work on that. In fact, Seb might just be his new favorite project.

"I'd like to work out with him again in the morning. I won't be there 'til seven-thirty, though."

"I'll leave him a note. I try not to deal with him from midnight to eight-forty-five."

"You got to sleep sometime, honey." He'd better get out of her hair, too. It was late. "I'll just get me a snack and head to bed."

"Sleep well. There's fruit and stuff in the kitchen on your way out." She winked. "You're welcome to sample the potato chip stash I keep, just don't give me up to Mister 'Do You Know How Many Calories Are In That?'."

"Never," he promised, before waving and leaving the room. Fruit would do just fine, and he would bet there were some nuts, too.

Fuck knew this place was full of friggin' nuts.

Sebastian had just hit the halfway point on his workout when Markus walked in.

Huh. Interesting.

"Hey."

"Hey, ba—man. How goes?" The towel got slung over a weight bench and Markus hopped on the treadmill.

"Good. Good." He started another set of squats, thighs screaming. "You?"

"A little tired." The slow chuckle was just pure sex. "Took me a while to wind down last night."

"Yeah. I bet." He'd jacked himself raw. By the time noon rolled around, he'd be ready to crash.

"Still, we had a good session."

Sebastian was in a perfect place to watch Markus' ass.

"It was amazing. Recording is going to rock." Up. Down. Up. Down. Ten more, then lunges.

"You know it. I'll have to watch it with the band there, though."

"Watch it?" Like he'd do anything to fuck up Markus' career.

"I said I would. Not you." Markus shrugged, muscles shifting in the wide shoulders. "I thought it would have gone away more in eight years, you know? The wanting you."

"Yeah. I know. We're good together, like that." They were like fire and gasoline, like that.

"We are." Glancing over his shoulder, Markus grinned. "We make good music, too."

"We make amazing fucking music." He dropped the barbell, grabbed the dumbbells. Lunges. Go.

Markus did a five minute warm up, then headed for the Smith machine. Sebastian went from lunges to push-ups to pull-ups, giving his legs a breather.

They moved around the room together, not talking much. He had to admit there was a hell of a lot of looking going on. Hell, there was a whole lot to look at, with Markus and that taut, tiny little ass. Every time the man got on the treadmill for an interval, those buttcheeks moved in a hypnotizing way.

He hung on the bar, staring, swinging, eyes on that fine backside.

Markus jumped off the treadmill again, turning to look at him. "You okay?"

"Huh? Yeah. Yeah, just taking a break." He started pulling up again, close to muscle failure.

"No falling." Markus picked up the heavy bar.

"I won't." Hell, he already had. Hard. Years ago. No one had ever measured up. It sucked.

He started doing leg lifts, working his abs. Fuck.

Markus was working on chest and arms, muscles flexing, sweat beading up. The hard on tenting the man's shorts was pretty, too. He groaned, licked his lips. He wanted that cock. He wouldn't go for it, but he wanted it.

"Stop it, man." Markus stared at him, the bar lowering to the floor.

"I'm sorry." He let himself down off the captain's chair. "I..."

Shit. He had to get out of here.

"Should I go, baby? I mean all the way. See you in the studio. I would understand." Markus didn't want to go. Not a bit. Those dark eyes said as much.

"I know. I want you to stay. I won't touch, but I can't not look."

"I'll work with that." Grabbing a towel, Markus dried off. "I got a half hour left of cardio, but I think I'll jog, huh? Can you pencil me in tonight for some writing?"

"I'm free to work from six to midnight."

"I can do six. I promise to eat before I come." Markus had taken to teasing him about the food.

"You're obsessed with food. Obsessed. Freak." He grinned and hit the treadmill.

"If by that you mean I eat..." Laughing, Markus smacked him with the towel on the way out. "See you at six, huh?"

"Have a good day, asshole." He turned the speed up, flipped Markus off.

The door closed, and he put his head down to run, not

sure if he was happy or furious that they'd dodged that bullet again.

It didn't really matter. He needed to focus on the music. Just the music.

Chapter Four

Markus wiped his hands on his jeans, as nervous as a seventeen-year-old on prom night.

He'd left New Zealand in early March, and he hadn't seen Sebastian since. They'd danced around each other for weeks, writing songs and working out, and it had been both heaven and hell. Truth was, Markus missed the man.

The house was ready for Sebastian and his band, though. The studio in the back was tricked out with new equipment, he'd put extra beds in otherwise empty bedrooms for the musicians—all nine of them, plus Seb and Bev, for fuck's sake—and he'd gotten a host of new shit for the workout room.

He even had a VitaMix for Bev to make Seb's Ensure mash-ups.

So why the hell was he so nervous now that the day had come?

A limo pulled up, his housekeeper Helen hollering up. "Baby doll, you want me to get the door for you? Your comp'ny's starting to show."

"No, I got it. Can you just get some drinks and snacks

going?" Seb would never eat anything, but the guys would, assuming Helen didn't make some kind of tofu log with raisins. That had been one epic fail in her attempt to health up his food.

"Absolutely. I got jalapeno poppers, chicken wings, and lots of fruits and veggies."

He went to the door, opening it to a tiny little girl, a spiky-headed kid, plus Abe and Dooley.

"Hey, y'all. Markus Kane." He shook hands with Abe, then Dooley, the huge black drummer who shook the damn house when he walked.

The wee girl shook next, her tiny hand all hard calluses. "Kerry Demoss. This hooligan's Jonny. Ignore him, no matter what he says. Is the boss here yet?"

"Nope, Seb's not here yet. Come on in, y'all. Helen has snacks and rooms and shit."

They cracked up. "God, no. We were talking about Beverly. She's the woman with the plan!"

"Seb convinced her to drive in from Houston. She's called me twice in tears. I'm going to take her for margaritas when they get here." Bruce, Seb's huge band leader who was a local, popped his head in, guitar and Markus' fiddle player in tow. "I grabbed Kyle for you, man."

"Thanks, buddy." Bruce wasn't one to blow smoke up anyone's ass, but Markus liked him. Kyle had been with Markus since the beginning, and he gave the man a hug.

"Hey, stranger! You're looking good." Kyle handed over a jar of jam. "Pomegranate. Sally made it."

Wow.

"Christ, man. Your little girl is old enough to make jam?"

"I know, right? Sucks to get old."

"Who the fuck you calling old, asshat?" Janet walked in, looking like Reba's older, harder, smoking second cousin. Her hair had gotten bigger over the years, and her eyeliner was still peacock blue.

"Markus." Kyle winked. "There's my woman."

"Kyle! Baby doll!" Janet squealed and tackled Kyle. "It's been a dog's age!'

"God damn it, someone help carry the fucking gear!"

Markus blinked as Evy walked in, loaded for bear, the stench of patchouli overwhelming, followed closely behind by a long, lanky sun worshipper.

"We're coming. Jeez. We all had to get all introduced nice." The lanky blond was an Aussie.

"Lord have mercy, bring all that shit in here before we know Markus has a place for it." Janet was a ball buster.

Kyle snorted. "Markus has a place. Come on, y'all. I'll show you the studio."

They all trooped out, leaving him feeling like a whirlwind had passed through. Markus stood there waiting for Sebastian. Sure as shit, a bright red convertible pulled up, Sebastian standing up in the passenger side, laughing hard.

Bev wasn't laughing. In fact, she looked ready to explode. God, the woman was either a masochist or a saint. He was leaning toward saint, after getting to know Bev some in New Zealand.

He headed outside, just in time to hear Seb cackle. "Let's do it again!"

"I'm going to tear your head off and shit down your neck."

Now, that was a pissed off Bev. Markus moved in, prepared to soothe, but Seb just grabbed her and hugged her, then hopped to come pinch his shoulder.

"Hey, man."

"Hey, Seb. How was the drive?"

"Fabulous! We had a blast!" Someone was flying, bouncing off the walls.

"You ready to come in with the guys or did you want to see your private entrance?" He'd set the mother-in-law up for Seb.

"I'd like to put my stuff down and take a shower, if you don't mind, man."

"Come on, then. They guys are all in the studio, wandering. Helen can take care of them." He gave Bev a warm smile. "Helen can show you where to take a load off. You can't miss her. She's the one with the 'Sexy Grandma' T-shirt."

Bev nodded, almost tearing up. "Thanks. Thanks."

Impulsively, he gave her a hug before steering her off to the front door. "Come on, Seb. You're this way."

"Hold up." Seb ran Bev's suitcases up to the house for her, then came back for his bag, the guitar. He was a good man. He really was. "How've you been, Candy? You're looking good."

"Been working out hard. Need to keep up with you."

"Everybody else here already?" Seb looked like a wet dream—tight T-shirt, faded jeans. Every bit of clothing faithfully outlined that hard body.

"Everyone I know of, yeah." His fingers itched to touch, so he put one hand under Seb's elbow, steering the man toward the side of the big house. The man's skin was warm, somehow heavy.

"Good deal. Your guy Abe make it in?" He could see Seb's tanned throat working.

"He came in with Dooley. They'll be wanting to settle a little, I guess. Bruce said something about Maudie's."

"He's going to get Bev drunk."

"Good for him." Better to take her somewhere else and not try to sneak it in his house.

"My guys all know your place is off limits. Evy will go stay at Bruce's, too."

Everyone knew Evy was old school and needed his green.

"I appreciate it." Maybe it wasn't reasonable, but he needed to have his safe place.

"Man, I wouldn't fuck this up for you."

He opened the door to the little one bedroom house. It was private, comfortable, and Seb could settle here. No one would interrupt his schedule, except maybe Markus. Markus was seriously considering interrupting Seb a lot. The man was getting a little intense.

"This work, babe?" It was so damned easy when they were alone to slip into old habits.

"It's great, thank you." Seb put his suitcase down, looked around. "Fucking cool."

"I had it put in for my folks, but since they moved to Corpus they don't come as much." He stared at Seb's mouth, wanting to take a kiss. He obviously still had impulse control issues.

Seb's tongue flicked out, wetting those pink lips. The man was trying to kill him.

"I--" Markus shook his head. "I told Helen to leave you be, but you know how she is..."

"Yes, the food-pushing grandma. I'll sic Bev on her."

Privately, Markus thought his money was on Helen. She was a barracuda when it came to keeping her singers healthy.

Seb plopped down on the sofa, sunglasses bobbing.

"You want me to dim the lights?"

"Yeah. Please. Thanks, man."

Markus would never tell Seb but he'd had the dimmers installed last week when he knew Seb would be staying with him and not on a bus or something. He hit the dimmer, and Seb relaxed.

"Fuck, that's good." Seb's head fell back on the cushions, the man seeming to melt a little.

"I stocked the fridge with that water you like." His whole body wanted to go over there.

"You think we're going to fuck while I'm here?"

His mouth dropped open so hard he swore his jaw cracked on his collarbones. "Seb! You can't say shit like that."

"Why not? It's a fair question, isn't it?"

"Hell, yeah, but what if someone had been here?" He laughed a little, his belly fluttering.

"Well, I wouldn't have asked." Seb nodded and rolled so he was sitting up again. "I get it. I won't ask again. What's the schedule here like?"

Markus tamped down his disappointment that Seb didn't push it. The man never had, even if he was way more vocal about what they both wanted. Markus had always had to initiate the action. Seb just didn't have any filters, didn't have any sense.

"I was thinking we could work in the studio from six to midnight? We could work out like we did before, maybe bang out some more songs in the morning?"

"Works for me. Where do you work out?"

"I'll show you when you're settled. I have an old sunroom I converted." He was pretty self-contained, really. When he'd bought a place in Austin after the dot com crash, he'd gotten an amazing deal, so he'd gone nuts and bought an eight bedroom monstrosity.

Seb nodded and suddenly, just for a half second, the man looked exhausted and old and sad, like he'd been drained, then Seb stood, grabbed a bottle of water from his backpack and the look was gone.

Impulse control. It was always his damned problem. Markus fought the urge for maybe two seconds, but then he just stepped up to give Seb a hug, holding on tight. Seb was stiff for a heartbeat, then melted into him, took a hitching breath.

Markus didn't bother making soothing noises or saying anything. His touch would say it all for him, and he knew it. He held on, needing to lean just as much as Seb.

They stood together, for a long, long time before he backed off and left, headed back to his house without a word. There wasn't anything to say. Not a thing. This wasn't going to happen, not for either of them, and they just needed to stop torturing themselves.

Music streamed from the little studio Helen pointed him toward, and Sebastian followed it. It wasn't anything but a crazy cacophony of a jam session, but they were waiting for him, so nothing serious would be going down yet. Markus had a great little set-up, all they would need until the final mix sessions, which they could still do right here in Austin. He wondered if that would affect the vibe of the record.

He'd recorded his last two albums in St. Maarten and the one before that in Rome. It had rocked. Maybe that was what he needed to do after they did the record. Go for a week and surf or dive or drive like a maniac. That might get the restless edge off before the tour.

He could disappear for a week, reappear a new fucking man.

Sebastian opened the door, waved. "Y'all."

"Hey, man!" His band was all smiles, but the lights were nice and low and there was no food smell, so he was able to smile back and saunter in like he wasn't dreading this.

Dooley came blustering over, grabbed him up. "Seb! God, man! It's been months!"

He groaned as Dooley squeezed him tight. They'd known each other since they were kids and Dooley forgot they were both getting old.

"Don't kill the man, Doo." Kyle came over to shake his hand, those scarred, callused fiddler's fingers strong, hard. "Thanks for letting me sit in, Seb."

He snorted. "Any fucking time."

He kissed Janet, ruffled Jonny's hair, and winked at Evy.

Markus came in from the back with a bottle of water in one hand. "Hey, you. About time."

"I'm not late."

"He's never late." The band spoke in unison.

Markus laughed, those dark eyes sparkling, and waved everyone off. "Yeah, yeah. So, Seb. What's the plan?"

"Let's play a couple of standards, get in sync, and then we learn the new stuff."

"Bruce?"

His bandleader grinned hugely. "On it."

Kerry strummed the opening chords to *Rocky Top*. Little redneck girl. They all knew it, though, just like they all knew *Fishing in the Dark* when Gator gave them the opening line, loud and raucous.

Markus yodeled through *Make It Through the Night* and Sebastian took *Sunday Morning Coming Down*, then *Jambalaya*, giving Markus the second verse.

"Good deal, y'all. Let's break for some water." Markus sounded a little raw, but Seb knew better than to count the man out. Some fizzy water and that throat would be good as new.

"Bruce." He got the man over, started talking over the scoring for the new stuff—the lyric sheets with their chording, the basic rhythm scribbled on it.

"Nice." Bruce nodded over *Fireworks and Old Flames*. "This is a summer anthem, man. They'll go crazy for this."

"Yeah. I want it nice and rocking, heavy on the blues." He started picking the opening chords and Bruce listened.

"Oh, I like that. What if we put a little thump in here?" Bruce gave a whack to the acoustic guitar he held, and boom, there was a nice added element. They'd add that into the drums. He nodded and then Janet was there, adding the bass line, dark and heavy. Damn. Markus came in on the chorus, and they sounded so good that it hurt, deep in his belly. This was what music was supposed to be.

Soon they were going, all of them, and the room was ringing with it. He propped himself on a stool, staying out of the guitars' way, just singing. Markus grinned at him from across the room, foot slamming against the floor, those pretty eye lines all crinkled up. Sebastian nodded, rocking now, upper body moving, happy as a pig in shit. He raised his voice a little to take the last chorus, feeling like he was soaring, his heart thudding in his chest.

The last note faded and they all sat a second, panting. It was Gator who broke the silence. "Fuckin' A! That fuckin' ROCKED!"

Laughter broke out, everyone relaxing a bit. It had rocked.

"Good work, y'all." Markus was grinning like a fool.

"What's next? I want to do another one." Kerry was bouncing, laughing, eyes dancing.

"Bruce has the day sheet." Seb winked, sitting back and letting it all flow. Never worked to herd cats with his band.

"Bruce! Next!"

They all cracked up—even Kyle and Abe—and they started with the ballad, everyone pushing to find their places. Markus didn't have any trouble, though, and Sebastian slid right in, his voice making love to Markus' right there in the harmony. He didn't meet Markus' eyes. He couldn't, not without embarrassing both of them.

The last note lingered, Janet's clear alto caressing it,

and that worked. Another one knocked out.

"So," Evy looked over at Markus. "You two are becoming the writing dream team. Tell me there's more. One with a killer keyboard part."

"We got about ten more right now. We have to cull it to six for the EP."

"It's not like the songs just disappear if we don't use them, right?" Jonny was so new to this he squeaked.

Markus chuckled. "Something will happen with them. Seb puts out more albums than God."

"Someone's got to pay all these hooligans." He felt that weight all the damn time, the push of how many people depended on the Longchamps machine for a living.

"No shit, man." Kyle waved his bow in the air. "It don't grow on trees."

"You sure about that? I hear they got money trees 'round California." They all looked at Dooley, then cracked up, the room ringing with it.

"Let's try the swing song next." Markus settled on his stool, long old legs sticking out. "If it doesn't make it on the EP, I'll cut it myself."

Sebastian nodded. That was totally fair. Texas Swing wasn't his schtick. It went rockin' well with the band, though, and Kyle's fiddle really got to shine. Kerry even joined in with a little twin fiddle action. Hot. Hot. Hot.

This EP was going to be killer. It really was.

They all started to drag around ten and people started to break up, leaving him, Markus, Bruce, and Kyle to work out some scoring. He was on the floor with his guitar, dabbling, as happy as he could remember being.

Kyle had kicked off his shoes, and Bruce was picking out chords, playing with arrangements. When Sebastian looked up, Markus was just staring at him, eyes dark, the need obvious. He went for a grin, but had to look down. Markus had been crystal clear. The man was off limits.

No looking. No touching. No asking.

It was going to be the longest year in history.

He heard the sound of Markus' acoustic opening up *Sun's Gotta Shine*, which they'd written damned near ten years ago in Mexico. It suited the mood perfectly. His fingers moved, knowing this song like he knew his own soul. He knew all the places Markus needed a stronger backup, knew all the places he needed to lead.

Kyle's fiddle wailed through the bridge, the sound making him tear up, making his heart ache.

Markus' voice broke on the last note, but that just made it right. Fucking perfect.

None of them spoke, Kyle's bow hand dropped, and Bruce looked over at him with knowing, sad eyes, and he stood, nodded to them, and left.

He needed his pills and one of those fucking protein shakes.

Chapter Five

This was going to kill him.

Markus just wanted to go down to Sebastian in that little guest house and tear his ass up. He didn't because it would end this whole process, and while self-torture was generally not Markus' gig, they were making amazing music. Fucking amazing.

He was on the phone with his manager, discussing logistics, when Bev came into his and waved him down.

"No, Tawny. I mean, that's just too small. Sure, I want to do a showcase for the EP, but you forget how big an artist Seb is. We need more than a conference room at the Hilton. Uh-huh. Okay. I'll call back in a bit."

He hung up, rolling his head on his neck. "What's up, honey?"

"Hey, Mr. Kane." He stared, and she pinked. "Markus. I, uh. Can you tell me where in town I can find better pineapple? That's the only thing he'll eat in his shakes and he threw two in a row at me. Also, I need a dry cleaner and Helen keeps making him food..."

"God forbid." He winked. "Let me get Helen's husband to take you over to the Whole Foods."

"Thank you." She looked exhausted, like Seb was riding her hard. He wondered why she stayed sometimes, but she sure loved Seb.

"What else can I do? I'll talk to Helen."

"Talk to Helen about what?" Speak of the devil, there she came, tray in hand. "I just tried to deliver lunch to Seb, he didn't answer."

Bev paled. "Helen. Please. It's twelve-thirty. He sleeps from noon to three in the afternoon."

"If he ate, he wouldn't need such a long nap."

"Nap?" Bev looked confused as hell.

"Why does a guy like him need a nap?" Helen just seemed stunned.

Markus snorted. "Because he doesn't sleep."

"He does sleep, from noon to three, and you can't bother him."

Helen's lips tightened. "He needs food."

"He doesn't EAT!" Bev actually stamped one well-shod foot on the tile.

"Time out, ladies. Helen, Seb isn't your problem. I know you want to mother, but he doesn't want it. Bev, chill. I'll talk to him." What good it would do, he had no idea.

"Not until after three p.m.!" Bev looked panicked.

"No, not until after three." He wouldn't do anything to make Bev so upset. Even if he did want to see if Seb was actually sleeping. Who fucking slept from noon to three?

Markus would be jacking off. Seriously.

Of course, Seb said he did that from midnight to three. The thought made him grin, which made both Bev and Helen glare at him. Damn, how did he get tag-teamed by the girls?

Markus spread his hands. "Hey, now. I'm not laughing at y'all."

"Uh-huh." Helen looked at the food in her hands. "You eaten, Markus?"

"Nope." His belly rumbled.

"Well, then." She handed him the platter. "Turkey sandwiches and coleslaw."

"Thank you, ma'am." He took the plate and bent to kiss her cheek. "Helen will be good and take you to her husband and not criticize you, Bev. Right?"

"Sure. Sure, whatever. I'm not going to be mean, Markus." Helen looked a little ashamed.

"I know that, lady." He gave them both what he hoped was a gentle smile. He wasn't used to dealing with this stuff. He was usually the only one Helen had to baby along. "I think Bev is just wore out."

Helen nodded, spoke low. "What happened to him, honey? He didn't used to be like this."

"I don't know." Well, he did, he was pretty sure, but what was he gonna tell Helen? "I just don't."

"I'm sorry, honey. It's so sad."

Bless her heart. It was sad. For both of them. "I think I'll go eat this, and you get Bev set up with pineapple, huh?"

"I'm on it. Supper is at five. I'm making lasagna."

"Oh, God." He loved her lasagna, but it meant an extra half hour on the treadmill. "Be sure to tell Bruce so he doesn't run off home."

"Will do." She went to catch up to Bev.

Markus stared down at the sandwich, wondering what the hell to do now. He wanted to check on Seb.

He snarfed the sandwich down, then headed outside, shivering against the wind. Man, spring was a fickle bitch. It'd been almost warm yesterday. Today it was a little raw. He paused at the door to his little guesthouse, wondering if Seb would take his head off.

What the fuck. It was his house.

Damn it.

He went inside, the place preternaturally clean, quiet. Cool and dark. There was no one in the front room or the kitchen, so Markus peeked into the bedroom.

Seb was there on the bed, bare naked, splayed out. Lean and inked—there wasn't a spare ounce of flesh on the man. Markus' mouth went dry, his hands clenching and unclenching with the need to touch.

Seb stretched, arched, one hand rubbing that flat, smooth belly, and that's when he saw the tattoo. It was a flowing musical score, curling over the man's hips, over the bare-shaved pubic bone. Feeling a little like a peeping Tom, Markus moved closer, trying to figure out the song.

He hummed a bar, frowning. He knew this.

Seb's eyes popped open. "Markus?"

"Shit." He took a step back, his face on fire. "Sorry. I'm sorry. Bev was worried."

"Oh. Sorry. Is it after three?"

Bev was serious. The little shit did only sleep from noon to three.

"I don't know." He had a watch on, but he couldn't look away from Seb's body.

"Is everything okay?" Seb's cock was filling, so fucking pretty.

"Helen had food for you." Where did he even set that down? Jesus, he was stupid. He'd eaten it, maybe.

"Yeah, she came by. She's a mother hen." Seb yawned, stretched, those muscles just rippling.

"She is. Tell me to go away, baby."

Seb's head tilted, blood-shot green eyes searching his face. "Do you want to?"

"No, but this is stupid." He knew it was so, so dumb, but it didn't matter.

"Okay. So go away." Seb didn't sound like he meant it.

"I can't." When he could make his feet move they

went toward Seb, not the door.

Seb sat up, eyes eating him alive. Markus reached out, knowing he'd have to be the one who did it, the one who touched first. As soon as he moved, Seb surged up, that beautiful body slamming against him.

Oh, fuck. He was in so much trouble. All he could do was kiss Seb's mouth, one hand sliding under Seb's body to hold him up. Seb cried out, tasting him, hands like iron bands around his upper arms.

They rubbed together until Markus' clothes got to be too much, an irritation and a barrier. Like they'd discussed it, they both pulled away and started on all that cloth.

"So pretty." Seb's fingers worked his jeans open, tongue wetting those parted lips.

"Uhn." Talking was almost impossible when his cock got loose. All he could do was pant and groan.

"Get back over here." Seb grabbed him and pulled him over.

"You're talking." He could think of other things to do with that porno movie mouth.

"You noticed." Seb leaned down, mouth dropping over his cock like a molten lead balloon. The suction was fierce and strong and viciously familiar, even after eight years. Jesus.

His head fell back, his hips humping up.

Seb's hands wrapped around his ass, fingers digging in as he was pulled in deep, that throat swallowing around him. Torn between closing his eyes so he could just feel and watching so he could commit the whole thing to memory, he finally chose forcing his eyes open. This would be his own personal movie reel. He reached down, hands on Seb's bald head as he watched his cock appear, disappear into that hungry mouth. His body shook, his belly hard as a board. Seb's eyes were closed, the look on the man's face so fucking fine. Seb was loving on him, fucking making him fly. It was like a time warp, like they were right back on that last tour, running off after every show to fuck like bunnies.

He started moaning, damn near singing for Seb, his balls heavy and aching. It would only take the slightest little thing to send him over the edge. Seb deep throated him, fingers rolling his balls in their sac, tugging just enough to make his eyes cross. Markus just lost it like he hadn't been jacking off a few hours ago, like it had been eight years since he'd come at all.

When the pleasure faded, Seb backed off, let his cock slip free from that amazing mouth.

"C'mere." Markus hauled Seb right up against him, kissing those swollen lips. Fuck, Seb tasted like him.

Strong arms wrapped around him, holding him close while Seb humped away at his belly. He helped, his hand on that sweet ass. Seb's fat, thick cock left burning wet kisses on his skin. Markus reached for Seb's cock, his fingers learning it all over again. Thick and fiery hot, it fit perfectly against his palm.

"Please." Seb arched, fucking his fingers furiously.

"I won't leave you wanting, baby. I won't." No, Markus wanted to see Seb's face when he came. "Look at me."

Those famous bright eyes looked at him, the need on the lean face so sharp it read like pain.

"Sebastian." He stroked hard, harder, giving friction, pleasure.

"Candy..." Seb's head fell back, spunk spraying over his fingers, over that ripped belly.

Markus couldn't look away. He took in every moment. Fuck, Seb was so fucking fine.

Seb moaned, leaning in to kiss his throat, his collarbones. He loved the way Seb touched him, made him feel like the only other man on earth. One hand trailed down his stomach, fingers drawing lazy pictures.

He could stay there forever, leaning his forehead against Seb's, sharing air. He really could.

Except he couldn't. Jack and Tawny were coming out tomorrow. The production people were already on their way. They were going to start recording. Oh, God. This could fuck everything up for Seb, and it was Markus' fault. He was the one who'd come looking, the one who couldn't stay away. He sighed, reality crashing in hard.

"This is where you tell me this was stupid, right?" Seb took a deep breath, not looking at him anymore.

"This is where I apologize. I'm sorry, Seb. This could ruin everything you've worked so hard for." He eased away, the separation actually painful.

"Don't be." Seb headed for the little bathroom, wet a washcloth, and brought it to him.

"Thanks." The scrape of the washcloth almost killed him, his skin so sensitive it hurt. "You're so much better than the booze, baby. You're my worst addiction."

Seb looked at him this time, long and slow. "What can I say? You're my one true thing."

He dropped the washcloth and reached out to touch Seb's cheek, tracing the lines beside that beautiful mouth. Those green eyes weren't hidden behind sunglasses, and it was almost too much to bear, to see how much this man loved him, and knowing he was going to have to walk away.

"I know the feeling." He had to take one more kiss. Had to. Markus pressed his lips to Seb's hard, filling his memory cup to the brim. Then he pulled back and got his clothes. "I'll see you in the studio tomorrow, baby. I--"

"Yeah." Seb nodded and disappeared into the bathroom, the water starting up, the door solid between them.

Markus got his shit together and his clothes on straight

and left without trying to say anything else. That would just make things worse.

God, he wanted a beer. He wasn't going to have one, though. The only thing he was that stupid about was Sebastian.

"Bruce, can you get your guy in tonight?" Sebastian was packed, he had his plane tickets, he just needed to lay down his tracks.

"Tonight? Are you serious?" Bruce frowned. "We're supposed to start recording tomorrow."

"You are. You don't need me for that." No one needed him in the room for that.

"What if there's..."

He shook his head. "There won't be. No changes. If Markus changes stuff, you guys go for it. I'll record the entire song set, just cut me in."

"Where are you going?"

"Away. Base jumping. I have to get out of here."

"I told you he was bad news, boss." God, Bruce looked about like he felt. Like the world was graying.

"It's not him. I just need to get out. You'll see me on tour, but..." He couldn't do this. He needed to be somewhere where he wasn't the one fucking people's lives up.

"Yeah. Yeah, I'll make the calls."

"Good. I'll be in the studio at midnight; I have to be at the airport at six a.m."

Bruce rolled his eyes. "I suppose you want me to drive you."

"Yep. I'll be back in the States the day of rehearsals. I'll deal with details online." Sebastian knew that Bruce would deal. It would be Bev who lost her shit. "Tell Bev she's got two weeks off, then I'll tell her where I want her to show."

Bruce stepped back, hands up. "Oh, no. No way. You do what you have to, but I'm not breaking that news."

"Fine. I'll email her." Tomorrow. From the plane. Or from LAX.

Somewhere.

Anywhere.

Anywhere but here.

Markus rolled into the studio six-fifteen. He knew he was a little late, but he had the devil's own scratchy throat, and he'd talked to Tawny about maybe getting someone in to give him a B12 shot or something. She'd told him to get off his lazy ass and get to work. Good old Tawny, she was like a shot of pure adrenaline, right to the heart muscle.

When he got down to the basement studio there was quite a crowd, but there wasn't a bit of music going on. It was silent as a tomb.

He looked around, raising a brow. "Sorry I'm late."

"At least you're here." Jack Michaels, Sebastian's manager and all-around money making master had a face like a thundercloud. Hell, when had he shown up?

Bruce sighed. "Just stop it, man."

"Why? Why the fuck should I?"

"What's up?" Markus tried to keep it light, but he had a feeling he knew. Seb was gone.

"Seb laid down all his tracks last night." Bruce shrugged, the move non-committal.

"The guy's a fucking machine." Harry Davis came in, wild white hair like a cotton swab. "Can I work with him again?"

"I have no idea." Markus waved at Jack. "He'll set it up. Sorry, I don't have his perfect pitch." He wanted to ask Bruce a thousand questions, but the whole band was watching him. "What does the schedule look like tonight?"

"Totally up to you, man. Seb said we were your bitches for the duration. He did each song three times, plus harmony before he left for the airport." Bruce looked over at Jack. "You might go talk to Bev. She's having an aneurysm about him disappearing."

"Well, are you going to tell us where the fuck he went, Bruce?" Jack looked close to stroking out himself.

"He said something about base jumping or some shit like that. Austin's a little airport, man."

Base jumping.

Lord. Seb was an adrenaline junkie. They were two of a kind. Addicts all the way.

"Well, Jack, you talk to Bev. We'll work out a song list for today. Seb is a pro. He wouldn't leave without doing the work." There. See him. See him be all adult and coping and shit and not screaming like he wanted to.

Kyle nodded, headed over to him. "Shit okay, man?"

"No." He shrugged, gave Kyle a smile. "We got a little stupid, but it was so my fault." He didn't want Kyle telling him Seb was bad news or not worth it or whatever.

"Ah." Kyle's voice was knowing. "Well, still want to do this tour thing? Tawny can so get you out of it."

"No, this will be good for all of us, money-wise." He gave Kyle a shrewd look. "Doesn't Ali need braces or something?" He knew it was more than loyalty that kept Kyle out on the road with him, though he sure appreciated it.

"Yeah. Yeah, she does." Kyle sighed. "Is he crazy, man? Like for real?"

"No. No, he's just beaten down a little. You remember

how I was right before rehab?"

"Yeah. Yeah. And I know how that is. Sunglasses at night, skinny. It'll be worse on the road. Everything is worse."

"Like a microscope, yeah." He'd have to watch Seb, even if it was from a distance. "Thanks, man. I appreciate that you got my back."

"Always." And Kyle meant it.

It was Gator who growled. "Come on, you sheilas! Let's make some music!"

Markus shook off as much of his funk as he could. It wasn't fair of him to expect Seb to stay and make music with him when all it did was lead to them wanting other things. It was better this way, to focus on keeping it all business.

Right?

Right.

Chapter Six

Sebastian rolled into the Bellagio at noon. His rehearsal time with Markus was twelve-thirty to one-thirty, with six interviews planned between two and five, then the performance tonight at eight. He had a flight out to Cancun at midnight.

He had two weeks before he had to be back in the States for rehearsals and the tour; he was going to spend every second he had in the air or on the water.

Bev ran behind him, on her phone. "I want fresh pineapple delivered to his room, and I need a laundry service."

His head pounded, and he thought maybe it might fall off, especially if Bev's heels didn't stop click-click-clicking. He'd been to Jack's doctor this morning, explained that the pills weren't working anymore. He was tired, hurting, and grumpy, so the man had written a new prescription and given him a shot and a bunch of samples. Hopefully things would ease up, soon.

"Sebastian. So good of you to show." Jack was waiting for him, a sheaf of dailies for the interviews in hand.

"Fuck off, man." He did his job. Always. He'd never

missed a rehearsal, a recording, a show. Nothing.

"Here. Don't let that little chick from *Independent Songwriter* ask one question that's not on the sheet. She managed to twist John Stylie's words, even."

John Stylie was huge in Christian country, and was as clean as they came. That was talent, if a reporter could make him look bad.

"I'll be careful." He wasn't the rambling type, really.

"Seb, I know you're not stupid. I'm just warning you; she's a barracuda."

"Did you get Rick Wilder to run the tour on my side?" They were running two entire crews, one in front of the other and Markus had hired Gray Michaelson.

"I did. I got your memo." Jack pulled a cigar out of his pocket and started chomping on it, but didn't light it. "A damned memo. You used to call."

"I didn't have time." He didn't really care. He wanted to go sit somewhere and make music with someone that couldn't be around him anymore.

"Too busy surfing and jumping off bridges. Christ, Sebastian, you made the evening news two weeks ago."

"I did." And he'd do it again, in Mexico.

"Just don't break your neck." Jack cracked up. "Or anything more important."

"Not going to happen." And if it did, it did. "I have rehearsal, man. Anything else you need from me?"

"No. I'll see you at the production meeting. Bev has the schedule."

"Of course she does." He gave his best friend and the person he trusted most in the world a smile. "You ready to listen to music, girl?"

"You know it." She led him toward the auditorium. "I'm trying to get you a shake for after, okay?"

"Whatever. I'm good."

"No, you're not." Bev lowered her voice, her icy

eyes warming for him. "You've lost at least five pounds, Sebastian. You need to eat."

"Shh. I'm fine. Is my guitar here?"

"Both of your acoustics are. Your electrics are ready for rehearsal, but the others are in your room."

"Good girl." Then he asked what he really wanted to know. "Markus here?"

"Yes. He got in yesterday, did a walk through on the staging. He had two interviews this morning, but no one has seen him since." Trust Bev to be on top of everything.

"Thanks." He headed in, made it to the stage, nodded to Bruce. "Hey, hot shot. ?Como estas?"

"Good. Good. The set looks good. You want to do a walk-through?"

"Let's do it. The single sounds kick ass."

"I do like it." Bruce sounded like he didn't really want to like it.

"Cool. The family ready for you to be on the road?"

"Hell, yes. They're sick of me."

Sebastian cracked up, his laughter ringing out, echoing in the auditorium. The place had good sound. He liked it.

"Hey. Y'all ready to get going?" Markus looked.... tired. Still edible.

"Hey, Candy." He nodded, staying far enough away that Markus wouldn't think he was breaking the 'don't touch' rules.

"Good to see you, Seb." Markus was very deliberately not looking directly at him, which was probably good. Neither of them needed to be doing the hungry eyes thing.

"Yeah." He grabbed his guitar. "How do you want to do this?"

How would they manage to seem like friends without actually touching? Or looking at each other?

"I figure we've always done pretty well just winging it." Markus got his guitar, too, and maybe that would

Fighting Addiction

work. If they picked, they couldn't glad hand each other.

"Sure." He and Bruce worked the opening of *Old Flames and Fireworks*, the notes already familiar as breathing.

It took them a few tries to figure out when Markus ought to come in, but they got it going on in no time. They ironed out all the kinks way too fast for his taste.

Markus put his guitar down, nodded, and that was that.

"See you tonight, man. Bruce." He grabbed his stuff, making himself just focus on the business. He had interviews to do.

Sebastian wasn't sure how in hell they were going to do a whole tour this way, but that was a matter for after Mexico.

After some parachuting and some long days waterskiing.

Markus sat in his hotel room and stared at the glass sitting on the table. The thing was pretty and crystal and filled with two fingers worth of the best bourbon the hotel had on hand. He hadn't touched it since the room service man had left it on the table, but it was there and he knew it. If he never had to do another day like today, it would be too soon.

Three interviews, a radio station visit, rehearsal with Sebastian, where they couldn't even look at each other... Then the damned performance, where everything had been fucking perfect except that he couldn't look or touch or even smile or anything without worrying that what he was really feeling would show.

Goddamn, he hated being a big old ball of drama.

His phone rang, Seb's number coming up and he

70

frowned. What the fuck did the man want? Markus almost didn't answer, but before the last ring ended, he clicked the talk button. "Hello?"

"Hey. I didn't think you'd answer."

"I almost didn't. What's up, baby?"

"I'm going to Mexico. I need you to tell me we're going to survive the tour without you hating me. I know it's a pussy thing to need, but I do. I can't stop thinking about it and I've got to stop. It was good, in January, writing, us, and I'm not sorry for Austin, either." Jesus, was the man high?

Hell, who was he to at ask that question, even to himself, when he was sitting there with booze in his room for the first time in two years?

"I don't think I'm capable of hating you, Seb. I'm not. And you're right. It was damned good."

"It was. I'm sorry. I shouldn't call. I know, but we're friends. We were friends, once."

"We are friends." Damn it, they were. Even if they never had anything else. "I'm not sorry for what we did in Austin, but I'm sorry I sent you running. I miss you."

"I had to go. You know I did."

Yeah, he did know. They would have done it again. And again. It was addictive as hell. "I promise I'll be more human when we're on tour. We'll work out together and all."

"Me too. I won't be... naked." Seb sighed. "I'm going to Mexico to stay out of trouble."

Markus laughed. "Stay in one piece, too. Okay? I saw how you almost broke your neck on your last trip."

"Yeah. That was totally fun." Seb's chuckle made him smile, eased something in his chest.

"You're a nut." He eased back in his chair, staring at the ceiling. "I might go to Galveston."

"Go get tan. Ogle mostly naked rednecks. Eat shrimp."

"Yeah. Not too many photographers and shit, either. People don't expect guys like us in Galveston." That sounded better and better, in fact. He did love to swim in the ocean.

"There you go. I'll draw the press, you relax. Sounds perfect. You flying during the tour or bussing it?"

"Depends on what other commitments we have at the time. I'll be on the bus, mostly. You?" It was good just to talk, not have to worry about the physical stuff.

"I'm bussing it. All the way. Hell, that bus is my home here in the States."

"Bev said." He wished Seb would commit to a condo, at least. It seemed weird to be so rootless. "I told Kyle I'd fly him home for Ali's birthday. Bruce is welcome to go with him."

"I let Bruce deal with his shit, the band. As long as they show up for rehearsal and shows, I don't mess with them."

"Well, I'll let him know when I see him." Markus had always been a little more hands-on with the band. Hell, maybe it was because they all had wives and kids and the shit he was supposed to have, so he got it vicariously.

"That's cool. They liked working with you. Hell, I bet some of them defect."

He hooted at the thought. Seb was riding the wave; no one would defect on the man. He was pure gold.

"Uh-huh. I'll be lucky if Kyle doesn't poison your Kerry so he can come in full time on the Horsemen."

"Shit, man. Kyle loves you almost as much as he loves potato chips."

"Oh, God. Don't say those words in front of him. He's still trying to convince himself that apple slices taste just as good." Markus knew better. The substitute was never as good as what you actually wanted.

"You have my word. No potato chips." Seb's laugh

made him grin. "Have a good night, Candy. It was good to see you."

"It was good to see you, too, baby. See you again in a few weeks, huh?"

They didn't linger over their goodbyes, and he was glad. Seb hung up before he could say anything really stupid, and Markus stretched, rolling his head on his neck before he got up to grab that glass of bourbon on the table.

He didn't even take so much as a sniff before he took it right to the bathroom and poured it down the sink.

Chapter Seven

Seb flew into Houston and rented a car, hitting Baton Rouge to say hi to his sister, then heading to Nashville for a few days of rehearsal. He parked the convertible in the hotel lot, texted Bev to let her know he'd managed to not kill himself, and then let the bellman take him up to the penthouse.

He needed a nap.

The penthouse smelled nice, like lemons and pineapple, and he pondered a shake. Bev would have left them in the fridge.

Nah. Nap first. He wasn't real hungry.

There was a sheaf of papers on the table, and his schedule would be on his phone. Seb managed to get his shoes off before he collapsed, the alarm on his phone set for three.

When it went off, he could hear someone moving around the suite. "If that's not you, Bev, I'm going to rip your face off."

"It's me. Jack's calling. He wants to see you. The band is ready for you at six. You have to eat."

He did love the organized little bitch.

"Tell Jack I will see him at four-thirty. Here. I'm tired of driving. Tell Bruce to come up at five-thirty. You got the rehearsal area ready? And what about Rick Wilder? When is our first meeting? I don't want any surprises on tour." He sat up, scratched his belly. "I need laundry done and a waxing appointment with Michelle."

"Got it. I'll make the calls. Your shake is ready."

"You're obsessed with feeding me."

"You're scary skinny, Seb. Like, whoa." She pushed the shake into his hand.

His mouth flattened into a thin line. He was sick to death of everyone from Jack to Bev to the press being obsessed with his weight. It wasn't like he was a supermodel or something. He grimaced, but he drank the damned thing,

"Thank you." She was actually staring at him with this hurt deer look, like she thought he'd keel over.

"Do you need to get laid or something?"

"What? No! I'm worried about you." The nascent tears dried up, and Bev whapped his arm.

"I'm fine. You don't think I'm a stud? What? Are you gay?" He flexed, pranced around like a gold-plated idiot, just cracking Bev up.

"Idiot." She sniffed and chuckled at the same time. "I'll go call Jack and get Bruce on the rehearsal."

"Good girl. I'm going to holler at Kane, see if the lazy son of a bitch is ready to work yet." He grabbed his bag with his laptop, plugged in his phone, and dialed Markus.

"Hey. You made it in one piece, huh?"

Bev slipped out just after Markus answered, so he could sprawl and talk.

"I did. The evil bitch woman already invoked Jack's name and fed me."

"Good for her. Helen wanted to come to Nashville with me. She says I'm not eating well."

They got a good chuckle out of that. Markus could flat out eat.

"You didn't gain forty pounds in Galveston did you? All those shrimp." He did enjoy teasing Mr. Hard Abs.

"Nope. She just thinks I ate too much fried stuff. Wants to feed me turkey burgers and salad."

"Ew." Just the thought made him gag a little.

"I know, right?" Markus' chuckle warmed his belly. "Man, I'm ready to get to work."

"Rehearsals tonight at six. I meet with Jack at four-thirty, Bruce an hour after that. You want to show up then?"

"Hell, yes. I'll bring Kyle. He'll want the extra time."

"Cool. Looking forward to it. Did you get the schedule and everything? The first eight shows are sold out."

"No shit?" He could hear Markus drinking and could just imagine that tanned throat working. Yum. "Well, go us."

"Yep. Money, money." Speaking of... He stretched, logged on and moved some money around. He liked having bits that Jack didn't know about. God knew there wasn't much.

"Yeah. Tawny likes that. I've squirreled away enough that I'm more about the fans. Hey, who did they get opening?"

"You got that guy you asked for—that Houston McMann?" Sebastian liked his shit well enough. "Fancy, that sister group? They're in for me."

"That will appeal to both our crowds." Markus yawned. "Okay, baby. I need a twenty minute nap."

"Have a good one. I'll see you at five-thirty." He clicked the phone off, got to work organizing shit that he needed to deal with. Like putting a new Stairmaster on his bus.

Markus watched Sebastian run through his set, which was full of fifteen years worth of amazing songwriting, tons of great musicians, and lots of flat-out running around the stage. It was their first full-length rehearsal, and Markus' first chance to sit back and just watch Sebastian perform. Markus was quickly learning two things: Seb was still a damned fine singer, and the man was too damned skinny by far.

After a week of staging and working with the openers and arguing with Bruce and Kyle and Rick Wilder, the tour manager, they were all getting in a groove, and Markus had lost two pounds. Seb, though, he looked like he'd lost another five, and that was five pounds the man couldn't spare.

Markus was beginning to see why the press were poking at Seb's weight every time they wrote an article.

The entire show was frenetic, Seb going and going, running from one end of the guitar-shaped stage to the other, the band trying their damnedest to keep up.

Tawny plopped down beside him, solid and red-headed and fierce. "You sounded great, hon. Solid as hell. And you look amazing."

"Thanks." He tried not to preen, but Markus knew he was fitting into jeans he hadn't worn since his twenties.

"He's like a bunny out there." Tawny's lips twisted. "I hate to be catty, but... Is he sick, hon? Like AIDS or something?"

"No." The word was instinctive, and came out strong. "No, he's just not eating well, you know? Bev is working with him." Damn. If Tawny thought Seb was looking too skinny it was serious.

"Oh, good. That would suck so hard." Tawny grinned, winked. "I have all his albums, but you know that."

Yeah, Tawny had kicked herself in the ass for missing that meeting with Seb way back at the beginning, leaving a young singer primed for Jack to sink claws into him.

"I know. He wasn't so scared of you, I'd set up lunch or something." He winked, and she thumped his chest, right above his nipple. "Ow!"

They cracked up, then looked at the stage. Seb was on his knees, humping the air, the movement natural and blisteringly hot.

They both groaned.

Tawny gave him a sideways glance. "You gotta watch that, Scooter." She'd called him "Scooter" since their first meeting. Markus had never known why. He didn't take offense to the other, though. He'd come out to Tawny right after he went into rehab, told her all about him and Seb.

"I know. I am. I'm not going to screw up."

"I know. I hate this bullshit." She didn't mean Seb; she meant hiding and lying.

Markus reached for her hand, squeezing it. She was a tough broad, but she was also pretty much his best friend. "Thanks for having my back, honey."

"Until the day I die, Scooter." She kissed his cheek, leaning against him, watching Seb sweat and dance.

It was easier to be... objective when Tawny was there. To just watch and love Seb's aesthetic.

And God knew he loved that man's... look. A lot.

Even if it was too damned skinny.

Sebastian settled into his bus, moaning in pure bliss.

Everything was perfect in his little home on the road. Paul, his driver, had no access to him from the cab; Seb had cable, exercise equipment, his bed, pillows, and a hot tub.

They were opening with the show here in Nashville, then heading out.

The band was tight, the set list was perfect, and he was ready. Hell, if nothing else, he could sit for an hour every night and watch Candy sing. In fact, he totally intended to. Every night. He stroked the ink worked in over his cock, like he was playing his skin.

He'd written *Silent Love* seven years ago, put it out under a pseudonym and, when Markus had recorded it, it had gone platinum. He was an idiot, but it was his love song to Candy, even though no one would ever know. There had been times, during rehearsal, when he'd thought about asking Candy to sing it for him, but that would have been a dead giveaway. When Markus had added it to the playlist for his encore, it had been like a wet dream come true.

Acoustic. Simple. It was perfect and Sebastian got to see it, every show.

Sighing, he tugged his cock a little, thinking about how Markus closed his eyes on that last, long note. About how the man meant every word when he sang it. Some days he let himself pretend that Markus knew, that the words were real. The memories.

He had to stop this.

Rolling up, he headed for the stair climber. He was about to step on when his phone rang. "'lo?"

"Hey, man. Looks like we're making good time today." Markus sounded damned cheerful. "You got a half hour you can spare me before we get to work? I have a hook I want to run by you."

"You know it. I'll pop over." He didn't allow people on his bus.

"Sure. Thanks, ba--" Markus stopped mid-baby. They'd talked on how it was a bad idea for Candy to call him that. "Thanks."

"Yeah. I gotta run, man. Bye."

"Later."

He put his phone down and stepped on the stair climber. Time to run and sweat and stop thinking.

Please God.

Chapter Eight

Markus was pumped. And sweaty. The first night out on the tour was usually full of headaches, but those worked themselves out in the opening acts, and the sound guys adjusted for him like a dream. Song after song had rolled out and the fans had screamed just like they were there to see him, not Seb. Jesus, that had made him feel ten feet tall and able to climb mountains. He knew he should go clean up for the end of the show, but he waited the twenty minutes until Seb came on. He had damned near two hours; he wanted to see what Seb was doing for his opening, really see it, not just the walk through.

The lights went down, the opening strains of *Cajun Cowboy* started up, and then Seb appeared from the floor, riding what looked like a huge alligator. Show off. The alligator started bucking a little, and that made Markus cackle like a fool, startling the burly security guy he stood next to. He was going to have to see if he could get a feed on his bus or something. He might need privacy to watch Seb's show.

The music sounded tight, the crowd was screaming,

Seb's voice was rocking—Markus could admit that the man put on one hell of a show. There were surfboards and BMX bikes and stuff all over, the extreme sports theme heavy this year. It was like a bizarre cross between those X Games things and a concert. It suited Seb to the ground.

The megatron lit up and the cameraman zoomed in as Seb was doing his "Hey, Nashville" speech and Markus frowned.

Jesus.

Was Seb wearing contacts?

Markus sure as hell hoped so. Those eyes were... wow. Seb's pupils weren't quite pinpoints, but they were small, and Seb's eyes twitched like he was looking for a predator. Somebody needed to back off whatever diet pills he was on. The only thing that had that kind of reaction was speed, right?

He watched Seb move across the stage, jogging and sweating, singing his heart out. The man looked flat-out amazing, but he also looked a little out of breath. Markus made a mental note to ask about how much caffeine was in those shakes. The camera zoomed in again, on Seb's hand, which was shaking the littlest bit. Lord knew the man didn't get scared out there.

Markus frowned. He'd wait and see how Seb was by the end of the show.

They still had to work out the weird-ass jam sessions that happened at three in the morning. Kyle was going to have a breakdown. Markus had thought about having one, too. It was just the craziest schedule ever. Hell, he'd even bothered to look up whether people could live like that, sleeping just a few hours. Markus was pretty sure it was unhealthy as hell.

Apparently he'd started muttering, because the security guy was giving him the fish eye and moving away. Markus shook his head, turning and heading back to the dressing room Tawny had gotten set up for them. The last thing he needed to do was draw anyone else's attention to Seb's weird little things.

There was a huge bouquet of white roses, a dozen Round Rock doughnuts, and a six-pack of Barqs root beer sitting there waiting for him.

God, Tawny was a doll. A pain in his butt, but a good woman.

Markus inhaled three doughnuts, knowing he had to scarf a bunch of them before Kyle checked in. He worked off enough on concert days to eat half of that dozen and not gain a pound.

He looked at his wardrobe choices for the encore. Jeans, naturally, but... white T-shirt? Black? The hat went without saying. He was wearing his summer straw...

Seb was in a wife-beater, bright red, so he'd go with white, mess with the camera man's balance a little bit. Those guys got bored.

Grinning, he toweled off, got his shirt off, and put some more deodorant on. Old Spice had never led him wrong. He was contemplating a nap when Kyle knocked and came barreling in like a freight train.

"Doughnut. Stat," Kyle grumbled, grabbing a pastry and stuffing half of it in his mouth.

"How many Weight Watchers points is that, man?"

Kyle flipped him off and grabbed another one, getting through two-thirds of it before slowing down. "Oh, God. I've never been so hungry, man. I get like a thousand exercise points for the show."

Rule number eighty-four: Don't mess with a dude and his doughnut.

Markus held his hands up. "Eat up. We have what? Another twenty minutes?"

Kyle nodded. "Something like that, yeah. He'll go off

stage, do his one encore song and then we're up again."

"Cool." Markus grinned. "You need to change your shirt."

Kyle glanced over at him. "You need to put one on. And wax, for God's sake."

He rubbed his chest, grinning wider. "You don't like it? I'm not sure the waxed-like-a-surfboard look is for me."

"So, what, you're going for gorilla?" Kyle ducked his half-hearted swing, grabbed one last doughnut, and fled.

Markus glanced down, tugged at the curls right under his bellybutton and winced. Yeah. No. No waxing. He'd leave that for Seb.

That thought had him thumping his cock before he pulled that white T-shirt on. He didn't have time for the hard-on right now.

He had to go do the best fucking job on earth.

Seb landed on his dressing room sofa like a hooked fish while they waited for the crowds to disperse. Christ almighty, that had been good. Exhausting and sweaty and if he didn't get a pill and a bottle of water and a bath, he might die, but good.

His muscles jerked and burned, the energy slowly seeping out of him enough that he could feel his fingers again. He didn't have the energy to holler when the door opened and someone slipped into the room with him, even. It wasn't Bev. Old Spice and the clack of boot heels.

Candy.

"Good show." He lifted one hand, waved, let it fall.

"Fantastic fucking show, man. You rocked it out." Candy stopped about three feet from the couch.

"Thanks." He squinted a little. "My shades over there, man?"

The lights were murderous.

"You bet." Markus grabbed them for him, handing them over, their fingers not quite touching. "Good job on *Dodging Bullets*, man. That really got the crowd."

"I love that one. I didn't get to see enough of your set, but I could hear the fans."

"It was pretty damned great. They sang all the songs." Candy bit his lip, which always meant he was working up to pointing out the bad now that he'd gone through the good. They did this after every show back in the day, tearing it apart. "I got to ask something, ba—Seb."

"Go for it. Was I flat?"

"No. No, you're Mr. Perfect Pitch, and you know it." Sighing, Markus shook his head. "Are you on diet pills?"

Oh, for fuck's sake. "Quit reading the fucking tabloids." He wasn't on any goddamn diet pills.

"Well, then, tell me what's going on." Finally settling on a stool he pulled over from the bar, Markus stared at him. "Your eyes are all messed up, and you've got the shakes."

"The meds make my eyes sensitive to the light, man, but they're not diet pills. Dr. Norman gives them to me." Antidepressants and stuff to help him focus, keep him clear-headed and from wasting his time.

"You were out of breath a couple of times, too." When he opened his mouth to growl, Markus held up both hands. "I'm just saying what it looks like on the Jumbo-Tron, man."

"They just upped my dosage in the last day or so. It's always hard. No stress." He needed it. Markus and his doughnuts and nine hours of sleep was just going to have to deal. Damn it.

Candy tilted his head, but didn't say anything else. Not about that, anyway. "I think we need to streamline the staging between openers."

"I talked to Rick about that. I want your band set up in the back behind Fancy, then my guys can set up quick while you're working it."

"Sounds good. You're the brains, baby." Markus winked, which just made him stare. Stupidly. The man was so fucking hot. So fine. He wanted to tackle the big son of a bitch and just lick and suck and rub.

Markus cleared his throat, cheeks hot. "Uh. Any tips for me?"

"Either lift your head up or tell the camera men to shoot lower. Your face is never on the big screen."

"No shit?" Markus shook his head. "I do work the hat too much, huh?"

"That and you pay a lot of attention to the kids on the floor." He was sensitive to that one because he'd been called on it. A lot.

"Oh, hell. I never even thought of that. I've never had a stage set-up quite like this." Nodding, Markus rolled his head on his neck. "Thanks."

"You know it." He stretched, wincing as his sweaty shirt pulled. "You okay?"

"Just wore out, I think. You okay?"

"Sweaty. I hate this part—waiting to go to my bus, shower, jack off. You know, let all this go somewhere."

"I..." Those dark eyes dipped to his crotch. "You know it."

"You guys want to jam with us tonight? We go from three to six." It was a bonding thing. A safer bonding thing than he wanted. He wanted to bond with a certain hard body.

Sebastian. Stop it.

"I'll bet Kyle sleeps tonight, but I'll sit in." Markus actually looked surprised.

"Yeah? It's more fun than you'd think. We call it rehearsal, but it's a jam session."

"Then I'm in." That grin was megawatt.

"Bring your guitar to the band's bus when we stop at three." There would be coffee, laughter, and music.

"I can do that." Markus stood, stretching a moment.

He let himself admire, knowing Markus couldn't see his eyes. "You glad to be on the road again?"

"I am. It's weird, to be without the band, you know? But it's good."

Seb nodded. He'd seen how choked up Markus had gotten singing *West Texas Town*. It had been the man's first hit, and the guys in the band had all been there for it. You got into a groove with the band, and Markus hadn't hit that with his new guys yet.

"It'll happen for you. Abe loves you already." He thought that Kerry and Jonny were considering jumping ship. Of course, Bruce thought Kerry might be pregnant, too.

"I know. The best part of the night is being onstage with you."

"Hell, yes." There was nothing like that—playing and singing, touching each other easily, the screaming crowd, the lights. It was sex, but better, because it could be real.

"I guess the buses will be ready, huh?" Markus shifted from foot to foot, looking restless as hell.

He looked at the clock. "Ten minutes or so, yeah. Bev will let me know. You want me to get security to walk you to yours?"

"No. No, I just don't want to bug you, baby. I know you like to decompress. I couldn't sit in my dressing room anymore, though."

"So sit, dork. We're friends, for fuck's sake. Have a fucking piece of pineapple, and we'll watch cartoons on the TV."

Markus could be so fucking complicated.

Blinking, Markus chuckled, then came to sit on the

couch. "I wonder if Bev could bring me a sandwich."

"Shit. Bev could bring you an entire cow dressed like a platter of fried chicken. What kind do you want?" He grabbed his phone, hit 'Boss'.

"Moo." Then Markus' eyes lit up. "Fried chicken."

"Hey, lady. The hairy-monkey redneck wants fried chicken."

"You got it," Bev said without missing a beat. "Breast or thighs?"

"Bring both and he doesn't like the weird gravy on his potatoes."

"Cole slaw?"

Man, he'd forgotten how complicated food was.

"No, just biscuits."

Markus grabbed the remote, started looking for something, a goofy grin on his face.

"Anything for you, honey? Something?"

He shook his head. "I'm not hungry."

"Okay. Okay. You—you have pineapple, right?"

"I do." He grinned, not even looking.

"Okay. I'm on it." She hung up, and he knew it would be less than fifteen minutes.

"Thanks," Markus murmured, settling on some pawn shop show.

"Have you seen the one set in Alexandria? That main guy looks just like my Uncle Beau."

"No shit? He always had the best hair."

"Still does. I went to see Maman a few months ago and me and Beau chatted." Maman didn't know him from Job, really, not anymore. It had been a couple of years since the dementia had taken her away. He sent money to Sister to keep her comfortable and happy and just stayed away, and Uncle Beau was local and all, so he knew she was being taken care of.

It confused her to see him and hurt his heart to see her like that.

Markus didn't ask how Maman was, and he was grateful. They just moved on. "I always liked Beau when he came to the show. Did I tell you who called wanting an interview? Wacey Carrol. You remember him? The guy from that rodeo show we did back at the beginning?"

"No shit? I was at his place... oh, shit. Three years ago? Four? He taught me how to ride bulls." Well, tried to. Sebastian broken his wrist, his collarbone, and his ankle before the label stepped in.

"Adrenaline junkie." He got an elbow in the ribs, sharp as anything, those long old arms covering the distance between them.

"Uh-huh. I seem to remember you damn near losing a thumb playing high school roper."

"What?" That gimme cap dipped to shade Markus' eyes just like the cowboy hat did during concerts. "I have no idea what you're talking about."

"Uh-huh. You can bullshit some of the people..."

"Oh, fuck you." Markus dug into Seb's ribs again

He cracked up. "You wish, redneck."

"Of course I do." Markus gave him a noogie before sitting up.

That made him grin. "Lord, look at that car, man. Can you imagine how fast that little thing goes?"

By the time Bev showed with Markus' dinner, they were fighting over the price of an anti-tank gun and planning to race speedboats in Florida.

Bev knocked and slipped in holding a bag. "Fried chicken, no weird gravy potatoes, and biscuits. I also brought iced tea. Here's your vitamins, Sebastian."

"Thanks, honey." He took the handful with some tea. "You see the show?"

"I did. You were great. Both of you."

"Thank you. You've told the drivers to..."

"Stop at three and at six. Yes, Seb. I know."

"It's important."

"I've got your back." She smiled, pushing her hair off her face. She was looking less put-together every day. Must be Candy's influence. "Anything else?"

"No, honey. Tomorrow we're in... Memphis? Get some sleep."

"Thanks." She looked tired, her ass dragging a little when she left.

Markus held up the bag of chicken. "You want me to go eat this somewhere else, right?"

"Why? I'm not hungry. Go for it." He didn't hate food; he just didn't eat it.

"I wasn't sure. Bev kinda led me to believe you'd have a fit if faced with real food." Sitting back, Markus opened the bag and pulled out a biscuit. "Tawny would have my hide for this."

"So long as you don't try to feed it to me or pull it on me in the mornings, I'm good." They should all have Markus' metabolism.

"Well, I won't say I don't wish you would have a bite." The other biscuit went next.

"I'll get fat." He had the shakes, the pineapple.

"Bullshit. You're all bone." This time when Markus touched his ribs it was gentle, almost tickly.

"That's because I'm on the diet." He stretched, the pills kicking in again, waking him up.

"Why?" The potatoes disappeared in three spoonfuls.

"Why what?" He stood up, got some water, a piece of pineapple. Itchy. God, the new dose made him a little itchy.

Frowning, Markus munched a chicken strip. "Why are you on a diet?"

"Because I get pudgy in the middle." He sucked down the bottle of water.

"I've seen you do crunches."

"Every fucking day, man." They were his warm up.

"I know. So don't bullshit me." Markus polished off the last chicken.

"I have to do it." He shrugged. "It's a thing."

It made him feel in control of a life that moved too fast to see.

"Well, I guess I can see that." Right. Markus appeared pretty dubious. Still, if anyone had no room to talk it was Mr. Rehab.

"If everyone would pay attention to their own damned pants size, they'd stop ragging on me."

"Well, unlike the press, Bev and I are just worried, baby." Markus leaned over and gave him a short, hard kiss on the mouth before getting up and heading for the door. "I'll see you at three. I'm willing to lose sleep for you."

"Then I'm a lucky son of a bitch." Although Sebastian knew it was for the music.

It was always for the music.

Chapter Nine

The music was still throbbing in his ears when he went looking for Sebastian. They'd been jamming on the band's bus, but they weren't leaving at six, since they had three days before the next concert. No, they were letting all of the crew have a breather until nine, and Markus figured that was the perfect time to beard the lion in his den. They'd done three and a half weeks of shows, and Markus had finally gotten to sit and watch Seb's show all the way through again for the first time in ages.

Jesus, the big screen was brutal.

Sebastian looked like a fucking famine victim. His eyes were all iris, no pupil to be seen, and every time the man ran from one end of stage to another, he looked like he was fixing to have a heart attack.

Then there was the phone call. He'd answered Tawny on the first ring, because she never called at six in the morning.

"Yeah?"

"I knew you were up. You need to talk to Seb," she'd barked, no hello, no good morning, nothing.

"About what?" Markus had put her on speaker because his ears fucking hurt, and he was shoveling a fruit salad up like there was no tomorrow.

"I got a call after the show. Reporter working on a project for *Country Expose*. Wanted a quote about Seb's weight loss and alleged drug use."

Markus stopped with the fork halfway to his mouth. "What did you say?"

"Told him my quote was 'fuck off' and called Jack. Wanna know what Jack told me?"

God, he could imagine. "Fuck off?"

"Pretty much. People are noticing, though, Markus. Lots of people. I did a vanity search online. It's a trend."

"I'll talk to him," Markus had murmured before hanging up and heading for Seb's personal space.

It was time to reverse the fucking trend.

Markus knocked sharply on the door of the bus.

"Bev, go back to bed and leave me be. I don't want another fucking SHAKE!"

He knocked again, knowing Seb would come up to scream if he still thought it was still Bev. The man was notorious about not letting anyone on the bus.

The door was thrown open, Seb's face bright red. "I said no, Bev!"

Markus shouldered his way into the bus, making Seb stumble up the stairs backward. "We need to talk."

"What the fuck? I don't... What are you doing?" Seb's bus was like a fucking guitar museum slash gym.

"I said we need to talk." He reached over and tugged the ever-present sunglasses off Seb's face. "Look at your eyes, baby. You're high as a kite."

"Hey!" Seb grabbed for his glasses. "What the fuck? What is your fucking issue?"

"My fucking issue is that someone called Tawny for a quote about your drug use. She tried to call Jack, but he

93

told her to fuck off." He caught Seb's wrist when the man made another grab.

"Drug use? What the fuck are you talking about? There's no fucking illegal shit on this bus!"

"I never said you were doing illegal. I'm sure your speed is prescription." So frustrated he could spit, Markus shook Seb's arm a little. "Press people are talking, baby. It's only a matter of time before we have a problem." He should fucking know.

"Get out. You don't have a fucking problem." He knew the look on Seb's face; that was panic.

"Oh, fuck that. What are you doing, baby? What's going on? You're gonna kill yourself." He held on when Seb started struggling, just determined to help. Something.

"You don't fucking get it! The old dose wasn't working! I'm fucking tired!"

"Well, maybe you should fucking sleep!" He got right in Seb's face, shouting back.

"There's no TIME!" Seb snarled and tugged away, heading back, deeper in the bus, and he'd be damned if the little fucker didn't go for those fucking pill bottles. No. No way. They were fucking talking, and Seb was high enough.

He slapped the bottle out of Seb's hand, tiny pills flying, hitting the wall, the floor, clattering in the sink like little teeth.

Bright green eyes flashed up at him. "You can't do that!"

"I just did. You're dealing with me now, not them."

"Them? Dealing with you? You, who can't even bear to let me stay in the same house as you! You can't trust me enough to... Get off my fucking bus!" Seb grabbed him, shook him hard and tried to drag him down the hallway, and the tiny fuck was stronger than he looked. Good thing Markus was in the best shape of his life.

And bigger.

"I'm not leaving until you talk to me." He wrapped Seb in a bear hug, mainly in self defense. Little shit could hit hard.

"Talk to you about what? What the fuck do you *want*?"

"I want to know what's happening to you! You're so OCD you've stopped eating! This is crazy."

"Don't call me crazy. That's what the pills are for! To help!" Seb stared at him. "Lay off about my weight. I know exactly what I weigh, you asshole!"

"Yeah?" His lip curled. "Well, it's not helping." He was so fucking worried about Seb that he couldn't be nice. Not now. Not with the man he'd fucking been in love with for ten years turning into a zombie in front of him and twenty thousand fans.

"Fuck you, you sanctimonious prick. It must be fucking nice to lay off the booze for a few months and then suddenly be at your fighting weight and perfectly goddamn happy! Some of us have to work a little harder at keeping it together!"

"Lay off the..." Markus saw red at that. The only thing he was more addicted to in the world besides the booze was Sebastian. Roaring, he pushed Seb back into the bus, sending the little fuck flying, staggering back to land on the cushy couch he'd had custom installed. Seb came flying up off the sofa, launching himself at Markus, like a waxed, hysterical, skinny torpedo. He hit like a ton of bricks, and Markus grunted, lifting Seb up off the floor, those strong legs kicking. "I swear to God, I will beat you senseless."

"You'll fucking try. You watch out, Candy. You might start touching me and then where the fuck would you be?"

"Jesus Christ. You think I don't want to every

day?" He forgot what they were fighting about, forgot everything but the feel of Sebastian's body against his. Seb wanted to know what he'd do if they started touching? Markus would show him. He mashed his mouth down on Sebastian's lips, taking the kiss he'd needed for weeks.

Seb cried out, fingers digging into his shoulders, hard enough to leave bruises. Like he was going to back off, back down. Not this fucking time. No way.

Little fuck, pushing him. Always pushing. Markus was about to push back. Hard.

"Get the fuck out of my bus." Seb growled the words against his mouth, then shoved back into the kiss.

"No." The word was muffled, but Markus meant it. He wasn't leaving. Not this time. He tore at Seb's tank top, the soft sweats.

He wanted to feel, damn it. He wanted to hear Seb scream. He wanted fucking access. Those ribs stood out a little too much, and he could feel Seb's heart beating way too fast, but he didn't stop. Didn't care.

"You've lost your motherfucking mind." Seb bit his bottom lip, hard enough that the sting made him growl.

He pushed the move, making Seb bounced on the couch, then climbed up to straddle that strong little body, his hips pressing down against Seb's. "Just hold still, would you?

"I can't." No, he could feel those muscles jerking and twitching, moving against him.

"Yes, you can." He lowered his chest to rest on Seb's, holding the man down. He wanted Seb to stop, to breathe with him, and this seemed so natural.

"Stop it." Seb took a deep, deep breath as they stopped there.

"No." He couldn't. His cock ached, but that was the least of it, really. His whole self needed Seb like a drug. He pressed Seb's hands up above the man's head, loving the stretch and pull of those lean muscles.

Seb arched under him, a deep sound filling the air as their skin slid together. Fuck, yes. Just stop for a fucking second and feel. His eyes rolled a little, and he bent to kiss that mouth again. He drank deep. Sweet bastard. Every time Seb tried to move, he bore down, squeezing Seb's wrists.

Seb kicked a little, but Markus held him down, his cock burning against the cloth of his sweats. There was an answering hardness poking at his belly, telling him that he wasn't alone in this.

Of course, need was never their problem. Never. Markus levered up just enough to pull off clothes. When Seb tried to slip out from under him, he pushed back down, keeping Seb trapped in place.

"Markus. Candy. We..."

"Shut up, baby. We are." He was fucking tired of lying, of not taking what he needed.

Hell, he was tired of not giving his lover what Seb needed, and Seb needed him. Now. He bit a little, down on Seb's shoulder, right where the tank top would sit.

"Fuck." Those lean muscles rolled, body bucking beneath him. "Markus."

"Uh-huh. I want, baby. I want so bad." They were skin to skin, his cock in the hollow of Seb's hip. Every time Seb pushed, he bore down, not letting Seb run the show.

"You're just going to feel guilty after. You regret me."

"No." His hand tightened around Seb's wrist. "I regret not brazening it out when we had the chance. That's the only damned thing I regret, baby."

Seb groaned low, body slamming up into him, slapping their skin together. The sound was insanely rhythmic, almost like the bass line of a song. Oh, fuck. A song.

He looked around the couch area, trying to find

something to hold Seb's hands. He wanted to investigate those tattooed musical notes.

Markus grabbed Seb's tank top, wrapped it around the man's wrists before Seb figured out what he was doing. That was perfect. The fabric stretched but it didn't let Seb put his arms down. That way Markus could slide down, his teeth closing on one flat little nipple. Seb offered him a little squeak, a groan, but the lean torso arched up against his mouth. So sweet, the way every move got a hot reaction, a sound or a slide of muscle under skin. This was about pleasure now, not power. Well, maybe a little power.

Maybe a little of both wouldn't hurt anything at all.

When he was done nipping at Seb's chest, he moved lower, pressing sucking kisses to Seb's too-flat belly.

"Don't, Candy..."

Oh, no. No. He was tired of stop and wait and don't. It was time to do. Definitely. He pushed down, chin rubbing Seb's hip, the low light almost too little to see the tats.

He hummed the opening bar, frowning as he recognized the tune. *Silent Love.*

That was his biggest hit, not Seb's.

Markus pondered that for a moment, tracing the notes with his fingers. Seb went still under him, barely breathing, and Markus closed his eyes. It was definitely time to stop fighting this, no matter what came of it.

"Candy. I."

"Shh." He rubbed his cheek along Seb's hard cock, letting his stubble drag. "It's okay, baby. Just stop and feel." He turned his head, licking that hard cock from base to tip.

Seb made the tiniest sound, belly flushing a deep red. It was hot as all hell, the way those little tremors shook Seb's body, the way Seb's heartbeat throbbed under his tongue. Fuck, that was his. This man was fucking meant for him to love on.

He licked, then sucked for a moment, just at the head. This was just the warm up. Seb's legs spread, knees drawing up sweet as pie. That was an invitation he couldn't resist. He turned his head, biting one thigh.

"Fuck you. You can't just come in here and make me need you."

Oh, he so could. "I don't need to make you, baby. You want me, anyway." He bit again, licking to ease the sting.

That sweet cock was proof enough, that song, inked into Seb's skin. Markus moaned, licking his way down Seb's thigh, heading for the heavy balls. All that bare skin was erotic as hell.

Seb sobbed for him, rocked, damn near dancing, pushing under his mouth.

Markus pushed at Seb's balls with his tongue, moving them in their sac. He'd dreamed about this fine body for months. Now he got to explore. There was a tiny scar over one hipbone, a smooth place underneath that made Seb jump and gasp. Markus liked that, so he nipped at it, wanting more reaction. Fuck, he wanted to leave his mark, so he bit down, letting his teeth sink in, bear down, and Seb cried out, the sound like the best crescendo. Seb fought him a little, but it was a weak attempt. More for show than anything, he'd bet.

Didn't stop him from slapping Seb's hip. "Stop it."

"Hey!" Oh, that made somebody growly.

"I said stop it." He did it again, just because it felt good and it made Seb's cock bounce. They'd never played this game, but Markus thought it was a damned good idea.

"You fucker. You can't do that." Seb's eyes were burning down at him, lips parted, a dull flush climbing up that ripped belly. The man hadn't ever been so fucking hot.

Ever.

"You think so, baby?" Oh, that was a say I won't moment if he'd ever needed one. Kneeling up, he flipped Sebastian over, so that fine, tiny ass was up, Seb's arms still hampered by the tank top wrapped around them. He pulled back and smacked Seb's ass so hard it stung his hand. Jesus, his hand was big enough it almost covered Seb's ass, and he'd be damned if Seb didn't arch up, back bowing to offer him more. His belly went tight, and he smacked Seb again, then again, needing to feel, needing the tingle and the heat of it.

His mouth was dry, his eyes feeling like they were burning in his skull. Seb danced under him, moans like music on the air.

Jesus fuck, he... how had he walked away from this?

Markus groaned, tongue rasping over his lips, and Seb surged back, ass meeting his hand this time, humping up toward him.

It was like the best kind of rhythm, his hand on that skin. It sent little shocks up his arm, all the way to his shoulder. He was moaning, too, his cock throbbing, balls aching with it. Not that he could stop. He just couldn't. His hand kept moving, his palm and fingers on fire, Seb's ass taking on a rosy glow.

"Markus... Please. Please, man. I'm so fucking close." Seb's thighs spread, the offer clear as day.

"I know, baby. I'm not sure I'll make it." If he could find a rubber, that might keep him honest, keep him from blowing the moment he slid inside Seb's body.

His fingers trailed over Seb's ass and the man cried out, jerked hard under him, that skin burning hot. "Please!"

"I need stuff, baby. Where do you keep it?"

"My bedroom. It's all in there."

A bed sounded like a perfect fucking idea. Markus levered up off the couch and hauled Seb up, arm around the lean waist. It took no effort to carry the man, and only a little to keep from bumping them into things.

Seb's bedroom was a wreck, blankets tangled, pillows strewn everywhere. It sort of made Markus feel better, like maybe Seb could live here. He tossed Seb down on the bed and started digging, watching out of the corner of his eye as Sebastian tried to free his hands.

He found a stash of rubbers and slick about the time Seb got a hand free. It seemed to take Seb a second to decide whether to reach for him, reach for the hand that was still caught up, or reach down for that fat, dripping cock.

The decision was really his, so Markus pushed Seb's hand back up above his head, bearing down on that beautiful body again. "Spread, baby. Let me in."

"Oh, fuck." Seb nodded, legs going wide, so eager, so fucking hot for him.

His fingers fumbled with the little tube of lube, but he got it open, got enough out to get Seb ready for him. He touched that tight little hole, circled it once before pushing two fingers in deep, not playing. Seb's eyes rolled and, just about the time he'd decided to back off, Seb started riding his fingers like a wild man, teeth bared, abs rolling.

For a long moment all he could do was watch. There was something free and amazing about Sebastian like this, something that had nothing to hide. Then Markus remembered where he was and what he was doing, and he worked his fingers, opening up that tiny space.

"It's you." Seb's whisper almost got lost in the sound of their skin, of Sebastian's body on the sheets.

"Well, I hope to God it's not someone else at this late date." He grinned, though, because he knew what Seb meant. This was really them. Together.

"Don't make me fucking beat your ass."

Oh, funny.

"Just let me..." He pushed his fingers in, then pulled them back, focusing on getting a condom open and smoothing it on. His hands shook hard.

"Look at you."

Seb's fingers brushed over the tip of his cock. Thank God the fucking rubber was on. Otherwise Markus would have lost it. As it was, he had to pull down on his balls to keep it all in.

"Now. Now, Candy. I need your cock stretching me. Need to feel that."

His breath whooshed out, and Markus gasped to replace it, nodding sharply. Yes. He needed it, too. He pushed up, his thighs under Seb's, his hips hitting that burning skin on Seb's ass.

Seb arched, body like a bow for a heartbeat. "Yes."

"Fuck." Markus pushed in, the head sliding against that tight ring of muscle. His eyes rolled right back into his head. Jesus, Seb's ass was rippling around him, vibrating like guitar strings against him and it was so fucking tight.

It had been so damned long. This was like coming home.

The burning skin of Seb's ass slapped his thighs, then those amazing abs rippled and he had himself a handful of man, Sebastian driving down on his cock.

Markus held on, letting Sebastian ride. That way he could try to breath and watch and touch what he wanted to touch. He slapped and pinched, grabbed and tugged, searching out those places that he remembered—the small of Seb's back, the left side, right under his ribs. The tip of Seb's cock.

Sebastian cried out, rocking on him, throat working. Yeah. Oh, yeah. He pinched the little slit closed, then let go, knowing it would make Seb crazy.

"Markus... oh, fucking hell, you bastard..." Uh-huh. He liked that.

"So fucking pretty, baby. I remember." He remembered everything, from the way Seb felt around him to the way those heavy balls slid when Seb was spread this way. The ink was new to him, and his fingers found it, tracing the notes.

That sweet ass jerked around him, went so tight at his touch that he lost his breath a second. Markus kinda lost it then. He was too far gone to let Sebastian control their movements, so he pressed down, pushing Seb back on the bed, driving into that hot, amazing body.

"Markus!" Sebastian groaned, body milking him as ropes of seed splashed over Seb's belly.

His mouth opened, but no sound came out. Sound needed breath. Markus came so hard his ears rang, his balls pulling up enough that it actually hurt for a few seconds.

His head spun, his throat working as he groaned, then Seb grabbed him, pulled him down into a hard hug. Markus let himself relax, let Seb hold him. God, he felt good. Fucking amazing.

Seb's rough panting evened out, became soft and slow breaths. For a moment, Markus froze, not quite able to believe it. Sebastian was asleep. At six-thirty a.m.

He moaned as he pulled out, dealt with the condom, keeping one hand on Seb's belly. What the fuck was he going to do now? He couldn't just leave, but Seb was notorious for not letting people on his bus...

Bev, though, was the only person who could possibly catch them.

Screw it. He eased away, watching Seb for any signs of waking. He'd call his driver, Heath, and let him know to go on without him if they got ready to go before he woke up.

Then he could slip back into Sebastian's bed, which was where he really wanted to be.

Chapter Ten

Something smelled good.
Really good.
Sebastian frowned, sliding on the sheets. "Sausage biscuit?"

"Hey, baby. I got Bev to get some. A treat." Markus looked rumpled, well-rested, and hot as all hell, naked but for his guitar.

"Mmm." He nodded, licked his lips. "A treat."

God, look at that hot motherfucker. Seb could ride him into next week.

"Yep. They're right there if you want one." Nodding at a covered plate, Markus strummed out a couple of chords.

"I shouldn't." He wanted to, though. He loved hearing that lazy picking.

"Hell, have a bite. If it doesn't agree with you, I'll finish it." Markus strummed some more, the notes shaping themselves into *Walkin' the Floor*.

He chuckled and gave in, snagging a biscuit, moaning as he took a bite. Oh, yummy. "Can you do *Waltz Across Texas* for me?" He liked that one. He stretched, body sore, but happy. He probably needed to see what time it was. Soon.

"Hell, yes." Markus sang for him, a little scratchy in the throat, but better than he'd been at the start of the tour. The man got stronger every day.

Seb ate another bite, then stopped to sing harmony in the chorus. God, that sausage was nice and spicy, the biscuit flaky and buttery.

As soon as the song was done, Markus reached for another biscuit and wolfed it down. "Somehow I worked up an appetite."

"You work out?" He ate another bite, chewing slowly.

"Today, you mean? Nope. Been lazy so far."

"It... Did I sleep long?"

"Well, define long, baby." Markus grinned for him, and there was something in those dark eyes that told him long had been longer than he'd like.

"Just don't tell anyone." He'd stress about it later. After another bite.

"No, sir. In fact, we were on a travel hiatus. The buses leave in two hours."

"Yeah?" He stretched, wiggled. "You talked to Bev?"

"A little. Nothing bossy, I promise." Markus licked those long fingers before reaching for him.

He went. He had to. There was all that fuzzy, tanned skin to explore. The biscuit had been tasty, but Candy was always sweeter. Markus drew him onto the strong thighs, spreading him like butter. His raw ass slid on Markus' skin, the rough hair on Markus' legs scraping like mad.

His lips parted, this noise leaving him. Oh, fuck. That was like the best kind of heat, ever.

"Damn, baby. Your skin is hot." Markus stroked his butt with one hand, humming.

"Uh-huh. Burns." So good. His eyes might have crossed.

"Love it." Those big fingers caught his skin, pinching a little.

"I..." He needed to get up. Work out. Work. Take his meds. Do stuff. But...

"Shh." Markus' kiss left him breathless, left him unable to think of excuses.

His fingers tangled in the soft fuzz covering Markus' chest, and he held on, lost in the way Markus' tongue fucked his lips. God, he hadn't thought he'd ever have this again. Ever.

He might not have it again after this, so he was going to feel every second. Markus' cock rubbed his belly, hot and wet and so good. If his mouth wasn't busy, he would have told Markus that he dreamed about that fat, long cock, about those hands and the way Markus touched him. Hell, he could probably tell Markus all that with his touch. Markus could read him like a book.

Markus moaned and grabbed his hip, fingers digging in, bringing his attention into sharp focus. Panting, he tugged at Markus' nipples, then the head of that heavy cock.

Markus jerked under him, teeth sinking into his bottom lip and tugging. "Baby."

"Uh-huh?" He pulled again, thumb teasing the slit.

"Don't tease me." Markus started rocking and rolling, hips starting to push up.

"Why not?" Teasing Markus sounded like a delicious idea.

"Because I need you too much." One big hand covered his, showing him what Markus wanted.

He groaned, playing Markus' cock, dragging all along the shaft, pulling on the upstroke. The flesh felt like fire against his palm, the skin velvety and soft, a stark contrast to the fuzzy balls beneath.

It felt amazing, to not be rushing, to not be wishing.

Not to be worried that someone would catch them.

Sebastian grinned, pushing at the soft skin around the head of Markus' cock again. That moan made him happy.

"Singing to me, Candy?" He let his thumb drag over the slit.

"Anything if you keep doing that." Those dark eyes were all pupil, Markus grunting and pushing.

"Going to, until you shoot for me." Playing games wasn't his thing. Feeling was.

"Oh, God." Markus' eyes blazed at him a moment, then those hands slid up to his shoulders, pushing him down. "Want your mouth, again, baby. I've been dreaming about it for eight years. Once wasn't enough."

"Never is." He moaned and went, hands sliding to the strong thighs as he wrapped his lips around the tip.

"Uhn." That was pure incoherence, and Sebastian went looking for more of those sounds, getting them when he licked down the underside.

Oh, hell yeah. He nibbled along the heavy vein, then left sucking kisses all around the ridged head.

"Seb. Baby. I need."

When he glanced up, he could see how much Markus needed. The ridged belly was tight, muscles standing out. Those tiny nipples were hard points, and Markus was clenching his teeth, tendons in his neck in sharp relief. Sebastian moaned, and dove down, taking Markus to the root, prick sliding in deep, into his throat.

"Fuck!" Markus jerked, fucking his mouth hard for a few short seconds. Then the man went still, a long, indrawn breath Sebastian's only warning that Markus was fixin' to come. He reached down, rolled the heavy balls, hard enough that Markus would feel it, had to feel it, and swallowed.

Markus came for him, just as he'd demanded, wet, hot seed sliding down his throat. The man smelled like heaven.

He pushed his hand down, grabbed his own, aching cock, pulling hard. Markus made him need.

"Seb. Baby. Come 'ere." Markus yanked him up so hard he dangled for a moment, but then he landed on Markus' lap, and that hot, callused hand closed around his prick.

Seb arched, pushing up into that touch. Yeah. Yeah, just like that. Fuck him raw. Well, maybe Markus had already done that. He'd take the hand job and be all over it. He balanced himself on his hands, his tender ass bouncing off Markus' thighs. He flinched a little, and Markus laughed, the sound dark, sexual as hell.

"Tender, baby?"

"Fuck off." It felt so frigging hot that he could scream with it.

"Don't make me beat you again. I might have to take after your thighs, and then where would you be?" Markus never let up on his cock, stroking from base to tip.

"Burning. Fucking burning." His teeth sank into his bottom lip, hard enough to hurt.

"Kiss me, baby." Markus nudged his chin up, lips opening his so that tongue could take him.

He bounced up into the kiss, coming so hard he couldn't fucking see for a second.

Damn. Just—damn. Yes. This might just kill him, but it would be worth it.

He slumped down, coming to rest against Markus' chest. Those long arms came around him, holding him there, squeezing a little.

"This cool?" Could he hang out here, rest, just for a minute?

"Hell, yes, baby. This is more than cool."

"'kay." He took a deep breath, humming under his breath, fingers playing on Markus' belly.

Markus hummed along with him, and he could feel

Markus' chest rise and fall in a steady rhythm.

He didn't question it, for once. He just let it go.

Life was coming as soon as the busses started. This bit was his.

Chapter Eleven

Y ou got the notes I sent on that bridge on *Shining Through*, right?" Markus asked, settling on his stool across from Kyle.

"I did. I like it." Kyle nodded, stretched. "You still having those crazed jam sessions in the middle of the night?"

"Some nights, yeah. You know I like my sleep." Not to mention that he had better access to the reason he'd been going to those jam sessions now.

He was careful—damned careful—but he'd spent a couple of mornings working out, watching, fucking that tight, tiny little ass. Markus had to admit, he was happier than he'd been in years. He thought Seb was, too, as happy as the man could be. He'd actually seen the man eat—one sausage biscuit, half of a pancake, and a scoop of ice cream—and he'd held the beautiful son of a bitch while he slept three times.

"Noticed you weren't on your bus the other day when we had that layover."

Markus met Kyle's eyes, refusing to look away, be

ashamed. Kyle had been the third person he'd come out to.

"Not that anyone else noticed but Bev." Kyle grinned, keeping it light, which he was grateful for.

Markus nodded. "Good. Good deal."

"Yeah? Rock on." Kyle rolled his eyes a little. "My kid says that. It's like a bad habit."

"How are the peeps, man? You haven't said much." Pulling out his notes, Markus grabbed a guitar.

"Good. Good. Janie is a little pouty that we're on the road again, you know. The kids are getting older."

"So are we." Not that he felt old. Things were going good. Real good.

"Yeah. I know." Kyle looked at him. "No one can ride the top forever. You either slide easy or crash hard. I... I think that sliding easy was a good decision."

"You think so?" He'd always been the crashing kind until recently. "You'd be okay with that?"

"Yeah, man. We've got a damned good life, you and me, and the music is always going to be there. Your buddy, though? He's on the runaway train plan, and there's hard core hurt when he hits the wall. I hope you can slow it down." The man was serious as a heart attack. "If not, you get out of the way, man. You worked too hard to get run over."

Markus gave that the thought it deserved before answering. "I'll be careful. You know I'll always take care of you and yours, right?"

"I never doubted that." Kyle grabbed his fiddle. "You considered doing *The Devil Went Down to Georgia* in the encore?"

"That would be good, huh?" It really would. It wasn't hard to sing, and it would show off Kyle's talent.

"It might be fun, huh? That little Kerry gal can join in. She misses playing her fiddle." Kyle's lips twitched.

"If she can manage between bouts of morning sickness."

Markus stared. "Morning sickness? She's pregnant?"

"That's what morning sickness means, Markus. I mean, I know you're a fudgepacker, but you did take basic biology in high school, right?"

"Oh, fuck off." Markus snorted. "I just meant I didn't know she had a fuck buddy."

"You been otherwise occupied. She's doing the rhythm guitar player. Lots of times in backstage during Seb's acoustic break."

"How very Def Leppard of them." Maybe that showing his age, but damn. Markus shook his head. He'd done that once. With Sebastian. Back when they were opening for Wacey Carrol at the rodeo.

"Yeah, well, we're old." Kyle's shrug spoke volumes. "At least she's not a screamer."

Oh, god. Markus remembered, back when Hank was playing keyboards for them and he had that little redneck blonde under the set up and...

Yeah.

Whoa.

"You remember that howler monkey girl, man?"

"Shee-it. Has *anyone* forgotten that crazy chick? I think Hank still has scars on his dick from trying to shove it in and shut her ass up."

They shared a chuckle over that one before Markus sobered up. "Well, you holler if you think Kerry needs anything, huh? She doesn't need to be putting her health at risk."

"Seb's already talked to them both, pretty hard. Jonny's got a ring for her. Gonna ask on stage in Detroit. His folks are going to be there."

How did Kyle know everything? Hell, how did Seb know? Markus guessed it was that not sleeping thing. "Good on them."

Kyle nodded. "Okay, I'll talk to Bruce about the song change. You talk to Seb. None of us need to run through it, I don't think."

"Sounds good. You want to work on anything else?" Sometimes Kyle just liked to play.

"Sure. *Fighting Monday*? *Counting the Days*?"

"*Fighting Monday* sounds good." He hit the opening chords, his foot already tapping.

That fiddle started wailing, right on cue.

Fuck, yes.

He loved his job.

"Sebastian? Honey? You okay?"

Seb stood in his dressing room, heart slamming in his chest. It had been a tough week—Kerry had collapsed on stage in Columbus on Thursday, and she and Jonny were still in the hospital, making sure the baby was okay. Jack had sent up this new kid—Ricky something—to do rhythm and it was all weird, just enough wrong that he couldn't relax. Thank God for Kyle and his ability to jump in.

Still.

He was just not fitting in his fucking skin. Maybe he needed to find a hotel somewhere, hide for the next couple days before the western states. Texas was going to be brutal and that wasn't including New Orleans, not that New Orleans was western, because it wasn't, but it wasn't deep South either and they started in Nashville and that was another part of the tour, right?

"Sebastian?" Bev called him again, knocking lightly. "Don't make me use my key."

"I'm fine. Fine. What do you need?" He sucked in a couple of breaths, trying to relax before he opened the door.

"Well, first, I need you to eat your pineapple and your shake. I know you didn't eat before the show."

"I'm not hungry."

She had a plate with spears of pineapple, right there, and he loved pineapple, but it just didn't sound good.

"You need something, Sebastian. What else would you like?" She was pleading with him, worry in her eyes.

"I'm not hungry, honey. Just a shake, okay? Just a little one. And some Excedrin Migraine."

"Okay. Promise you'll eat that shake."

"I promise, okay. I promise. Excedrin. Please."

"It'll be here in a few minutes. Okay?" She touched his arm, and it was almost more than he could stand.

"Okay." He nodded, shut the door, and then ran to the sink, scrubbing until it burned or until the fucking shake got there, whichever came first.

He was taking his pills, damn it. Why weren't they working?

Chapter Twelve

Markus rolled his head on his neck, wishing he had some damned headache powder. There must be something in the air, because no one was up to snuff.

There was a weird sound, then a tap on his door. He knew it wasn't Heath, because there would be the sound of bagpipes or something to preface his driver's arrival. That Scot had no shame.

When he opened the door, Bev stood there.

"Hey, honey."

She looked up at him with a near-hysterical expression that looked completely foreign in her normally so-put together face. "Mr. Kane, I'm sorry, but... I need your help, please."

"Anything you need." He was exhausted, but she looked so damned worried, heading into scared.

"He won't eat anything. He threw his shake up. He hasn't slept in two days, he's washing everything. Whatever you did, before, when he slept, please. Do it again."

"What?" He pulled her up into the bus, just in case

someone was listening out there. "Seb?"

"Yeah. He doesn't like the new rhythm guy, he's worried about the kids, it rained. You know."

He'd never even thought on how all that would ping Seb's OCD tendencies. He'd been dragging ass and dealing with a hysterically pooped Kyle, who was playing two shows a night and two encores now...

"Okay. Get me a piece of pineapple upside down cake and a carrot cake from Syd's Bakery on Farmer Avenue." She'd be cutting it close. They closed at one a.m. to make the doughnuts for the next day, but they were the best bakery in nowhere Kansas. "I'll go see Seb."

"Thank you." She hugged him, the act impulsive, but so sweet.

Markus kissed the top of her head. "Thanks for having his back, honey."

"Always. No matter what. He's my best friend, even if no one sees it. You, too, huh? I promise I got yours, as well."

"Thank you." He patted her back a little awkwardly because she was so small. "Tell Heath to go on if I'm not back by pull-out."

"Okay. Let me get the cake and I'll be at Seb's bus in... twenty?"

"Half hour." It would take twenty to get Seb to let him on the bus. Of course, he had a key now.

"You got it." She was on the phone before she was out the door.

Markus changed into sweats and grabbed his phone and his keys. He didn't bother to knock; he let himself in to Seb's bus.

"Seb?"

"It's my time off. I can't see anybody right now. I'm tired."

"Baby, it's not just anybody." He found Seb in the

116

bathroom, scrubbing his hands. Oh, man. Okay. Okay, this was crazy, now. The man's fingertips were starting to bleed, scratches showing on the man's arms.

"Seb." He put his hands on Seb's shoulders. "Stop."

"Candy? What's wrong? Is everything okay?"

Seb had to stop this shit. Right now.

He whirled Seb around, staring down into those bright green eyes, which looked feverish. God, how did this happen so damned fast? "Baby, you need some rest."

"It's not time. What do you want?" Seb blinked at him. "The pills aren't working, Markus. I called the doctor and they're not working like they're supposed to."

"I want you to breathe." He wanted to shake Seb, actually, but he didn't. He guided the man toward the back of the bus. Seb was trembling in his hands, muscles jerking and twitching like they had minds of their own.

"That's it, Seb." He eased down on the bed, pulling Seb down on his lap. Seb stayed for about, oh, half a second before he started twitching and shifting, muttering.

"Shh." He kissed Sebastian's neck, let his hands run up and down Seb's back.

"Markus?" Seb moaned, pushed back into his hands. "Fuck, you're warm."

"Uh-huh. It's been too long, baby. Next time you have to tell me." If he could just get Seb to come to him when this happened he could help. This shit was insane, and all Seb needed was somewhere to breathe, a place to settle so his brain stopped eating itself.

He hugged Seb tight, kissing whatever skin he could find. Seb's body moved like there was music playing, like he was strumming the lean body. It made him feel ten feet tall, that he could ease his lover out of the hardcore freakout.

He heard the bus door open, heard footsteps, then a soft "I left the pieces on the table." Good woman.

Seb frowned. "Pieces of what?"

"Don't worry about that right now." He kissed away the frown.

"The pills aren't working anymore." Seb's face chased his lips.

"No? Well, maybe we need to work on something better than pills." Markus kept it light, non-judgmental. He'd self-medicated a lot over the years.

"Touch me." Seb brought their lips together in a hard, suddenly hungry kiss.

Yeah. God, yeah, he could lose himself in Seb for a little while. He kissed back, pushing hard, daring Seb to make it even better. He wanted that sweet motherfucker focused on nothing but him, nothing but how much they needed each other. That was all Markus could think on, all he wanted in the world.

His brain skittered away from those thoughts, focused instead on what he needed, right now. And that was Seb—all of him, right at this moment.

Moving slowly, he eased his hand down Seb's belly so he could push into Seb's sweats and grab that hot, hard cock. Wet-tipped and swollen, Seb's prick pushed right into his fingers. That was it. So fucking perfect. Addictive. He pushed his fingers deeper into the sweats, rolled the heavy balls, jonesing on Seb's need. The way that head fell back, the cords standing out in Seb's neck, made Markus want things, made him want to hear Seb scream.

Markus surged up, pushing Seb right back onto the bed, slamming the lean body into the mattress. He wasn't sure what he wanted to do first: slap, bite, or fuck like crazy.

"Damn it." Seb's fingers dug into his shoulders. "Markus, come *on*."

"I got what you need, baby." He pulled back enough to reach down and tug Seb's sweats off, just so he could pull those heavy balls. That would sting a little.

"Uhn." Seb's shoulders left the mattress, their lips slamming together.

The kiss left his head spinning, his body jerking. He smacked Seb's thigh, finally figuring out what to do. A sharp sound pushed between his lips, Seb rolling into it. So Markus did it again. He moaned when Seb jerked, and he flipped Seb over, that tight ass right there for him to work on.

"Don't you dare, you fuck." Seb's cock was hard as nails, driving against his thighs.

"Don't you dare me, baby." He smacked that round, tight butt, his hand bouncing back.

"Uhn. You can't..." Seb rocked up, pushed back into his hand.

"Oh, I so can." He was going to beat that beautiful, needy ass raw.

The talking stopped just about then, because he started laying down blows, hard and steady, meeting each and every one of Seb's motions. Seb bucked and rocked and panted, and Markus gave the man everything he had.

"Candy. Candy, love. Please." Seb was moaning now, steadily, breath hitching.

"Anything, baby. I know what you want." He hit the backs of Seb's thighs, knowing the thin skin there would be so sensitive.

"Fuck." Seb curled up, knees pulling up underneath, nudging his thighs.

"Soon. Not done with this yet." His hand tingled, his arm starting to tire.

His Seb was going to feel this—tonight, tomorrow. They had four days. Four days to fucking chill out. God, that sounded so good. Time away. Time that didn't belong to anyone else.

"Please..." Seb leaned in and bit him, hard.

"Shit!" He smacked that ass so hard his palm went pale, then red. Seb cried out, the sound so musical that he wanted to scream.

Seb sucked in a sobbing breath, hips rocking up, and come sprayed over his thighs.

"Oh, baby. Love it when you come. You smell like heaven."

"Fuck me. Markus. Candy. I need you."

He knew. He fucking knew. Shit, he was risking his entire fucking career for it.

"Just let me..." He knew where the slick was now, where the condoms lived.

Seb moaned, hips still moving in random, jerky motions. All Markus had to do was stroke Seb's skin and hum, waiting for the aftershocks to die down before he moved. His lover relaxed for him, though, tremors easing enough that he could move from under Seb, slide behind the man and drag his burning fingers along the blistered heat of the man's ass.

"God, if you could see what I see right now, baby. You're on fire for me."

Seb's hips rolled up, that still-stiff cock fucking the air. "Please. Please, Candy. I'm losing my mind."

"So am I," Markus murmured, leaning to reach for the lube and the rubber. "I need you, Seb. Need you."

Seb pushed up, lips wrapping around one of his nipples, the suction sudden, fierce, and Markus moaned, his body jerking hard. It was almost too much. "Want to fuck you."

"Please." Those green eyes blazed at him, bloodshot, hungry, wanton.

"God." Markus handed Seb the lube. "Get yourself ready, baby."

Seb didn't argue, the man fumbled the tube open and slicked those clever fingers, two of them disappearing into the tiny, needy hole. Markus watched, his teeth in his mouth, his moan shocking him with how loud it was.

Jesus, look at that. Seb worked himself furiously, lips open, eyes rolled back. It was like Markus' own personal porn reel, only so much better, more personal and amazing. He slid the rubber down over his cock, slicking himself up as he watched Seb's fingers appear, disappear, then Seb added a third finger.

He reached out and tugged Sebastian's hand away, pushing between those muscled, spread thighs.

"Are you finally ready?" Oh, little shit. Pushy little butthead.

Markus slid in so fast it left him breathless. "I'd say so, yeah."

Seb's response was a soft little cry, that burning ass slapping against his thighs. They rocked together, their skin slippery with sweat and Seb's come, the feeling so good that Markus wanted to write the dirtiest song ever. He buried his lips in Seb's shoulder, humming hard as they moved. Yes. Fuck, yes. This was better than coming home. This was everything he'd ever wanted. He watched Seb, keeping his eyes open when they wanted to close.

Seb's groan made his mouth dry, or he'd answer it, sing his own fucking harmony, and Markus moved faster, harder, Seb's skin so hot it almost burned. A wild cry split the air, and suddenly Seb was right there, again, needing.

"That's it, baby. That's it. Come on." He reached for Seb's cock, loving how it filled his hand.

He felt Seb's hunger, all around his cock, and when he pulled that hard prick, his eyes crossed, Seb's ass like a vise. It made friction so much hotter, so much better, and all he could do was work back and forth against it. Nothing so good could last—it just wasn't possible, but damn, it was like time stopped for a little while before his balls tightened, his rhythm lost. He grunted, his breath whooshing out when he came, his body wracked with shudder after shudder.

Seb was sobbing low, bucking on his cock when he came back into his own head, and he started stroking, the sensations of Seb's body around his dick almost too much. He stroked hard and fast, wanting Seb to be right there with him.

It only took a few tugs before heat splashed on his wrist, Seb's little moans fading.

He waited for Seb to stop shaking before patting that spent cock and flopping down on the bed. Fuck, he could live on that for years.

Fucking stunning part was, when Seb came to him, cheek on his chest to rest, that was even better. There was no more shaking, no more scratching. Just sleep.

Next on the agenda was food, then him and Seb, they needed to chat. At length.

That he wasn't looking forward to nearly as much.

Sebastian ached—his head, his ass, his chest.

What the fuck?

He blinked, trying to understand. The bus was moving. That was good. There was a warm, heavy body next to him, and he could smell waffles. Sebastian muttered. There weren't supposed to be food smells on his bus.

"Hey, you." Markus kissed the corner of his mouth. "How do you feel, baby?"

"Sore. A little blinky." He pressed closer. "Do I smell food?"

"I made waffles. Did you know you have a waffle iron? I ate the cake, I'm afraid." Candy looked so... pleased.

"No. Why do I have a waffle iron?" Maybe they'd stolen one from a Waffle House, a long time ago.

"Hell if I know. I got Bev to get me some Bisquick and some eggs and shit."

He pondered that. He shouldn't. Waffles were fattening. Butter. Syrup. They smelled so good, though. His stomach growled, rumbling and snarling like a living thing.

"See? Waffles good. Come on, baby. Come get a plate and we'll eat. I know you don't want crumbs in bed."

"Okay." Seb rolled up, following that tempting body. Markus was naked and easy, moving through his bus like it was nothing. Those muscles—it just wasn't fair how easily Markus stayed in shape. Maybe it was about being tall.

"I missed my workout, I think."

"You needed the sleep. We're stopping tonight at this amazing park. We'll take a run."

"Outside?" He liked that. A lot. "Okay."

"Yeah. There's miles of trails and not a lot of folks and the weather is good." Markus looked so pleased that Sebastian had to grin.

"The waffles smell pretty good." This whole eating thing was just... weird.

"I'll just make you up one to begin with." Markus moved around his little kitchenette like it was actually functional.

He nodded, wandering a little. He needed to find his phone, check his messages, see what time it was. Take his meds. Where the hell were his meds? He always kept them in the kitchen.

"Did you move my pills, man? I missed a dose." And his hands were a little shaky.

"Yeah. I put them in that cabinet. Want some juice?"

"No. Yes. I mean... calories."

"Well, you've missed two rounds of pineapple." One dark brow rose, Markus waiting patiently.

He looked down at himself. "I guess." God, his head hurt.

"Here, baby." Guiding him to a seat at the table, Markus got him apple juice and pulled out his pills.

"Thank you. I'm sorry. I'm off my schedule." And weirdly confused.

"I know. I'm an expert at rolling with it, man."

While he took his pills, Markus made him a plate. He swallowed his pills down, then looked at the waffle. The butter, the syrup... uhn. All of a sudden he was hungry as all hell. He dipped his finger in one of the squares, then licked the syrup off. Damn. Bev had good taste in groceries. Only the best for Markus. She couldn't be buying for him. She knew he didn't eat.

"I don't eat." He dipped and licked again.

"I know." Markus slathered butter on a waffle.

He nodded, cut a square out of his waffle, nibbled. God, it was good, crunchy on the outside, soft in the middle. Carb heaven. He smiled, licking his lips. Markus stopped, fork halfway to his mouth, staring at Seb.

"What?" What was wrong? It was just one bite and it had been good.

"Sorry." Candy's cheeks went red. "That was hot."

"Oh." Oh, now, that was okay. "Do you want me to stop? We're naked. Avoiding hotness like this will be hard." Hard. He snorted.

Markus laughed, too, the sound low and sexy. "Nope. Don't stop on me. Lick away."

He grinned, took another bite, licking his fingers clean, again. Markus watched happily, smiling that way. That way Sebastian knew meant he was in for a world of fun.

"I'm going to have to do a thousand crunches." He ate another square, this one rich, buttery.

"I told you, we'll run it off." There was something fierce in Markus' eyes. "Course what we got up to earlier will burn calories for at least another hour."

"That was..." Hot. Fierce. Amazing. "...intense."

"It was. I liked it a lot." Markus wolfed down two waffles.

He ate a quarter of one, then got up and started wandering, restless, horny.

"What's up, baby?" Once the dishes were in the sink, Candy followed him.

"I'm horny. I'm a little itchy. Do you want to write?"

"Sure." They got out the guitars, got settled. "What does itchy mean?"

"Hmm?" He grabbed a pen, some paper. "It's like... I don't know. My skin doesn't fit right. I keep telling Jack and Dr. Norman that this isn't working, that I'm still tired, but I itch. What are you in the mood for?"

"Something bluesy for you. Something... caramel."

"Caramel?" What a great fucking word.

"Yeah. Smooth, creamy, but with that bite of burnt sugar."

Seb grinned. This was why Markus was a good lyrics man.

"You should make breakfast more often." He started picking, fingers moving over the strings.

"Yeah?" Those long fingers started picking in turn, Markus right there with him. "Maybe I will."

They found a melody pretty quick, then Markus started laying in the lyrics, working hard while he dithered out some of the rhythm section. It was going to be a good song, all about whiskey and sugar and how nothing eased the pain. He liked it.

He got up for coffee after they hammered out the bridge, needing the hit of caffeine.

"That smells good." Markus got up and wandered over, looking all tall and naked and fuzzy.

"You want a cup?" He licked his lips, eating Markus

up. He had to stop this. They had a handful of shows left, damn it. He couldn't just fall apart.

"I do." They bumped hips, and he almost moaned at how hot Markus' skin was.

His hands were shaking a little bit as he poured the coffee. God damn, he needed to put on pants.

"What is it, baby?" Markus moved even closer. He shuddered as Markus' hand slid down his back, over his aching, still-warm ass. Those long fingers searched out every tender spot, pushing him a little. Maybe a lot.

"Markus." His hands landed on the little counter. "Oh, fuck, you can't do this." He spread a little though, wanting it more than he wanted his next breath.

"Why not, baby? We're here. We have time." Markus spun him around, dropping to the floor behind him to lick his too-hot skin.

Oh, sweet fuck. His eyes crossed and he pushed back, that tongue like a flame and he wanted to beg. He wanted all sorts of things, but he just rocked back and forth, panting. Then Markus spread his asscheeks and licked at his hole.

"Candy!" It felt like every muscle in his entire fucking body went tight.

Markus didn't answer him out loud. The only answer he had was Markus going at him, harder and faster.

His thighs began to shake, his legs muscles trembling as he spread and went up on tiptoe. The feel of Markus' morning stubble was intense against his spank-tanned hide. He gasped, so freaked out he didn't know what to do. He stumbled forward, slamming against the counter, grunting deep in his chest.

"Baby?" Markus paused a moment, hands spreading him wide.

"Please. You're making me fucking crazy!"

"No worries, lover. I got you." Markus moved back to

Sebastian's skin, licking, pressing.

So big. So big and he was burning and he needed like nothing else. His blood throbbed in his veins, his heart pounding. His skin felt like the tiniest scratch would break him right open.

When Markus pulled back his mouth and fingers slammed in, Sebastian threw his head back and bit out a scream. It was huge, this feeling, and it took over everything else.

"Mmmhmm. That's it, baby. You gotta breathe."

Breathing was overrated. The way Markus' tongue worked him was the only thing in the world that mattered.

Sebastian grunted, then found himself writhing, dancing like he was on stage and the lights were beating down on him. His hips rotated, his chest dipping toward the counter, his belly hard as a board. Markus didn't let up on him, either, fingers and mouth moving in concert, that tongue sliding down to his balls.

"Please. Oh, fuck. Please, don't stop." He wanted it to go on forever.

He felt as much as heard Markus' chuckle. That vibration almost made him crazy.

"Bastard!" The swat to his thigh made him jump, made him cry out.

Markus just did it again, slapping just below the burning skin from last night's marathon round.

"Don't. Don't. Fuck." So close. He was so fucking close.

"No?" Those fingers inside him moved, pegging his gland, and another slap rang out, making him jump.

"Please." Markus was like music. Like the best kind of late-night jam session, smoky voices at three a.m. music.

"Please what, baby? What do you need?"

"Everything." He always had. He needed everything.

"In a heartbeat." Markus stood, rubbing against his ass.

The words made him dizzy, made him need to write them down, find them a melody, but more than that, he needed Markus to prove the man meant them. Markus wasn't hesitating. Not one bit. He could hear the man slicking up, the sounds wet and amazing, then the head of Markus' cock was pushing against his hole.

He went to drive back onto that fine prick, but Markus had his hips, slamming into him so that fuzzy body slapped against his skin. His ass was so sensitive he swore he could feel each and every hair. Sebastian could definitely feel Markus' breath on his nape a few seconds before the man bit him.

"Oh, fuck!" His eyes rolled and he heard Markus grunt as his muscles clenched.

"Seb. Tight." Markus pinched the hot flesh right where his ass met his thigh.

That bright sting zipped down his thigh, burning him perfectly. He panted, his arms shaking from holding him up, his breath heaving in his chest. The noise in his head was fading, only Markus and his song there.

He nodded, encouraging Markus. Don't stop. Not yet.

"Gonna ride you until you scream, baby."

"Please. Fuck, Candy, I need it." He always had.

"Yes. Gonna scratch that itch so good." The thrusts came, long and deep, the rhythm completely unstoppable. Sebastian burned, melodies flashing in his brain. Fuck, yes. He could stay, right here. Forever.

Not that it was going to last. Not when Markus grabbed his cock and started stroking.

His head fell forward and he humped, pushing hard as he used every bit of strength he had. The move drove Markus deeper, deeper than ever before maybe, their bodies straining for every bit of leverage.

"Markus!" The word tore out of him.

"Fucking love the way you say my name, baby. Love it."

Those words and the slam of Markus' cock against his gland pushed him right up to the edge. He only needed the tiniest shove. He came, his vision fading out, the only sound in his ears Markus calling him "love".

It was the most perfect moment, and he wanted to hold on to it.

Those strong arms held him up, kept them stable, even as the bus moved. Markus thrust a few more times, jerky now, losing the thread. Then the man came for him, moaning his name like it was a chorus to a really good song.

Sebastian held on to the sounds, soaking them up. Drinking them in. He had to remember this.

"Damn, baby. That was a hell of a way to start the day."

"Uh-huh." It had been... stunning.

Markus pressed a soft kiss to the back of his neck, making the bite mark there sting.

"We're not being careful. You good with that?"

Leaning against him, Markus nodded, He felt the way that bristly chin rubbed on his skin. "I tried to be good with the rubbers, but I got to tell you, man, it's been a long time and I've tested clean since." Candy wouldn't lie to him. Not about that.

"I'm clean, Candy. I wouldn't give you anything." Shit, he loved the man. And that hadn't been what he was talking about anyway. He was talking about their lives.

"Well, there you go." Markus didn't seem worried.

"You mess up my schedule these days."

Markus palmed Sebastian's butt, making him wiggle. "Does that give you stress?"

"It probably should, more than it does. I'd scream at anyone else." Was that normal?

"Well, if I start giving you too much, you say so." That hand squeezed, making his toes curl. "I know just the way to relieve it now."

"You're crazy-making." He meant that in the best possible way. "We should shower. We're all sweaty."

"Sure. I like your shower. Need to get one of those on my bus one of these days." Stepping back, Markus stood and pulled him up.

"What do you have?" He hadn't been on Markus' bus.

"Pretty standard shower with a fancy jet head." Laughing, Markus muscled him into the bathroom. "I had to get a new bus when we contracted this tour."

"I live in here, when I'm in the States."

"You don't have a place here at all, right?" Markus stopped, stared, Seb's lack of roots still amazing him. "Didn't you have a place in Nashville once upon a time?"

"No. I stayed here or in a hotel. Mostly here."

Markus stared until he ducked his head. Then Candy started the water and got them into the spray.

What was he supposed to say? Do? "I'm not a freak."

"I never said you were, baby. That just sounds rootless." Markus started washing him, voice carefully neutral. Not like humor the lunatic or anything. Just plain old even and calm.

"I am rootless. I'm a musician. We don't get roots."

"Hey, I get it. I like my house, though. It has my studio."

"I liked your house." He would have liked to have seen more than the studio, really.

"Next time you'll stay with me, huh? We'll go and I'll even make Helen leave you be."

"Stay with you, like in your house?"

Markus pulled back to stare at him, dark eyes serious as a heart attack. "Yeah. You'll like my bedroom."

"They'll catch us. It'll happen. You know that." And when it happened, Sebastian wasn't sure he could walk away again. He was older now, more in love. Sebastian laughed a little. He was more OCD or whatever. If Markus worked into his routine, it would kill him when it changed.

"I'm willing to chance it for you, baby. This time I know what the stakes are."

Sebastian's mouth went dry and he just stood there. What the hell did you do when someone offered you the thing you want most? He thought he might fall over.

"You don't have to say yes or no right now, baby. We still got tour dates." Those hands started moving again, soaping him up.

"You're the one. You. No one else. Eight years and I never once found anyone close." Sebastian fought to breathe. "I'm dreaming, and you're in your bus, right?"

"Nope. No dreaming." Markus kissed him hard enough to let him know this was real.

Shit, Sebastian wasn't sure he was ever going to sleep again. He didn't want to miss anything, and he might just have to prop his eyelids open with toothpicks, like in the cartoons.

"Baby?" Markus washed Sebastian's belly. "You okay?"

He thought about the question, for a long time. "I don't know. I. I've lived a long fucking time running from wanting something and now you say I can have it. Shit, I've built a whole career on lying about everything and trying to feel something."

Did that even make sense?

He was fucking exhausted and more than a little scared. What if this wasn't real? What if he was making it up? Shit, Markus had made him sleep in a whole other house in Austin. Markus had been the one to say they couldn't do this. What if he was making this all up and he did something—touched the man or said something and then Markus lost his shit? What if Markus walked off stage and just left him there with all those people staring at him, wanting a piece of him? Like monsters, all just wanting to tear a piece off of him and eat it, so they got their pound of flesh.

He could see that, clear as a bell, the mass of people with their claws and their teeth, hunting him and the guys, hungry for a bite. Just one bite. And then one more and one more and one more and one more and one...

"Hey, baby. You're shaking. Seb? Come on. Let's go sit." Turning off the water, Markus dried him off and led him back to his bed, easing him down. "What can I do?"

"I just... I missed a dose of my pills, I think. I'm just..." He was on a schedule. Pills. Work. Music.

"You had some. Do you need a shake? Some pineapple?" Those eyes were almost black, staring into his, Markus looking worried, but not scared or frantic or anything. That was good, right?

"I don't know." He sighed and looked at Markus. "This whole thing, with the meds, it's complicated. They stop working and they just give me more, but the working part doesn't last as long anymore." And he was so tired, all the time.

"Maybe we ought to back off the meds, then, try something else. I think I can help."

"I don't know. I don't..." His voice lowered. "I get a little weird, without them."

"Oh, hell, baby. You missed it when I quit drinking." Markus held up a hand when he opened his mouth. "I ain't saying it's exactly the same, but I was pretty sideways."

"I start imagining shit. Doctor says I just have to take them, but... man, it ain't supposed to be like this, is it? Either flying so high you can't see or just having to have every second be full?" He snorted. "And shit, I'm bitching. What the fuck can I bitch about? Everybody wants to be me."

Everybody but him.

How spoiled was that shit?

"Yeah, but you can burn out, baby. Everyone can, even with the best job on earth." They snuggled, the world seeming less abrasive all of a sudden. "We'll work on it."

"Oh, God. Okay. I need to close my eyes a minute."

"Then close your eyes, baby. I'm right here." Markus held him, and somehow it made the world go away. Sebastian chuckled. He'd write that, but it was already a song.

Chapter Thirteen

Markus counted pills, putting them back into the bottles with tiny clinks.

Sebastian had cut back by almost a third in the last few days, and Markus couldn't be more proud. Hell, Bev seemed torn between relief and abject panic. She didn't know what to do with a sleepy, eating Seb.

Of course, Bev hadn't been dealing with the paranoia, the night sweats, the hysterical phone calls searching for a goddamn paraglide company in Arizona that did full moon flights at two a.m.

Markus figured she deserved three days off. Hell, he'd decided to take a night off the bus and get them a goddamned hotel room. In-room hot tub, giant bed, room service delivered to the antechamber where no one could see anyone but Bev sign for it...

Sebastian was sleeping in the Jacuzzi right now, head back and bubbling away. Markus could see those cute as hell toes bobbing on the other side of the tub from Seb's head. He grinned, thinking of going and tickling those toes, when he heard his cell ringing back in the bedroom.

That was his girl, and he needed to talk to Tawny

anyway. He hadn't seen her in days and he missed her face. He scratched his belly, making a mental note to fish Seb out before his blood pressure dropped through the floor. Twenty minutes maybe. He shut the bedroom door halfway and grabbed his phone.

"Hello?"

"Hey, Scooter. How's it hanging?" She sounded like a slice of home, husky and somehow always laughing.

"Not bad at all." The last few days had been up and down, but he'd gotten to spend them with Seb, so he wasn't gonna complain. "How are you, lady?"

"I'm doing okay. Chilling out, working. Normal stuff. How's the tour going? I haven't heard any complaints from anyone lately. It's sort of creepy. I'm waiting for disaster."

"Lord, don't say that." He chewed his lip, trying to decide how much to tell her. Thing was, he'd found it was always best to be honest with Tawny. His manager had always had his back. "You ought to know. Seb and I, well, we're, uh—running hot."

"Yeah?" He didn't hear a lot of surprise in her voice, but there wasn't any censure, either. "Well, it is good? I mean, you're happy?"

"I am. I think he is, too, but this is a messed up thing he's got going, Tawn. He's running on fumes."

"Is he... Is there... I mean." She sighed and he could see it, her blowing her hair out of her face. "What's he into? I can't help if I don't know."

Markus listed the names of the drugs he'd read off the pill bottles. "Anti-depressants and ADHD stuff. All prescription. It's a hell of a cocktail, though."

"Uh-huh. You. Look, I hate to be awful, you know I do, but... Is someone prescribing them?"

"His doctor, yeah." Markus peered out to make sure Seb was asleep. "Tawny, he never needed this stuff before.

Remember? When I was self-medicating like crazy, he was the sane one."

"Honey, the schedule he's on... I've talked to Jack. Did you know he has another eighteen shows booked immediately after y'all are done? He won't even get a single day between y'all's curtain call and a slew of outdoor venues. Then he gets something like four days before he's supposed to go to Japan or somewhere and do promotion for a crazy tour right after Christmas and there's supposed to be the promo for y'all's album, a new album for him, contract negotiations for the label." She sighed softly. "A normal human can't live like that. It's not possible, not and be sane."

"No. I know." Sebastian needed a break. "Can you talk to Jack again, get him to back it off?"

"I'll try, but you have to figure that he knows, at least a little."

"I know." He hated that. Jack was part of the machine. But the man wasn't evil. Was he?

"Do you want me to call around, see what you're dealing with, I mean, health-wise?"

"I'd rather you went to Dr. Michaels." He had a doctor who had helped him out a lot. A naturopath. The man was extremely discreet.

"You got it. I'll get back to you a.s.a.p. Now, is there anything you need, Scooter? Doughnut delivery? Massages?"

"Oh, God, I could murder a doughnut. Or a kolache." Surely they were close enough to Texas to get one of those amazing Czech pastries.

"You got it, honey. You know I love you."

"I know." He wasn't one for big emotional things, but he cleared his throat. "I'm glad you have my back, Tawn."

"Forever, Scooter. Go relax and recreate."

"Thanks, hon." He hung up, feeling less overwhelmed, less alone. It was probably time to go fish his lover out of the tub, too.

Seb was still in there, sound asleep, body twitching restlessly.

Markus went to him, drawn to that beautiful body, and to the obvious distress. He had a feeling Seb was coming down some, and he remembered detox all too well. He slid into the hot tub, hands sliding along Seb's legs.

Seb's eyes popped open, the look panicked for a second. "What's wrong with the bus?"

"Nothing, baby. We just had one extra night, so we decided to live it up, remember? We hit the road tomorrow." He petted, trying to get Seb to relax.

"Right. Right. I was dreaming." Seb shivered. "I need to go for a run or something. I'm always asleep."

"You're okay." He tugged, watching as Seb floated up. Then Markus pulled the man into his lap.

"Mmm. Hey." Seb looked surprised, every time Markus touched him.

"Hey, baby. Nothing wrong with catching up on some sleep." They would work out a little later on, just to keep things going.

He'd made sure the fucking scale was left on the bus. God knew Seb could stand to gain a pound or... hell, fifty? Maybe? The body he held was too light by far, all skin and muscle. Markus thought maybe the bones had been replaced by pineapple.

"I guess. Things will pile up. God, you feel good." There were almost normal-sized pupils. Almost. Hell, Markus had turned the lights on in the hotel room once, even, and Seb had just blinked like an owl instead of hunting sunglasses.

He just kept touching—it wasn't sexual, just giving

Seb sensations that were good, easy. Reminding both of them how much good could come from just being.

Seb leaned, cheek on his shoulder. "What's your favorite song?"

"To sing, or of all time?"

"Yes."

Markus chuckled, giving that some thought. "I love to sing *Silent Love*. My favorite classic is *Blue Eyes Crying in the Rain*."

Seb nodded. "That song was written for you."

"What?" He pulled back to look Seb in the eye.

Seb went bright red. "It was written for you."

"How do you--" Markus stared. Hard. "You wrote it, *Silent Love?*"

Seb wouldn't meet his eyes, red face going purple.

Markus traced the ink worked into the skin of Seb's belly. "That's why this, huh? Jesus, baby, I never knew."

"That pseud is a secret. I needed to write it. I needed to hear you sing it."

"I've always loved that fucking song." He squeezed Seb hard, moved beyond words, really. That was his song—now more than ever. Meant for no one else.

"Let's get you out of here, huh?" Markus felt incredibly protective at the moment, unbelievably tender. He stood, lifting Seb out of the tub. Seb dangled for a second, then they headed for the towels, the heavy, thick soft robes.

They settled together on the bed, the couches just not comfy enough for both of them. Markus wasn't feeling the need to get busy; he was more interested in just holding on.

Seb turned something on the television, something silly and mindless, quiet. They piled up the pillows and rested together, bodies heavy and lax, murmuring nonsense to each other. It felt like they were a couple. Like a real couple.

Markus thought he should be scared. Worried. This was what he'd been hiding from, for damn near ten years. Oh, not from Seb; that was always easy. No, from people possibly finding out, from having to deal with the fucking logistics of their lives, and from not being brave enough to see it through back then.

"You're thinking hard. Do you think that guy on the TV was born looking like that?"

"Like what?" He looked, and the guy bore a striking resemblance to those eighties puppets with the weird long faces. "Huh."

"I know! It's creepy." Seb laughed and Markus sort of basked in it. Seb needed to laugh more.

Markus let the TV lull him, let his thoughts slide away. He needed to relax, too. Stop worrying so much. This whole thing, it was eating away at them.

Markus just hoped there was something left when they got around to settling down. If that ever happened.

Sebastian stared at the scale, his heart pounding.

Oh, fuck. What had he been doing?

Three pounds. Three pounds and he'd... Oh, God.

Sebastian ran his fingers over his belly, searching for proof that he was getting heavy. There wasn't so much as a new bubble, not even a tiny roll or bit of bumpy skin. Surely three pounds ought to cause a bubble.

There was a knock on his bus door and he frowned, headed over. "Who is it?"

"Bruce, man. Are we rehearsing tonight?"

Was he that fucked up? Really? "Nine to midnight, full band. Three to six, jam session, just like always."

"Okay. Sure. Just checking." When he opened the door, Bruce was grinning. "Man, you look great. Rested."

"Thanks." He found himself grinning back, actually really pleased to see Bruce. "You get home during the break?"

"I did. Ate a lot of Tex-Mex. It was good to crash a few days."

He nodded, heading out to sit, visit. He pulled out a couple of chairs, stopping as Bruce stared. "What?"

"No sunglasses?" Bruce peered at him, then shook his head. "Go you, man. Daylight is your friend."

He flipped Bruce off. "Fuck off, asshole." He eased himself down into the chair, leaning back. "You heard from Kerry? She okay?"

"She is. You sent her flowers. She was tickled."

Sebastian nodded. That hadn't even been Bev. He took care of his people. Loved them. "The baby?"

"Still in there cooking. Jonny is looking like a ghost, a little."

"I bet it's still a shock, huh?" When he thought about it too much it freaked him out. He couldn't imagine Jonny's feelings.

Bruce chuckled. "It's what happens, when boys and girls do the dirty."

Yeah, like he knew anything about that. He was the only man he knew who never had even tried that. Thank God Markus was all man. Sebastian smiled, thinking of Markus' man parts.

"Boss, we got to talk."

His smile faded. He hated those words. "Are you quitting?"

"Fuck, no." Bruce snorted, eyes rolling. "But you got to talk to Jack. He's got you slammed after this tour for fucking months. I know you don't need us for most of it, but it ain't right. You got to take time off."

"I--" What was he supposed to say? He was used to being busy. "I'll talk to Bev."

"Good. Good. You have to protect yourself, man. This whole thing, it's a machine."

"I know. Shit, I've been in it with you since the start." He wasn't a fool. He wasn't. Sebastian knew the score.

"Yeah, but... I just think you have to pay attention."

He tilted his head, pondering that. "I'm more awake these days, huh? I'll look at it."

"Yeah." Bruce grinned at him. "You want to play a game of one-on-one, man?"

"Fuck, yes." He laughed, heading back into the bus to get a ball, feeling pretty good in his bones.

He needed to sit with Bev, talk. First, though, he needed a hat and a better pair of shoes. Sure as shit, Markus and all the other tall fuckers would be out soon, kicking his fun-sized ass.

He couldn't wait. They hadn't played a pick up game in years.

The door of the bus clicked behind him, on the way out at this time of day.

Who would have thought?

Chapter Fourteen

Markus toweled off, his dressing room ringing with quiet, which was just what his poor ears needed. His set had gone like butter, smooth and slick, but he was a little wore out from being back on Seb's rehearsal schedule.

Maybe he could squeeze in a nap before Seb's set ended.

The banging on his door was sharp, panicked, almost furious. "Markus? Mr. Kane?"

Bev. Great. She was in full-on emergency mode, too. He could tell the difference now, in her voice. "Yeah, honey?" He opened the door, his ass dragging.

"He's lost his mind. He says he won't go on, that they're demons. Demons, for fuck's sake!" Bev was the color of milk. "Do I call Jack?"

"What? No. No, don't call anyone." Markus turned and grabbed a hoodie, shrugging it on to cover his bare chest. "Show me."

"Hurry. Hurry, we've only got a little bit. I'm tempted to call 911. He's scary." She led him down under the stage, the roar of the crowd floating overhead. Seb was pacing, one arm bleeding, eyes crazy.

Markus waved Bev off and gave the security guy the fish eye until he turned his back. "Seb? What's wrong?"

"Candy, they're going to eat me. I saw them." Seb wasn't fucking around; the man's face was serious as a heart attack. Pale, too.

Shit. Markus touched Seb's cheek. "No, baby. I was out there. They didn't bother me at all."

"Something's wrong with me. I can't do this. I dreamed about it. They ate me, tore me in half."

"No." He moved closer, lowering his voice. "It's detox, baby. It's just coming off the pills." Markus had done a lot worse than Seb with that, in fact. Screaming, puking, relapsing.

"De...detox?" Seb blinked at him, eyes huge. "You think so? I swear to God, Candy, it feels real."

His thumb rubbed at Seb's cheekbone. "I dreamed I was being smashed between the dock and a cruise ship once, baby. Woke up with a splitting headache. It will be okay."

"Will you watch? Just to make sure?"

"I will. I'll go back behind the main stage, be right there if you need me." He would do anything for Seb.

"Okay. I believe in you."

That was the scariest fucking thing ever—that this man believed demons were out there and only needed his word to go out into it.

Markus squeezed Seb's shoulders. "Okay, baby. Just sing and do your butt shaking and remember I'm right there."

"Okay, Candy. Don't let them get me."

"Never. No one will hurt you." He glanced over at Bev, who had managed to give them some privacy. Then he kissed Seb hard on the mouth, just a quick peck.

Then he pushed Seb into place.

Please, God. Don't let Seb fuck this up.

He'd done it.

He had.

The hallucinations had backed off about three quarters into his set and he focused on nothing but singing, running around. It was hard, though, to keep from jerking, flailing his arms like they wanted to.

It wasn't until Markus came out at the end of the set to do the encore that his heart had stopped pounding like he was being chased by an axe murderer. Markus, with his wide shoulders and long old legs and serious Texas twang made it all better.

The glad handing had almost done him in and he'd stumbled back stage, the sound of the crowd rushing, pounding at his brain. His savior had been Bruce there, hauling him to his dressing room while Markus handled the meet and greet folks and the press-pass people.

He looked at Bruce, blinking, staring as sparkles grew around the edges of his vision.

"Seb? Man, your eyes look bad, like you're gonna pass out." Bruce squatted in front of his chair. "You need some water?"

He nodded. He was. He was going to just lose it.

"Seb? Sebastian? Did you not eat?" Bev came in, fluttering. "I have him, Bruce. I bet he didn't eat. Silly man."

"Oh, man. Bottoming out? I got glucose pills."

Bev waved Bruce off. "I got it. Really. Can you make sure the band gets dealt with?"

"Sure, lady. You want me to keep Rick out of here?"

"Please."

Seb nodded, too. "I need Candy."

"I know, but you have to wait." Bev sighed. "I want a doctor in here. I want you looked at. I don't like this."

The door opened, Markus walking in. Thank God. Markus knew. He knew that the doctors wouldn't really help. Seb was trying so hard.

"Hey." Markus smiled, coming to hand him a bottle of water. "Here, baby, drink this and then we'll get some food."

"Okay." He tried to reach for the bottle, missed, then tried again.

"This is bad," Bev murmured, but Markus never wavered.

"Here." Markus took his hand, helped him take a drink. The water felt shocking. Cold. It was cold. Bright. Good.

He swallowed hard, and his stomach thought about rebelling, but he managed it. Then he took some more in. God, that was amazing. His abs clenched and he frowned.

Bev was hollering at Markus. How had he missed that? "...obviously fucked up? He's my friend. He was telling me the fans were going to EAT HIM!"

Markus looked at him, those dark eyes searching his. Maybe asking for permission?

"I'm trying to back him off the meds, Bev."

"Oh. Oh, thank God."

"It's just making things squirrely. And he's been eating, which he forgot today."

Sebastian nodded, closing his eyes as he swallowed the pills.

"You two can't do things without keeping me in the loop. I can help!"

"It wasn't intentional," Markus murmured. "We had that time off. We need to get him to the bus, okay?"

"We can't, not for another forty-five minutes. The

crowd's insane out there."

He shook his head, heart slamming hard. "We'll wait. Turn on the TV."

"Sure, baby." Markus turned on the TV, and damned if Bev didn't produce a protein bar from her bag.

"It's good. Chocolate. You'll like it. I need you to eat at least a bite."

"I..."

She stared at him. "Now."

Sebastian took the bite she tore off and chewed. It was like sawdust, but it did make his head feel better. He managed to eat one more bite, the noise from the TV cutting the roar of the crowd. The noise in his head eased off, too, and he was able to look at Bev and try for a smile. Markus was there, close, but not interfering.

"I'm going to go see how the crowds look. Markus, do you want food?"

"Oh, God, yes."

Sebastian chuckled softly, and Bev's eyes met his. "I could order breakfast in, or..."

"I'm not hungry, honey. Get Candy whatever he wants." He was too tired to eat.

"Okay." She gave up way too easy, but that was all right. He could say no again when the food came.

"Don't think it's that easy, baby." Markus gave him a knowing look. "You gotta eat."

"I'm getting fat."

"Bullshit. Which one of us has gotten a write-up in the rag mags about being porky, raise your hand." Markus dared him to say anything and thrust one hand in the air.

"Not yet. I ate a meal with you!" More than one. It was... insane.

"Well, hell, baby. You might just explode. Boom." Those eyes took on an evil sparkle, Markus just laughing.

"Laughing at me! Fucker!" He threw one of the

pillows off the couch, starting to feel more like himself.

"Uh-huh. Bev, why don't you go ahead and order that breakfast. No eggs. Just biscuits and sausage and fruit and maybe some kolaches. And a doughnut for me."

"You got it. Orange juice?"

Sebastian nodded. That actually sounded good.

When she left, leaving them quiet and alone, he looked at Markus. "I really thought they were going to hurt me." Candy had to think he was an idiot.

"I know, baby." Markus checked the lock on the door before coming to him, pulling him up for a long hug. "I'm proud of you."

"For being a psycho?" He held on a second, loving the way the fine son of a bitch felt.

"No. For going out there and busting through it. I know how scary coming down is." Markus was warm, solid, like a rock, letting him lean. Then they turned in a lazy circle, Markus easing down with Sebastian on his lap.

"I'm on your lap, Candy. Someone's gonna notice, if we keep up. You know that." He wasn't going to hump Markus on stage, but there were photogs everywhere.

"I know. I've sure thought on it." Markus shrugged. "I was always more worried for you. Still am. But I'm too selfish to live without you now."

Sebastian just sat, taking the words in for a long minute. "Okay."

"Yeah?" Markus smiled for him, and it was like sunrise over the bayou. "Well, good deal."

"Yeah." Yeah, it didn't suck. His phone rang, buzzing on the table, and he stared at it. "It's Jack."

"So, don't answer it. What can he possibly need at this time of night?"

He knew the answer to that. "He'll just keep on. I'll grab it." He grabbed the phone. "Jack."

"What the fuck is wrong with you?"

Sebastian looked for photographers instinctively, eyes moving. "What? What did I do?"

"The fucking Internet is already buzzing, kid. Longchamps lackadaisical. Low-energy Longchamps. What is up? You're not interacting with the crowds, now? You're running off the stage?"

He shook his head. No. No, the crowd had been... vicious. They'd been ready to eat him. He'd believed that. "Bad night, I guess."

"Bad night. Shit. Those people paid good money for you. You don't get a fucking bad night at front row seats going at twelve hundred a piece online. What? Are you getting fat or something? Bored?"

His hand went to his stomach. Two pounds. It had only been two pounds today. "What do you want?"

"For you to remember that you have to fight, kid. There's always someone waiting to push you off. You think Houston McMann isn't working his ass off? Talking to the press? He's featured on the Top 20 show this next week. What are you doing?"

"Writing. Playing three shows."

Markus frowned, grabbing for the phone. The move surprised him so much that it worked, Candy just plucking the phone out of his hand. When he tried to get it back, Markus just held it up where he couldn't reach it.

"Candy?"

He could hear Jack, still bitching. Markus shook his head, grinning, and hit the off button, cutting Jack out of the conversation. "No, baby. No more tonight. He can call during daytime hours."

"Can... can you do that?" He sort of blinked, then felt a grin just growing. Okay, yeah. That was hot.

"Just did, right? I swear, baby, if you were feeling a hundred percent I'd be all over you right now."

"I get that." He touched Markus' throat, just letting his fingers trail. "I so get that."

He didn't have words.

Good thing he didn't need to.

Chapter Fifteen

"H ey, baby, you sure you don't want some toast?" Markus was the picture of patience. He wasn't letting Seb's sudden refusal to eat again get to him. Right? Nope. Now, if that big vein in his temple would stop throbbing...

He wasn't sure exactly who said something or what happened, but the fucking chart was back, the scale, the six hours of sweating a day.

"I'm good, thanks."

"Have you had your shake, at least?" Bev asked, coming over with her clipboard. It was damned near time for their production meeting.

Seb's nose wrinkled but he took it, drank about a third. "So, talk to me, girl. Tell me wonderful things."

She shook her head, grinned. "The new single is number one on iTunes. There's a concert footage video coming. You've got to glad-hand with the local media in Vegas, you're scheduled to be at some fancy-assed bar having drinks with showgirls after the show."

"No." Seb looked stubborn. "I told Jack no. I told

Penny no. I'm telling you no. I don't drink. That time is mine. No."

"But."

Seb's eyes flashed. "Bev. Don't. I said no."

Bev sighed. "I'll talk to Jack. I told him that was a bad idea."

Markus made a mental note to get with Bev. Jack had been pretty squirrelly the last few shows.

"Thank you." Seb's hands were shaking, that hideous fucking shake put aside. "What else?"

"Uh... Bruce needs to know if Hank Bitters is really stopping by for a cover, mid-show."

Seb nodded. "Yeah. He called this morning and gave the nod."

Huh. Hank had known them both for years and years. Markus hadn't even known he was in town.

"Do you know what song?"

"Hank said to let Markus choose."

No pressure. Markus pondered that for a few, wondering what the hell they could let Hank in on.

"Bruce loves to play *Fishin' in the Dark*." Huh. The crowd liked that one, too. Even non-country fans loved that song.

"Sounds good," Markus said, still watching Seb close.

There were cracks, all in the walls Seb had, those eyes twitching, a fine sheen of sweat covering the newly shaved tanned skin. "What else? Is my sister able to come out?"

Bev shook her head once. "No, sir. I'm sorry. Your momma needs her, she says."

"Well, that's a shame." Damn. Seb had been looking forward to that.

"Yeah. I'm going to put some time in on the treadmill. I have a headache."

"You need a little more food before you do that, Seb." Markus was starting to dig his heels in and growl.

Bev looked at him, looked at Seb, looked back. "Call me if you need me?"

He did love that woman.

Seb nodded. "Sure, Bev. Sure."

He watched Seb head back to the weight equipment, the treadmill, the scale, the damned numbers. It made him a little crazy, made him want to snatch the man up physically and run off. That wasn't going to solve shit right now, though, and he was a fucking master of solving shit.

Markus was getting better and better at it.

Bev touched his arm. "Jack asked him if he was fat. I know it. He gained three pounds."

Shit, the man could put on fifty pounds and look good. "Jack and I are fixin' to have a war." The man had to know Seb was unhealthy. Had to.

"I... Yeah. Seb and I need to talk about the money. I. We just do."

"Your money? Is Jack stiffing you, baby girl?" Okay, Markus was going to eat the man's face.

"Not me. Sebastian pays me." Her eyes cut to him, something real worried in them. "But... things are different than they have been."

"Okay. I'll ease him into it today." If someone was cheating Seb, Markus would take them down. Period. Sebastian was the most generous man Markus knew. No one had to take him to the cleaners; they just had to ask.

"Just get food into him. He's not fat."

"I will." He gave her a hug, needing to let her know how much he appreciated what she did for Seb.

"I'll get your laundry delivered and your boots shined while I'm out."

"Thanks, honey."

She walked out, and Markus squared his shoulders and his jaw, gearing up for battle.

The fucking treadmill was going ninety to nothing, Seb's head down, sweat covering the muscled body. Markus knew he couldn't just unplug it, but he was sure tempted. Then he grinned. He just needed to get a guitar.

There was something that Seb needed, even more than breath, more than pills or running or sweating, and Markus knew it. Shit, he was right there.

He found an old acoustic propped up against the wall and started strumming, sinking down on the couch. The rhythm on the treadmill stuttered, and he grinned. Oh, yeah. Now he just needed to find a new hook. A melody Seb hadn't heard before.

It took him about five minutes, but he knew when he got it, because the treadmill slowed to a crawl. *Come on, baby. You know you want it.*

Sure enough, Seb's face appeared in the doorway. "What's that?"

"Huh? Oh, just twiddling." Still, it was a good melody.

"Oh." Seb wiped himself down, padding closer. "Can I hear it again?"

Score.

"Sure, baby." Markus picked it out again, humming along.

"I like that." Seb picked up another one of the guitars. "Can I?"

"Hell, yes. We collaborate well."

There was a plate of cold cuts, cheese, fruit in the fridge and he'd grab it during the bridge, while they beat out the lyrics. First they needed a hook. Seb picked up the melody, dropped it half a pitch and, fuck, pure gold sex. They had a smooth, sweet song and all they had to do was drop in lyrics.

"Mmm. How about a hook like... you got to know the rules?"

"Oh, I like it." There were a hell of a lot of rules

153

floating around. It had endless possibilities.

"Yeah." Like magic, they were going, playing and laughing, scribbling down lyrics and beating out rhythms. It was easy, to get lost in the swing of it, in the rightness of this. Markus forgot everything but the music, and how inextricable Seb was from it these days.

He stood up while they were working on the bridge, grabbed two bottles of juice and the tray, put it down between them without fanfare. Seb kept playing, but when he picked out the counter melody, a piece of ham disappeared, as well as some grapes, a slice of cheddar, and half the juice.

That was the ticket. Seb just needed to be. No thinking, no worrying. Breathing.

Being.

They could do being. Together.

"What do you think of switching the second and third verse?"

Markus shook off his wandering thoughts and got back to songwriting. "Let's try it."

They laid that one out, then took a break, both of them grinning like idiots. God, he loved making music with this man. Fuck, he just flat-out loved Sebastian.

"You look at me like that, Markus, and I can't breathe." He got a grin. "Which, okay, isn't true because I'm talking, but you know what I mean. It's true."

"I know." The words were right there, hanging on his lips, but he didn't say them. Seb was the one with the mind-mouth connection. Markus chuckled. "I want you."

"Yeah?" Music started up again, low and easy, familiar. "Sing for me?"

He knew that song, sunk deep in his bones, and he closed his eyes, his fingers picking out the rhythm line. *Silent Love* slid out as easy as hot butter on toast.

Seb's voice picked up the harmony, the sound wrapping around his own voice, making him ache. He was never going to sing this fucking song alone. Not ever again. They sang the last chorus twice, the ringing of the last chord seeming to go on forever. The silence after was almost impossible to break.

Seb's eyes glittered at him. "I've wanted that, a long, long time."

"You have. I won't make you wait again, baby."

"Okay." Seb touched his wrist, fingertips hot, swollen from playing.

"Oh." The touch jolted him to his toes, his cock lifting in his sweats. "Seb."

He got this smile—slow and fucking wicked, like something he'd have seen ten years ago. "Yeah, Candy."

Markus stood, going to lock the door to the bus, not wanting Bev or Bruce to interrupt. "Come on, baby."

The touch to his ass was gentle, then Seb's cheek landed on his shoulder. "Let's go."

Laughing, Markus lifted Seb up, carrying him. The man weighed next to nothing. They were going to have to figure this out. Soon. Before Seb disappeared.

Chapter Sixteen

Sebastian sat at his desk on the bus, staring. "What do you mean, Bev?"

"Something's going on with the money. I've tried to fix it, to figure it, and I can't. I tried to wait until the tour was over, but..." She shrugged. "You've got three dates left in the biggest tour of the year. The album was number one before it released and still, it just doesn't add up to what you ought to have. You know?"

"Okay. Okay." No way. No way Jack would fuck him over. No way. They'd been together for almost a fucking decade. There was no way.

Her face crumpled a little, but she held it together. "I'm so sorry, Seb. I mean, what if Jack isn't the one? What if it comes from higher up? But he won't take a meeting."

"Well, it doesn't matter who it is right now. What matters is that we'll figure it out. Good job for catching it. You rock, girl." Sebastian was going to be sick.

"I—did I do bad, Seb? Should I have waited?" Bev rubbed her arms, looking very small.

"No, ma'am." He reached out, squeezed her hand. "Lady, you're my best friend and I can't do without you.

You have my back, and I know it. Thank you."

Tears shimmered in her eyes, but she held them back, and the will it took to stop her lip quivering showed in the lines bracketing her mouth. "I love you, Seb. I'm not going to let them take advantage of you."

"Well, good. Now we just have to figure out what the hell to do next."

"Yeah. I—Markus would let us talk to his manager."

"Tawny? She's not on my side, honey. Hell, she's the reason I hired Jack on. Or Jack took me on, or something."

"I bet she's sorry." Bev grinned for him, putting a hand on his arm.

"I bet she is." God, his head hurt. "Okay. I need bank statements, all the things. You know." He didn't know what else. Bev would, though. She always had the ideas.

"I got it. I'll get it to you in the morning. Just in case Jack comes for the show."

"Good deal. I want everything. If we're going to wage a war, we have to have everything in a row." He wanted a pill, for the first time in days, he *wanted* one.

"Do you need me to get anything? Should I call Markus?"

"No. No, I can't just run to him whenever things get weird. I'm a grownup." He'd been doing this on his own a long time, right?

"Of course you are. I just—He loves you."

"I know." He dropped his head in his hands. He knew.

"I'm so sorry, Seb." She patted his arm, and then she was gone, the door closing only a whisper of sound.

He sat there for a long time, looking at the paperwork. He couldn't do this. He wasn't smart enough, wasn't with it enough. All he needed was to go get his pills and he could forget it all.

And if he could forget, he wouldn't care.

***

One more show.

They had one more show to do, and the tour was over. Markus felt like his head was in a vise, being squeezed down like someone was trying to make brain lemonade. His jaw hurt from clenching it, and he hadn't even seen Seb today.

He headed for Seb's bus, the little area where they parked providing just enough privacy to slip through the diesel soaked air. Maybe they could work out together. Maybe talk about what happened after the tour.

Bev was running around like a ghost, flitting around with tight lips and serious eyes. "Mr. Kane."

He was back to Mr. Kane?

"What's up, honey?" He tried a smile.

"What's not up? You should probably leave him alone. He's... Fuck, he's had a bad day and he's high as a kite, trying to fix it. He says everyone has to leave him alone."

The smile fled, chased off by the immediate frown. "Oh, no. No, I think I need to see him."

"He's really... Some bad shit happened." Bad enough to make Bev cuss.

"Has he eaten?"

She shook her head. "He flushed the shakes."

Markus' mouth flattened into a tight line. "You go do your pre-show stuff."

"Okay. Okay. Please don't fight."

At this point, that was fucking inevitable. If Seb was freaking out and tweaking, it could kill their last show, and this was the one all the press would attend. He geared up to go in there and tear up Seb's ass, even if he didn't want to.

The music in the bus was blaring—AC/DC screaming out. If that son of a bitch blew his voice...

Markus slammed in, not giving Seb a chance to meet him at the door. "Are you crazy?"

Bloodshot eyes stared at him, the bags under those green eyes big enough to pack for a three week trek. "Yes!"

"Baby--" He reached out, trying to get Seb to hold still a minute.

"I can't do this shit! Everything is fucking falling apart! Do you fucking hear me? Everything." Seb was just... wild.

"Seb." He caught those flailing hands, pulling Sebastian to him. Then he shook the man a little. "What the hell is going on?"

"She brought me the papers. I thought I could trust them, but I can't and I can't deal with all of it without the pills and I'm fixin' to lose you, too and I'm NOT A FUCKING CHILD!"

"Then stop acting like one. Goddamn it, Seb, I won't be able to be here all the time. Not until your contract is up. I have to know you can take care of yourself." His chest hurt from the emotion pushing up in him.

"I've been taking care of things. I have. I work hard." Seb spun away from him, and a chair went flying, crashing into the wall. "I had it under control. I was doing it."

"Then why aren't you doing it now?" He fought the urge to chase Seb around the room.

"I'm stupid without the pills! I sleep all the time and I'm fat! They're stealing from me!"

Christ. Markus didn't know what to yell about first. The silliest thing, maybe. "You're so far from fat it's a little scary, baby."

"Jack asked me! I'd gained three pounds! People can tell!" There went another chair.

"Bullshit. Jack is an asshole. So are the fuckers in the press." Damn, he was tempted to toss a chair himself. Instead he pulled up to his full height, making himself a target.

"I'm starting to need you, you fuck. Like all the time. You let me love you!" Seb came after him, almost roaring with rage.

He caught that hard little body when Seb slammed into him, lifting the man right off his feet. "I had to. I love you too much not to."

"I'm so fucking scared, man." And there is was, just as fucking bald and simple as could be.

Markus found himself nodding. "I know, baby. God, I know it. Tell me who's stealing from you." Time for the bigger worry. Then the biggest. What the hell were they going to do about them? He'd been so careful over the years, had been the one to pull away.

Now there was no way Markus could let go.

He just had to pray Seb was with him, willing to work it, because losing this now would kill him.

"We can't figure it out, but there's way more than ten million gone, man. That I can see."

The air burst out of his lungs with a surprised grunt. That was a drop in the bucket to a big machine like Sebastian Longchamps, but it was a huge amount of brazen stealing. Jesus. "Who?"

"I don't know! I don't fucking understand." Bloodshot eyes stared at him. "Fuck, man. I don't know what to do. I don't have time."

He resisted the urge to hug Seb now. First they had to figure shit out. "You think it's Jack?"

"Why would he fuck me? I've made him a shitload of money."

"People do stupid things." He wasn't making excuses. If he found out it was Jack, Markus would rip the man's head off and shit down his neck.

"I'd have given it to him."

That was the bad part. He knew that. Everyone knew that. Sebastian was generous to the level of ridiculous. He never turned down a friend. Never.

"I know, baby." He sighed, finally lowering Seb's body to rest against his.

"I had to take them, man. I had to. I can't make it."

"I wish to fuck you had called me." The urge to shake Seb teetered on the edge of his consciousness.

"I can't just lean on you for everything."

"No? It's better to take pills?" Shit, he knew it. He was the one who'd just been screaming about how he couldn't be there soon. What the hell were they gonna do? "I can call Tawny."

"I'm just... I'm not a fucking weakling. I was doing it. I was. And now I'm not."

"You're not weak, baby. You're overwhelmed." Rehab sucked hairy donkey balls when you had nothing better to do than sit on your ass. When you had to keep all your balls in the air at the same time? Christ.

Seb was the strongest son of a bitch he'd ever met.

"Tell me I can call Tawny in, baby. At least she can help us look at shit and no one will ask why she's here."

"She's your manager, Candy. Is that like a conflict?"

Markus shook his head, "She's my friend, too. And she worries. I'm out to her, baby."

"I told Bev about you." Like Bev didn't know. Seb rolled his eyes. "Look, I know she knew, but I told her."

"That means a lot to me, baby." It did. "Kyle knows, too. About you, I mean. Not just about the other." Silly, but he needed Seb to know he wasn't ashamed.

"Are... What happens next? I mean, not with the money. With you?"

"I don't know." He looked around, blinking at the mess in the bus. "Can we go sit?"

"God, yes."

Seb led him over to the sofa, the man's clothes hanging off him, everything too loose, too odd. This whole situation was going to kill the man, and Markus didn't know whether to scratch his watch or wind his butt. Maybe he could figure out how to travel with Seb a bit.

How the fuck did this happen, that he ended up in love with somebody as fucked up as he was? It wasn't fucking reasonable, damn it, but he still... Shit, he couldn't just say he wasn't in this, ball's deep.

Like Seb had heard him, read his face, the man sighed. "I'm not a fuck up. I'm not. I know you think I am— that I'm a goddamn weak loser, but I'm not. I just..." Seb's shoulders slumped, his lover shrinking in front of his eyes. "Too many balls, too few hands. How long until the show starts?"

"I don't know." He looked at his watch. "I'm on in about four hours. That gives you damned near seven."

"Okay. Okay. Okay."

He shook Seb a little, hoping to... shit, he didn't know, reset the little fucker. Shake the brain in Seb's head until something in the loop of "I suck" came loose.

"Right." Seb stopped, eyes closing. "Call Tawny. Please. Tell her I need... help. I have to figure out what to do. I'm supposed to fly out tonight, right after the concert."

"No. No, that we'll change. I'll get Bev on it. And I'll call Tawny. Promise me no more pills tonight." That was important. Seb was almost vibrating in his arms.

"I promise. You'll be there, here? Tonight?"

"I will." Come hell or high water, he would be there and they would put their heads together and figure this shit out.

"I'm not a loser. I just... I'm tired."

He bit back the fact that maybe if Seb ate, if the man wasn't a good sixty pounds underweight, maybe he'd build energy... That would just be bitchy right now, and Seb didn't need that at all. "I hear you, baby. It's been a long couple of days."

"Shit. It's been a long couple of months. Damn good music, though."

"I've written more in the last two months than I have in two years." They shared a smile; music was worth the pain.

"We're good at it." Seb nodded. "Just think how well they'll sell."

"Hell, yes." As long as no one stole their shit right out from under them.

He had to get Tawny down here, tonight, and he had to figure out how to get Seb out of whatever he was supposed to fucking be doing tomorrow. That was the only way this whole mess was going to work.

Time to call in the reinforcements.

The crowd was wild, and they played an extra three songs before finally shutting it down. Given how shitty his day had gone, Sebastian would have sworn that the show was going to suck. Somehow it hadn't.

Markus brought the house down, he did his shit, and then they got on stage together and... fuck. Fuck, yes. There was something about the energy between them tonight, something amazing and scary and wonderful. Bruce had figured it out; the man couldn't seem to stop grinning at him.

He wiped his face, took the shake from Bev and downed it. "It was a good finale."

"You sounded fabulous." Like Bev wasn't totally tone deaf. She was still his number one fan, though, and she meant what she'd said. He could tell.

"Thanks, sweetie. I'm going to get cleaned up."

She nodded. "Uh. Markus—Mr. Kane—his company is here. Waiting."

"His manager?"

That got him another nod.

"Good deal. I'll be in my dressing room."

"I'll tell Mr. Kane. Right?" She gave him a searching look, like a puppy needing reassurance they were a good dog.

"Yep. Then just keep your phone close, yeah? I might need you."

"I will. Don't let them mess with you, Seb. Call me before Jack makes you do anything." She clicked off, her "it's showtime" heels making the best noise. Like castanets.

He cleaned up, changed shirts, drank three huge bottles of water. The need for the pills buzzed at the back of his skull, but he resisted, pacing instead. He chewed his thumbnail, a habit he'd given up three years ago.

When Markus—and he knew that rhythmic sound like he knew his own heartbeat—knocked, he damn near jumped out of his skin. He practically ran to the door, his hand shaking when he opened up.

Markus stood there, smiling, looking relieved as hell. "Hey, baby."

"Hey. We did it." He let Markus in, shut the door behind him.

"We did. It was a hell of a tour." Markus hugged him, the motion easy as breathing.

Sebastian snuggled in, hummed, stealing this second. He needed to soak up Markus' solid strength to do this. Shit was fixin' to hit the fan, he knew it, like he knew the melody to *Pretty Woman*, and he wasn't ready.

"So." Markus paused, then sighed. "You ready to talk to Tawny?"

"No, but I bet I don't have a choice." He took a deep breath, then stepped back. "Do we do it here or in the bus?"

"The bus, I think. Unless you want to go to mine."

"I do, but everyone will notice. Bev said she cleaned up from my shit fit earlier." He'd been on the far side of stupid. Go him.

"Okay, baby. We'll go to yours." Markus winked, taking his hand.

"Tell me that I'm not a paranoid idiot." He knew he was, just like he knew that Bev wasn't. At all.

"Well, you're not an idiot." They laughed, Markus squeezing his fingers.

"Fuck head." They headed to the sofa, waiting out the crowds, the chaos. It felt so good, to sit there, held in Markus' arms. He clung a little, so afraid this was going to end, that it would all be ripped away.

"Hush, now. We're gonna fix this."

Sebastian could hear his maman in his head. "Chile, chile, we gon' fix it." It made him smile. Helped him believe, too. His maman, the old Cajun witch woman.

"Mmm. That's better. I like when you smile."

"I like it when I smile, too."

"Imagine that." Markus kissed his neck, just below his ear.

He shivered, his cock filling with a rush that left his hands shaking. "Be good, Candy."

"Sorry?" Markus didn't sound sorry. The man sounded evil. Like incarnate.

"Uh-huh. No kissing."

Markus answered him with a bite that might just leave a mark. Maybe that was okay, though. He didn't have anywhere to be for two days, so long as he made tomorrow's little show. He'd argued for that one until he was blue in the face.

Finally, finally they were going to be able to stop a second. Breathe. Figure shit out.

When the knock came at the door, Markus sighed, but

let him slide off the couch. "It's Tawny, baby. I'll get it."

"I got it..." The door popped open and Bev stood there, pale as a ghost.

"Seb?"

"What?" He backed up a step.

She held out her phone. "Your sister's been calling, honey. I'm so sorry."

His knees buckled. "Oh, shit. Shit, no." He'd just been thinking on her. His maman. Not now. Oh please.

"Seb?" Markus caught him when he staggered. "Seb, you need to talk to your sister."

He reached for the phone. "Sister?"

"Chou? Chou, she... it's over. About fifteen minutes ago. I been calling."

Seb figured he was gonna puke. "I'm sorry. Oh, God. I should have been there."

"Oh, Chou. Lord, she's not been awake in days. She was gone-gone. Shit, you know she ain't been Maman in two years, easy." His older sister chuckled, and the sound was so Maman that it burned. "I reckon she waited for your big tour. She always hated messing with folks' schedules. I need you now, though, huh? Just to help for a few days and maybe to give this old girl a hug."

"Anything."

"Well, you just get here as soon as you can. The funeral will probably be Wednesday."

"I'll pack now. I'll be there by morning. I promise." Shit, he didn't even know for sure where he was. Michigan? Wisconsin? Somewhere. "Love you."

He pushed the button and handed the phone back. "Bev, I need..."

"I'm on it."

"Thank you." He didn't know what to do. His hands kept fluttering, his mouth opening and closing. Finally, he turned to Markus, who immediately grabbed him.

"Oh, baby. I'm sorry."

"Me too. I think. I mean. I have a show tomorrow. I have to bring Jack in." Could this whole fucking nightmare have come at a weirder time?

"No. No, you need to go home. I can take your show tomorrow. I bet Tawny can swing that." Markus chewed his lip. "Bev, we need to get a schedule worked out."

"Let me get a private plane booked for Seb, and I'll get with you and Jack and Tawny." Bev looked at him. "Your job is to be with family. All this crap—all this politics and bullshit about family and values—everyone has to understand or expose themselves as assholes. Grab your bag. I'll have a suit delivered to your hotel for the funeral."

"What would I do without you, girl?"

"Be painfully disorganized and skinnier than you are. Get your go bag."

"Thank you." He hugged her hard, just needing to hang on to her for a moment so she understood how much he loved her.

He headed to the back and he heard Bev talking to Markus, then the big man filled the doorway, looked at him. All in the world he wanted, right this second, was to hide in those arms, but it wasn't going to happen. Shitty, but true.

He found a smile for Markus, knowing it wouldn't be true. "I guess I should be happy she's out of pain, huh?"

"That's what they say. I think you should feel what you feel, huh?" Markus knew, too. Those dark eyes looked a little haunted. "I'll take care of business. You take care of family. We'll meet up after the funeral."

"Okay. I'm sorry." He wasn't sure what he was sorry for, but he was. This whole situation bordered on ludicrous in the extreme. He might just start laughing hysterically and not stop.

Markus moved close enough to touch his shoulder, fingers strong, warm. That was all they were gonna get, because security was there suddenly, ready to take him to the car so he could head for the airport. Markus held on, though, long enough for him to look the man in the eye.

"I'm not," Markus said softly. "Not about anything except your mamma."

"I love you."

He didn't wait to see if Markus said it back; he didn't wait to see if Markus had even heard him. He'd said it, he meant it, and, God willing, one day he'd say it again.

Right now, though, he had to head home.

Markus went to his bus, needing to get away from the media frenzy. Hell, he needed to get away from Bruce and Kyle and the opening acts and the damned photographers who all wanted to know what they could do or if there was some way to get more information.

Christ, what a zoo. At least Seb had managed to get out, get on a plane.

"Hey, Scooter. How's he doing?" Tawny was sitting there, like she belonged on his bus, looking cool as a cucumber in a pretty little white dress.

"He's freaking out." Markus went to the fridge and stared inside, wanting a beer so bad he could taste the sour goodness of it on the tip of his tongue.

"I brought us strawberry milkshakes." She stood, pushed one into his hand. "And of course he is. Poor baby. We'll send flowers to his sister."

"We will." He took a sip of the shake, closing the fridge. "Someone's stealing from him, Tawn. We need to figure this shit out."

"I've got your back. You have all the files for me?"

"Bev got them to me, yeah." He knew he should try to wind down, but he was too damned worried. "I agreed to take that Vegas thing for him."

"Okay. I'll call Jack, arrange it. You don't worry about Longchamps' money. I'll figure it out." She put her shake down, hands on his shoulders. "Jesus, you need a real massage. I'll get you one first thing in the morning."

"I worry about everything to do with him, Tawny. He's all I want." He hugged her just like Seb had hugged Bev, like he needed to absorb strength.

"Well, looks like you got him. And I got you. No matter what happens." The words sounded...full of portent.

"You know something I don't, lady?" He sure as hell hoped he wasn't about to get ambushed with a full-on expose on one of those news shows or something.

"I do. But it's not about you, or Seb."

He hated games. She knew that, so what she was up to was a mystery. "You gonna tell me or do you want to sweep for bugs?"

"We caught pregnant." The grin he got was as scared as it was tickled. "It finally happened, Scooter. We tried for so long, but... I'm due in late January."

His jaw dropped, his heart swooping before taking up a hard beat of happiness for her. "Oh, honey, that's great!" Markus hugged her tight, thinking better of spinning her like he wanted to.

"I know! You're going to be a godfather!" She squeezed him, cackling. "Jim's going to stay home, full time. I'll have a house-husband. Crazy, huh?"

"That's something else." Lord, when it rained it poured. This was good, at least.

"The doctor says I'm great, she's great. I'm not leaving you, you know that, right?"

"I know. No, I know." She'd be hard pressed to keep up with him and Seb, though, if Seb was gonna have to fire Jack.

"I know what you're thinking. Two singers ain't too bad."

"No? Seb is more popular than me, honey."

"I love you, Scooter, I really do, but Sebastian Longchamps is in the center of a nuclear breakdown. He's either going to have to back off or it's going to kill him. You know this. I think he does, too."

"I do." His shoulders tried to pull up around his ears. "I mean to stop him."

"Then I do, too. There's life after stadium shows, and y'all need to start planning one."

Hardassed bitch. God knew he loved her. She was solid as a rock, too. "We'll need your help on that. Can you get me to Vegas?"

"I can. I'll run interference with Jack, too, get these numbers run."

"Thanks." He sighed, his urge for a beer backing off enough that he could enjoy the strawberry shake. He was starving all of a sudden, too.

"Doughnut?" She grinned over, winked. "Or we could just get in a car and drive. It's a beautiful night and I ended up with a luxury."

"That sounds like a plan. Everyone else can just catch up." Most everyone else would go their own way, once the tour was cleaned up.

"Yeah. We can be in Vegas by dawn, sleep all day. It'll be great."

"Let's do it." He had his go bag and she could stop and get him a chicken biscuit or something.

"Hey, Scooter."

He looked back, "What?"

"I love you, honey. It's going to be okay."

Markus nodded, trying to believe it. He'd do what he had to do, and by Christmas, come hell or high water, he and Seb would be giving up the stadium life. He'd damned well see to it.

Chapter Seventeen

He sat at the funeral home, in one of the alcoves where nobody could see him. The photographers had been dogging him—at Sister's, at his hotel. Everywhere. Now he was waiting.

Maman's casket was already there, closed and waiting for Aunt Laney to wail over her and all of Sister's kiddos to say goodbye. Sebastian wasn't sure he knew how to. Shit marthy, it wasn't supposed to be like this. She was supposed to wait for him, let him say goodbye, take her last breath clinging to his hand.

Sebastian snorted at himself. Jesus, drama much? Nothing went like you planned it to, and she was in a better place. He believed it. Alzheimer's was no way to live.

"Where you at, Bubba?" Sammy's voice rang out, too loud as always.

"Here, Sister." He stood, peeked on the other side of the curtain. "Hiding."

"'Course you are." God, she looked tired. Eight years separated them, and she looked every one of them. "You need to eat."

"You need to sleep." He scooted over as she sat, her curves settling beside him. "How are the kids?"

"Bitchy. One's with her boyfriend, the other's playing video games. Did you pick music and stuff with M'su Thibbedeux?"

"Yeah." That had actually been easy, almost fun. Maman had loved her some music. She'd had a fondness for hymns that were more Southern than Catholic. They'd argued a bit, and Seb had agreed to have *Ave Maria* if they'd let them play *Just a Closer Walk with Thee*. Either way, the music would play here at the funeral home, not at the mass or at the graveside.

She leaned against his side. "It don't seem real. I keep getting up of the mornin', looking 'round for my glasses, so I can call up to the home, check on how her night went."

"You're a good woman, Sister."

"Shit, you paid for everything. You're the one that got out." Sammy hadn't done bad for herself—marrying a vet, having babies, even getting a pretty damned successful fabric store going when her quilting habit had tried to take over. Still, Sebastian got it. He was the one hiding from the press, after all.

"I miss her." It was so strange, being home and not having her.

"Yeah. I get that. It's weird."

They sat there, together, just sorta...breathing. In a way, that was a good thing. Seb couldn't remember when he last took a deep breath and stayed still. The world moved slower once you crossed into Cajun country.

"Can you stay for a while?"

"I can. At least a week or two." He had to. Sister needed him to help her clean stuff out, deal with the big picture like she'd dealt with the little shit all this time.

Hell, probably it was more he needed her.

"*C'est bon.*" She hugged on him a moment, then patted his leg. "I got to go make sure the aunties know where to take the food later."

"Okay. I... I'm just gon' sit here with her a bit." Maybe sing to her.

"You do that, Chou. I love you." She left in a cloud of lemon-scented perfume, humming a lullaby he'd heard all his childhood but not since.

Sebastian sat there, staring at nothing at all, then he stood, feeling ancient, feeling like he couldn't breathe deep. He rested his hand on the smooth wood, eyes on the picture that had been on the wall of the front room since the beginning of time. It was both his folks on their wedding day—a skinny little soldier with a pretty girl with a miniskirt and long, ironed hair. Did this make him an orphan?

He smiled at himself, then whispered. "I did it, Maman. I really did, and I think it's going to be real this time. I think... God, I need you to pray for me, because if it goes bad this time, there ain't gonna be no rescuing your boy anymore. If I screw this up..." He shook his head, gritted his teeth.

He knew the truth, damn it.

If they did this for real—him and Markus—and they got caught, it was over. The ride was done for them, for the band, for Bev. He knew that.

But how many love songs did he have to write before his came true?

And what kind of sick, crazy fuck thought about his love life while he was leaning on his mother's casket? He rested his head on his hands and let himself cry—for him, for Sister, for Maman.

Wasn't nobody here to listen on it and so it just came on, his personal storm. When it was over he just felt tired, wore to the bone. He just felt like his whole life had taken a left turn when it should have gone right.

Of course, taking left turns was sort of what he did.

He rolled his head on his neck, his shoulders like frozen rope. "I don't know what to do, Maman." He didn't have to work out, or sing or rehearse. He was lost.

"Lawd, bebe, you don' have to know. You 'sposed to be a little lost." He turned, saw the familiar face of Maman's best friend, Cece, broad and dark and sad and right there. "Come here and let me love on your baby body."

She tugged him in, surrounded him in the scent of baby powder and cayenne and apples.

Sebastian hugged her tight, the tears threatening all over again. The only people in his life who didn't want something from him were Bev and Markus. Being home like this, there were hundreds of people just like Cece who just needed to comfort him.

"Made you pralines, bebe, and made up the bed in the doghouse."

He chuckled; he'd always been fascinated by the little one bedroom house built behind Cece's home. She'd called it the doghouse because she'd sent Warren to sleep there when her husband had pissed her off. It was private, simple, and...perfect. "Yeah? You don't mind?"

"No, bebe. I insist."

"Thank you. I just don't think I can stay at Sister's." Or another hotel.

"No. No, there's energy in there that got to ease, huh?"

"Not to mention all of the clocks are stopped. I'd be late for everything." He gave her a watery smile. "Thank you."

"Anytime, bebe. You mine, jus' like mine's hers."

"'kay."

She nodded. "Come home, now. Rest. Folks will sit with her and tomorrow we'll sing and the good Father will send her home."

Sebastian could handle that. After that was over, well, he had no idea what he would do.

That thought terrified him, down to the bone.

"Let me buy you a drink, Markus."

Markus turned to stare down the record exec who had insisted on taking him to dinner to talk about some award show or another. He would much rather be by the phone in case Seb called, and he sure as hell didn't want a drink.

"Just water, please."

"Are you sure? They make an exceptional martini."

"No, thanks. Look, I hate to be in a hurry on your dime, but I'd like to kick back at the hotel for a few hours. Can we cut to the chase?"

"Absolutely, man. We want you to do the CMAs. Closing act. It's a good spot, you could parlay an encore into something with all the performers."

"Oh." Well, hell. Tawny would shit a pink Twinkie. Markus frowned, wondering why they hadn't just taken it to Tawny instead of catching him in Vegas. "My manager knows my schedule better than me, man."

"Are you with Jack Michaels, now? Or are you still with Tawny?"

"Tawny is my girl." He forced a smile. "Jack is pretty busy with the Longchamps machine."

"Yeah. I heard he had a death in the family. That sucks. I hope the family's okay."

"Last I heard they were holding it together." Thank God Seb's sister was as solid as they came.

The dude—who, Markus had to admit, had a name he didn't even know—just nodded, all sympathetic and shit. "So, I'll contact Tawny, tell her that you agreed to the gig and we'll discuss compensation. Do you think that Longchamps will be available for the show? I know you two have the EP."

"I don't know. If he is, it would be great to do the show with him." That would be just fine, in fact, allowing him and Seb to come back together.

"Excellent." He got another of those slick grins. "You sure you don't want anything but water? I won't tell."

"No. Thanks." Markus tapped his fingers on the table, wondering how soon he could duck out after a steak dinner. If this was a date, he'd know. Tawny always gave him the signal at business things.

His phone vibrated in his pocket. Twice.

"Hey, can you excuse me a moment?" Markus slipped out of the booth, heading out toward the casino floor, where he might be able to get a steady signal. Deep in the steakhouse it was harder to keep a call going.

He called Seb back, as soon as he got a good signal, keeping his ball cap pulled down low.

The first thing he heard was, "You busy?"

"Nope. What's up, baby?" He started walking. He'd call Tawny later, tell her to apologize to Mr. Industry, that it had been an emergency.

"Jack says I'm out of bereavement leave. I'm supposed to be in... New York in the morning? Some morning show? How's wherever you are?"

"I'm still in Vegas. Tell Jack to fuck off. This isn't an option. This is your mamma we're talking about." He was going to call Jack personally, set a meeting, and pull the man's teeth with a pair of pliers.

"Vegas, huh? Don't gamble, it's bad for you."

"No gambling, no drinking. Is Sister feeding you?" Please God let Seb be eating.

"I'm staying with Cece." Seb sighed softly. "I miss you. Is that a pussy thing to say?"

"God, no." No, he missed Seb like a lost limb. Hell, he'd decided to chuck all caution and be with Seb, and now he wanted the payoff, damn it.

"Oh, good. I can't write. I don't want to sing. I just run a lot and read. Cece really likes vampire books."

God, Seb made him laugh.

"Are they the sexy books, or just bitey?"

"Mostly biting, some fucking." He could hear Seb's smile in the man's voice. "Tell me you've been having fun. I heard your show went well."

"Touring with you has done wonders for my career." Ironic, since he was really retired.

"Yeah. You were rocking it, without me. You look amazing."

"Shit, baby, I was just trying to live up to the show you would have given." He found a quiet alcove near the bathrooms off the lobby.

"Still." Seb sighed for him. "Are you going to be somewhere day after tomorrow, maybe?"

"I'm sure I'll be somewhere," he teased, then relented. "San Francisco."

"I'll see if I can come, if you want. I've got New York City tomorrow morning, then Nashville tomorrow night, but I can fly out late."

"Oh, baby, I want. I'm getting antsy for you." That was putting it mildly, but he knew they would have to work through obligations.

"Good. I need to see you for a bit, just sit with you. Maybe have a sing."

His fingers itched for his guitar, just like that. "God. Please."

"I'll bring my acoustic."

"Then I'll be waiting." They needed to write together. They were turning out good songs.

"Cool. You...you talked to Tawny?"

"I did. She says the rabbit hole is deep, baby. We need to talk in person." His teeth clenched, just thinking about what Tawny had already dug up, which was the tip of the proverbial iceberg. Somebody'd been fucking Seb for a while, but it was getting worse, getting blatant.

"Yeah. Yeah, we will." It seemed like every time he spoke to Seb, the man sounded a little older. That whole tired and sad thing needed to stop.

"Over cioppino and sourdough, huh?" He might be from cowboy country, but he could eat local when he was on the road.

"Listen to you, eating food that you have to chew." The words were fond, teasing.

"I know. We can always get you a nice broth." Chuckling, he checked to make sure no one seemed too interested in him.

Everyone was busy, smoking, drinking, working the slots. Suddenly, painfully, the scent of addiction was everywhere, like it was in his fucking skin. Markus closed his eyes, ready to just—something. Explode, maybe. Tawny had left yesterday, and the rental car was gone. "I need to get out of here, baby. I need to..."

"Okay. Okay, like now? Do you have a room?"

"I do, but it's here in one of the casinos. It's--" Markus laughed a little, his throat feeling raw. "It's a bit much."

"Shit, it's like temptation distilled into fucking neon lights."

He croaked out another laugh. "I know, right? You think someone would come get my shit if I just left? I have my wallet."

"I think someone would, yeah. Get in a car and drive, man."

"I will. God, baby, why is this so hard? We did this for years, you and me. Being apart."

"Because we got spoiled, maybe. Mostly, though? We got hope."

179

Hope was as painful as it was wonderful. "You know it, baby. You know it. Thanks for saving me from the shark."

The *Jaws* theme song came over the phone line, making him chuckle.

"I'm heading out. I'll call you when I get a car and figure out where I'm staying tomorrow."

"I'll have my phone. Have fun driving. Sing a lot."

"I will. I have a lot of Longchamps on my iPod." He headed for the doors, intent on getting a cab to the nearest car rental place, which was probably at McCarren.

He managed to slip into the cab before the pair of teenagers discussing whether or not he was him got the courage to ask. Better to leave them wondering than snarl at them and end up getting bad press.

Soon he was in a Mustang, flying through the desert, the moon huge. He thought about calling Seb again, but the man had to sleep, and Central time was way ahead of him, now. Still, he'd gotten out of Sin City without so much as a cigarette, which he thought was a triumph of sorts.

He'd head for San Francisco and find an amazing boutique hotel, let the one Tawny had chosen be the decoy. If he was going to spend some time with Seb, he wanted to do it right.

He wanted contact, privacy. He wanted Seb. They needed to touch and sing and just be. The rest could just go away.

Chapter Eighteen

Sebastian flew into Half Moon Bay, sitting close enough to Justin to see out of the front of the little plane. There were benefits to being him—lots of them—and he'd made a couple of calls and found an old friend who still had a pilot's license and a free schedule who was willing to take him to Cali.

He loved surfers.

"Thanks for the short notice, man. Things are..." Weird. Awful. Insane. "...crazy busy."

"No worries, mate. I need to hang on this side of the world a bit. I'll go see my sister, you call when I'm supposed to take you wherever, deal?"

Sebastian nodded. "I have to be in Nashville day after tomorrow at eight a.m. for a business meeting. When's the latest we can leave here?"

"Be here at midnight. We'll make it happen."

"Rock on."

He got out of the jet, grabbed his guitar and bag, and headed toward a little red convertible waiting by the hangar, a familiar grin under the brim of that gimme cap.

Long arms unfolded and reached for him, Markus

coming to meet him just inside the hangar door. "Hey, baby. Nice ride."

"It's good to have friends." He admired the Mustang. "I like it. Can we drive? I have until midnight tomorrow and my phone's turned off."

"Anywhere you want to go. I got nowhere to be and I'm rested up."

Markus had told him about the long sleep, about how Vegas had worn him out, just resisting temptation.

He put his guitar in the back seat, slid in the passenger side. "Somewhere we can write and I don't have to pretend to be somebody else."

"I got us a house on the beach. Tawny rented it in her name and I picked up the key last night." Markus pushed into the driver's seat, hand landing on his leg. "God, I missed you."

"Ditto. You look good." Three weeks and Markus looked like magic still, somehow. "Cece sent me with pralines."

"Oh, man. I remember those. They're like heaven." Markus leaned over to give him a lingering kiss, which made him a little stupid. "Thanks."

"Drive. Tell me everything you've done." He blinked, achingly happy to be there, with Markus.

Markus started up the car and got them going, heading out toward the highway. "Mostly I did those Vegas shows and met with label people. How's your sister holding up?"

"I think she's a little relieved, cher. She can focus on the kiddos, on doing her thing. She looked less tired when I left." He sighed. "Lord, I don't know. It's a damn strange thing."

Markus laughed, patting his leg again. "Such a Cajun once you've been home a while."

"I stayed up at Cece's. She makes me remember where I come from." He'd told her about Markus—her and

Sister both—and they'd both laughed at him, teased him unmercifully. "Sister says you have to come sing her happy birthday in February."

"I can do that. Especially if she makes me etouffe." Markus looked over at him. "They... What did you tell them?"

"The truth." That he'd been Markus' for a long damned time and he didn't know how it was going to work yet, but he knew who he wanted.

The smile that broke over Markus' face made it all worth it. It was beautiful to see.

They were going to have to talk about things—mostly Tawny and money—but this was enough for right now. It had to be.

Sebastian leaned back, let the air wash over him. The interview had gone poorly this morning, the makeup on his newly shaved face too heavy, the lights too bright, the newscaster too toothy. They'd forgiven him, he thought, offered condolences about Maman. Jack hadn't been happy, though. Had been hanging too close, hovering over him.

Markus let it ride for a good while, just humming along with the radio. That kid who'd opened for them, Houston, had a new single out. Go him. He'd known the kid would hit; there just had to be a catalyst.

"Not bad," Markus said when the song ended. "Not as good as any of the ones we wrote."

"Nope. You going to do a video for *Running on the Wrong Side*?"

"If I have to." They got going on the highway, getting up to speed, which was just fun as hell.

He slipped out of his seatbelt and got up on the seat, letting the wind hit his torso as he swayed on his knees. God, he wanted to fly. Really fly.

"No jumping, baby." Markus sounded amused, though, not worried.

"No. I'm just..." Breathing. Soaring. Free. "...happy."

"Good."

Yep. Good. It was a fine thing to hear the satisfaction in Markus' voice, too.

He plopped back down, breathing hard like he'd been running. Immediately he felt Markus' hand on him again, stroking his arm. "You want to stop for some food?"

"I'm okay."

He felt Markus' eyes on him. heavy, looking hard.

"Maybe a milkshake?"

"Sure, baby. I bet you'd eat some fries, too." From the way Markus' smile went a little strained he thought he'd failed the test.

He sighed, rubbed his forehead to ward off the headache that was threatening. He hated fucking up.

"Stop it." Markus flicked his arm with one finger. "I worry. I'll be good, though, huh?"

"I just... I don't want to think about that part right now, cher. There's enough to think about." Maman, Markus, Jack—he couldn't do anything else.

"Then I'll think on it for you." The next exit rose up and Markus pulled off. "Get your sunglasses on, baby."

He nodded and pulled on his cap, glasses, relaxing back into the seat bonelessly. He knew he looked nothing like his concert/ photo shoot self. It would be Markus people recognized. Markus was stunning and unique. He was a Cajun in a T-shirt.

"Hey, there," Markus said to the kid at the drive-in. "A double bacon burger, two fries, two vanilla shakes and a fried apple pie."

"Sure, man." The kid nodded and dealt with the order, giving Markus a fish-eye only a couple of times. "Cool ride."

"Thanks. She handles real well." Markus grinned, and Seb was thankful Markus had sunglasses on. Those eye crinkles were the stuff of legend.

The smile made his cock jerk, try to fill for the first time since Maman had died. He'd had it turned on him, more than a few times, and it was breathtakingly effective. They got their food without anyone making the connection, though, and Markus hit the road again, whistling a little.

"You might have to feed me French fries."

"I can do that." He pulled out one of the containers, pulled a fry out. "Open up."

"Ahh." Markus opened up and let Seb pop a fry in his mouth, licking the salt off his lower lip. "Yum."

Seb moaned, eyes on the dark stubble, on those now slick lips. "You want another one?"

"I do." Markus opened up again, slowing the car down just a tiny bit.

He fed Markus another, then licked his own fingers clean.

"We might have to find a place to stop before we get to the rental, you keep doing that."

"Feeding you fries?" He liked it, that he felt like he could tease a little bit.

"Licking things." That voice was just a low growl.

"Fuck, cher. You got things way more lickable than my fingers." He was addicted to that fat, heavy cock.

"Don't make me wreck the car, now." The sideways look he got damned near burned him to the ground.

"I won't. Drive. I'll feed you." He ate a fry; they were good. Greasy and salty and hot.

"Thanks, baby." Markus ate another fry before grabbing one of the shakes.

Sebastian played with the radio, landing on a classic rock station and lighting there, singing along as he unwrapped Markus' burger, set it up so the man could eat on it. He also downed a half an order of fries and a quarter of his shake before he slowed down, which made him blink in surprise.

Markus didn't say anything about it, and neither did he, because they were singing with Pete Townshend and Paul McCartney and Paul Simon. Sebastian kinda forgot about it halfway through *Mother and Child Reunion*, and by the time they'd yodeled their way through *Hocus Pocus* with that Focus band, they were turning off the highway again, the GPS pinging softly.

The place was gated, Markus digging out his phone for the code. It had that California look to it, like it would be all tile and hot tub. Private, too. His fingers found Markus' thigh, traced the seam of those soft, ancient jeans.

"Oh, now. Good thing I'm done with my food. I'd be dropping stuff everywhere with you distracting me."

"And all you have to do is get to the garage."

"Yeah? Gonna ride me right here in the car?" Markus gunned it through the gate, keying the garage door opener hanging off the visor.

"Fuck, no. I want you naked, sprawled out on a bed. Maybe in the pool."

"Jesus." They almost hit the back wall of the garage, but the door shut behind them and Markus jumped out of the car. "Last one to find the master bedroom is hauling in the suitcases later."

He grabbed his guitar, noting with a grin that Markus did too, and they headed in, running. The cases were left on a kitchen table, then they made a beeline for the huge staircase. Masters were always upstairs, right?

"Look at that, baby." Markus opened a door, but it was a bathroom. It had an amazing tub.

"Mmm." He tugged Markus in, turned on the water. "I can handle slick and hot."

"I like the way you think." Markus started stripping

down, clothes flying everywhere.

He stripped down, all nice and waxed, bare. He stepped into the water, moaning at the heat.

"That's fucking decadent, baby." When Markus was naked he joined Seb, pushing his legs out of the way.

He let his fingers trail all up along Markus' legs, tugging at the short hairs.

"Mmm. Hey, baby. Missed you." Markus floated a little closer, legs sliding under his.

"I hear you." He pushed forward, ending in Markus' lap, legs wrapping around the man's waist.

Markus laughed for pure joy, grabbing his ass and pulling him so close they pressed together from chest to groin.

"Hey, Candy." He rolled his hips, cock sliding on Markus' abs.

"Feels amazing." They rocked together, Markus bending to kiss him like there was no tomorrow. The music started up in his head, deep and rich.

He loved it, this slow, lazy touching, the way neither one of them was in a hurry, when they both knew they needed to be. The kiss literally made his head spin, and he had to break to breathe. They grinned, then dove back in.

Markus' hands were huge, covering his ass, cupping the back of his head, fingers teasing one nipple. The man was constantly moving, touching him everywhere. Stroking his cock, Markus hummed, licking Seb's lower lip. He opened, laughing as their tongues touched again, both of them playing.

A low, rough noise came from deep in Markus' chest, and the water splashed over the sides of the tub as Markus lifted him, lips sliding down his chest. His ass was in Markus' hands, the man's strength stealing his breath.

"Love the way you taste, baby."

"You're so fucking strong." He looked down, fingers

sliding through the heavy, thick hair. "And hairy."

"Hey, not all of us can be waxed like a surfboard." Markus rubbed one cheek against his chest, the stubble burning him a little.

"No. No, but you like it." Just like the mat of hair over Markus' chest made him dizzy.

"I do. I love pretty much everything." Those lips moved against his skin, leaving little patches of warmth.

He looked down, loving how dark Markus' skin was against his, how Markus lifted him to lick at his ink. That hot tongue traced practically every note, Markus openly fascinated with the song he'd written.

"For you." He meant the music, the song, his body. He was in a giving mood.

"Mine. I like that idea." Markus lifted him a little higher, biting his hipbone. The little sting made him grunt, made him bare his teeth. Fuck, that was fine. It got even better when Markus rubbed that bristly cheek against Sebastian's cock.

"Fuck. Candy." That little burn made his toes curl, made his balls draw up.

"That is the idea, baby." Not that Markus was letting him back down. No, Sebastian dangled, feet in the water, his cock sliding into Markus' mouth. Oh, fuck, those lips were like the best wet dream, the way Markus' tongue slid on his shaft hot and slick. It made him arch, trying to get more, trying to hump that amazing mouth.

"Uh-uh. You take what I give you, baby." Evil bastard. Fine, hot evil smiling bastard.

Sebastian loved him.

Markus gave him more, but not enough. He wanted to find that place where all he could hear was Markus' song, but Markus kept changing the rhythm.

"Please." He reached out, balanced himself on the marble tiles.

Sucking him in deep, Markus swallowed around him. Finally he got the friction he needed. Damn. His legs were resting on the broad shoulders, his entire body shivering with his need as his hips rolled, fighting to move between lips and hands.

Markus helped him now, pulling him in, keeping him safe. The man was just so fucking strong. Maybe strong enough for a fucked up guy like him.

"Need you. So bad, Candy. Need this. Your mouth. Your hands." It was like something cracked inside him, let him pour himself out. And Markus was like a machine, loving him so hard, so good, taking him in, every inch.

Sebastian drove in, crying out, begging with every single inch of his body.

Markus finally just propped him up with one hand, the other sliding down under Sebastian's ass to push at his hole.

"Please."

One finger became two, then three, the stretch making him burn. He was flying with it, and Markus wasn't holding back a bit. He pulled away, groaning, teasing them both, playing for a few seconds. Then he sank down, took Markus' cock down to the root, the burn wild, fierce, perfect, as perfect as the expression on Candy's face—a study in pure need.

"Fuck. Seb. Holy..." Markus bit off a moan, hips rising in sharp punches.

Yes. He leaned down, driving himself faster, harder, taking everything Markus gave him. The kiss he got rocked his world, leaving his ears ringing as he fought for breath. That music started, ringing in his head, erasing everything but them.

"God," Markus moaned, adding lyrics. "Seb."

He nodded, wanting to say so much but all his fucking breath control was shot to shit. He was panting too hard, his body working at light speed. They sloshed water all over the damned place, Markus pushing and pushing.

All he needed was a little something, something to shove him over the edge. Markus gave it to him seconds after he had the damned thought, hand closing over his cock, that heavy thumb pressing into his slit, and he came so hard it hurt, the tension leaving him in a rush.

"Uhn." Markus made this amazing noise, face red and hot when the man came inside him. He felt every pulse of Markus' cock.

"Oh, God." He rested his head on Markus' shoulder. "I feel you."

"That's good, right?" That chuckle moved all sorts of things in fascinating ways.

"That's good, right." He couldn't stop his grin, it just grew and grew. Before he knew it he and Markus were just laughing like fools, clinging to each other. It was a little hysterical, at the end, both of them at the end of their rope.

"Come on, baby," Markus said when the gasping laughter ended. "Let's dry off and get some popcorn."

"Sounds good." He caught his breath, stood, muscles trembling with little aftershocks.

"It does. And we got a few days." Those strong hands caught him, helping him.

"I'm supposed to leave for Nashville midnight tomorrow night." Maybe he'd call Jack, postpone for a day or two.

"Well, that's a day and a half." They got dried off, but Markus didn't head for the suitcases. The man just wandered around naked. "I had them stock the kitchen."

He poured two big glasses of water as soon as they got to the big kitchen, then found a stereo system while Markus rummaged. The Eagles would be good right now. Sebastian put them on, starting out with *One of These Nights.*

It felt good to sing, easy, and he took harmony on the chorus, giving Mr. Lead Singer the melody. Markus grinned at him when he took up the words, knowingly, even. The popcorn started popping and man, it smelled good.

He explored, found them both terrycloth robes that were obviously meant for post-hot tubbing, and wrapped one around him, took the other to Markus before settling on a bar stool.

"Thanks, baby." Markus poured the popcorn in a bowl and grabbed a couple of napkins.

He took a piece of popcorn, looked at it, turned it over in his fingers. Weird, how something so little and hard and uniform could explode into something big and white and unique. He supposed there was a song in that, if he wrote children's songs.

"What are you grinning about?" Markus asked, grabbing the popcorn from him and munching it.

"Writing kids' songs like Raffi."

"No way. You have too many good big people songs in you."

Sebastian chuckled, but he nodded. "I... The songwriting is the best part. The actual writing and playing."

"I like it, too. That and the jam sessions." Markus ate another handful of popcorn.

He didn't know about the performing, so much. Everything seemed so big, so overwhelming without the meds, and he knew that it was fake. He did, but...shit, he needed some balance in his life. That's what the pills had given him, balance from the craziness that life was and now...

Shit, he didn't know what to do, how to do this.

"What is it?" Markus knew. The man could read him like a book. One long finger traced his cheek, Markus waiting.

"I don't know how to do it without the pills." He just blurted it out, bald and raw. "I'm not talking about the rush. I'm talking about the fucking hallucinations, the paranoia. Is there something deep wrong with me, man?"

"No." The word was definite, and knowing. Markus stood, coming to pull him off his stool so they could go sink together on the couch. "No, baby. This is normal. It sucks, but it's part of the detox."

"You're sure?" He held one of Markus' hands. "You ever feel like it's all gonna just break apart on you?"

"All the time." Markus' hand turned in his, squeezing. "I mean, it gets way better as time goes on."

Sebastian nodded, but he wasn't sure he believed that. He was tired, and that wasn't getting any better. He just wanted to rest. His head felt huge, like it was stuffed with all sorts of things: cotton, weird clowns, too many musical notes.

"I'm sorry, baby, but I can't be sorry."

"I just... I don't know if I can do it. I think I'm going to lose my mind." He wasn't going to lie; he didn't understand what to do and he was scared to go to his doctor, scared to go to his manager. And how fucked up was that? These were supposed to be his people.

"No. No, we'll talk to some of the folks I worked with first. I mean, I can tell them I'm having hallucinations."

"Because having you lie to the doctors is good." Sebastian looked at Markus, his head pounding. "Do you think they did this to me on purpose?"

"No." Markus pulled a face. "I mean, yes, but no. I don't think they thought it was going to go this far."

Finally he asked what he didn't want to know. "What did Tawny find out? Is it Jack?"

"I think it goes higher than Jack, baby." Markus hugged him close. "But he's definitely in deep."

In deep? "Okay, okay. I guess I... I guess I need to talk to Tawny."

He had a lawyer, but Jack had hired him. Maybe he just needed to get in a room with Jack and the guys from the label and just have a conniption.

The look on Markus' face told him it was way worse than he thought. "I—Tawny thinks major skimming is going on, baby. We're talking millions."

Sebastian stood, not able to sit there any more. Millions. Millions. Shit.

"Okay." He needed to go. Run. Something. Millions.

How many millions was he making if he was missing so many and not even knowing it? And how could Jack do something like this? They'd been through so damned much together. If Jack needed money, all he had to do was ask. Sebastian hadn't ever turned the man down.

Twenty years almost, they'd worked together.

Sebastian walked to the window, looking out at the water, at the ocean, forcing himself not to just totally lose his shit.

"What can I do?" Markus didn't crowd him, but that gravelly voice carried.

"Nothing." He'd let someone else deal with things enough, it looked like. "I'll have to deal with Jack day after tomorrow."

"Okay. Be careful. Call me if you need me." Markus came to him, hands sliding around his waist.

"I will." He felt like something inside him had just turned off, like his soul had hit a dead spot.

"Come on, huh? I think you'll feel a million times better if you lie down a little." Markus took him back to the couch, which was way closer than those bedrooms back upstairs.

Sebastian didn't think so. His world was broken—everything that had been a truth three months ago wasn't

193

anymore, and somehow he had to figure out how to fake it until he had his feet underneath him again. Markus couldn't do that for him.

Still, he sat, leaned against Markus and listened to the man's heartbeat. It was the one solid, steady thing in his world. Thump, thump, thump. He could make a rhythm out of that.

"Sing for me a little, man?" Please, God, of everything, let that be the one thing that was still what it was supposed to be.

"I can do that." Markus kissed his neck. He half expected *Silent Love*, but what he got was *The Cowboy's Lament*, and oh, it sounded good.

He started singing along about three quarters through, and if they moved onto *Honkytonk Angel* and then wandered into *Sad Songs and Waltzes*, no one seemed to mind. By the time Markus was halfway through *Cheater's Waltz* Sebastian's eyelids were drooping and he felt like he could sleep.

Markus' hand was on him, solid and sure, and he trusted in it.

He had to; he didn't have a lot left to believe in.

Markus paced.

He couldn't help it. Seb was sound asleep, which he was grateful for, but Markus was full of nervous energy. Maybe he should go out to the pool, swim some laps. Oh, man, he hadn't done that in ages. That sounded good. He got his trunks out of his bag, left Seb a note so the man wouldn't panic, and headed down.

The crystal blue of the heated pool beckoned, and he tossed the towel he'd grabbed aside and hopped in.

He'd expected panic yesterday, screaming. Possibly

a temper tantrum of mammoth proportions. What he'd gotten was this quiet, lost hurt that had terrified him a little. Seb was aching, and there was nothing he could do about it. Not a goddamned thing.

It wasn't right, damn it. Seb was...shit, the man was good, decent. Real. Mostly.

He stroked through the water, head down for all but every third stroke, so he could breathe. The water made it easy to lose focus, to just drive and exercise. All he had to do was keep his body going. He could begin to understand why Seb worked out so hard sometimes.

There was a bottle of water waiting for him when he made one of the turns, like it appeared by magic. He grinned, spitting out the water he'd taken in. Two more laps and he'd stop.

When he pulled up, he could hear the whirr of the treadmill in the little home gym, the thrum of the bass just under that. Damn. He'd bet Seb hadn't eaten anything. His turn to get a little something together for when Seb slowed down.

Fruit, cheese. That kind of thing. Something.

His arms were shaking when he got out of the pool and he sucked the water down, then cracked up at the little pile of powdered doughnuts waiting for him. Someone had his back. He inhaled them, then headed to the kitchen, peeking in on Seb on the way.

Seb was running hard, wearing a tiny pair of shorts, sheened with sweat, skin bright red. So damned pretty. Markus stared for a little while, enjoying the view. Then he took note of the time on the treadmill. He'd give Seb ten more minutes. Ten more minutes, then food. Water. Rest.

He hustled to the kitchen, singing under his breath. The song fit the bass, but he didn't think it was the same as the one Seb was listening to. Seb tended to listen to some hardcore hip-hop when he was running hard.

By the time he'd sliced apples and bananas and cheese, adding blueberries, the microwave clock told him it was time to go retrieve his Cajun. Who sounded a hell of a lot more Cajun since going back to Baton Rouge. He grabbed apple juice, too, loaded for bear and ready to battle. He needed to see Seb eat more than one fry. The man was running hard, eyes closed, just soaked.

Clearing his throat so he didn't scare the man, Markus waited for Seb to glance over. "Time for a break, baby."

"H...how was your swim?" Seb slowed down the treadmill to a jog.

"Good. Cleared my head some." He watched Seb's hands shake. "Cool down, baby. Walk a minute. You need some carbs."

"It was good, to watch you sleep last night." The treadmill slowed more.

"You got a little rest, though, right?" He knew Seb had slept a few hours. At least as many as he usually got.

Seb nodded. "I'm good. Really. I even dreamed."

"Good. I guess, as long as they weren't bad dreams?" He hated the idea of Seb being blindsided in his dreams.

"Nah, jus' Maman. I dream 'bout her a lot these days."

"She would come visit you at night, huh?"

Seb's walk slowed even more. "I wish things had been different there. Not so bad."

"I'm sorry, baby. I know she loved you so much." Seb's mom had been a good woman.

He got a grin, warm and truly tickled, and it made Markus feel better, that Seb could do that, smile that way. "She did. She loved the music, the whole thing."

"Did you sing a little for her?" Markus had, in the privacy of his sterile Vegas hotel room.

"I did. Maybe a lot. We talked quite a bit, the two of us, about things."

He'd bet Seb had just babbled at his momma. There was no pressure in talking to someone who didn't talk back. Hell, Seb probably needed that, just someone to jabber at and spill out all the things in that wildly spinning brain.

The treadmill finally slowed to a stop, and Seb hopped off. Markus handed him a towel.

"Thank you." Seb's muscles were jerking wildly, belly hard as a board.

"No problem." Not that he couldn't relate. His shoulders ached from the swim. He was happy enough to stare at that fine body though, the sheen of sweat making the man glow.

"I might hop in the pool, do some laps. Burn off some energy."

"Nope." He reached out and snagged Seb by the waist, pulling him close. "You need to rest. Eat."

Those beautiful, famous green as glass eyes stared up at him.

"I know. I said eat." He grinned, dropping a kiss on Seb's mouth. "You're worn out, baby."

"I think sometimes that's going to be permanent."

"Maybe, but there's no sense making it worse right now." He tugged Seb with him. They'd eat on the couch.

He wasn't fixin to blow sunshine up Seb's butt. The man had done too much for too long and no one's body could do that forever.

Markus knew. From experience. It had taken him three years to get back to feeling almost normal, and he knew he could never drink again. He wasn't sure what the fuck Seb was going to do. The choices there seemed...harder.

Definitely more complicated than going to rehab. The man had to rehab his whole team. People he trusted had done him dirty. "Want some banana?"

"They have a lot of calories." Seb chewed his bottom lip and Markus stared.

"You've burned off at least ten bananas." He kept it light.

"Can you imagine eating ten bananas? You'd puke."

"Hey, I used to be able to mainline a twenty-four pack of beer. Ten bananas was nothing." Now, raw eggs? That Markus couldn't hack.

"I went ten days only drinking black coffee. That's when I hired Bev." Seb's denial was the weirdest addiction.

"She's a good friend."

"She's a harpy." Seb's grin was warm, though, happy, and a piece of banana got eaten.

"She is. I mean, Helen has nothing on her."

"I bet she's ready for you to be home."

"Maybe? Maybe she wants to have a retirement." He grinned. "I bet Bev is losing her shit."

"You know it. She's uber-efficient."

"She also worries about you, maybe more than I do." At Seb's raised brow, he shrugged. "I know more about your life. The way it is. From personal experience."

"I don't know what to do about it, my life. I don't know if I want it any more." Seb wouldn't meet his eyes. "That's selfish, huh?"

"No." Hell, no. Sure, they both had a lot to love about their lives, but everyone should have a chance to move on.

"I have everything everyone wants."

"But if it's not what you want anymore it can't make you happy." Markus hated platitudes, but he couldn't help himself.

"I'm not sure some people get to be happy."

He popped Seb's hip. "Stop it. You deserve it as much as anyone."

Seb pinched his nipple. "You stop it."

Markus jumped, barking out a laugh. That was kind of shocking. "Why?"

"Because you can't just randomly whap a guy."

Oh, this wasn't random. "You're not just a guy. You're my lover, and I wasn't being random."

"Your lover, huh?" Seb looked over at him, one eyebrow arched.

"Mine." That was the one thing that was certain in all of this.

"What are we going to do, Candy?" And there it was. Simple. Bald. Just put out there. Finally. "I mean, are we going to keep finding places to hook up when we get lonely? The press will find out, if we do it more than a couple times a year, so I need to know."

He chewed on that a moment, not wanting to blurt something out that had no thought behind it. "I don't want that, baby. I have no idea how we'll do it, but I want you. Not just part time, you know?"

"I want to watch you sleep when I can't."

God, that would be a great song hook. His fingers itched for his guitar, the music already starting to run through him. "That's a good song, baby."

Sebastian looked at him, then the smile busted out. "Yeah. It's one hell of a hook. I'll grab the guitars."

"Cool." They could work, scribble out the basic shape of the song. And talk. It was easier to talk through the music. They'd been making love through the music for years. This was no different.

"No, that should be the chorus, not the opening line." He made a notation, grinning when Seb snorted, obviously not agreeing.

"So, then how does it start? This great love affair?"

"How about with them knowing each other for years?" He gave Seb a slow grin, raising an eyebrow, feeling like he was issuing a dare.

"Watching each other? Working together?"

"That's it. And now they've been together, and there's

all this stuff they have to figure out."

Seb nodded. "Details. It's all details."

Now there was a first line. "I like it." He scribbled, plucked, and they had half a song. And a title.

"How do you figure out what to do, when you don't have a home to leave?"

It was a lyric, but Markus knew the question was real. He strummed a little on the guitar, not sure if he needed to answer right now. Then he nodded. "Find a place to lay your head."

Those green eyes looked at him. "Promise me a place to settle."

Markus gave up all pretense of writing a song and set his guitar aside, reaching for Seb. "I promise you that, baby. You'll always have a place with me, and if the spot I chose isn't it, we'll find a new place together."

Seb pushed into his lap, arms wrapping around his shoulders. "I liked your house." He got a soft, chaste kiss. "What I saw of it."

"I know. I want you to see it all." Guilt was overrated, but he had it for keeping Seb at bay then, keeping him isolated, just like everyone else did.

"I'm tired, Markus. Like in my bones, huh? I never used to be, but I am now."

"It's been a long road." There had been a hell of a lot of hills, too. They wore on a man.

"It's going to be longer, for a few days, then I'll come home, huh?"

Home. Home, yeah, that sounded good. A home they made together. It wasn't just a pipe dream. Markus had beaten so many of his demons. Surely he could help Seb fight these last few.

Then the huge ones, well, they'd just have to bash them together.

Chapter Nineteen

T ell me why you did it." Sebastian stood in front of Jack's desk, staring the old man down, trying to figure out when Jack had gone from dapper older gentleman to a hawk-like scary bastard sitting behind a huge oak desk like he was qualified to pass judgment. Sebastian had kissed Markus goodbye last night and flown back to Nashville. Six espressos and three energy drinks later and he was here in this familiar, yet somehow strange fucking high-rise, facing down another demon that he'd always thought was one of his angels. Part of him wanted to cry, wanted to shake Jack and beg for reassurance, answers, stability. Peace.

It wasn't going to happen, though. He knew that.

Sebastian figured he needed to start out like he could hold out, because this man had been a friend, a father-figure, a confidant for years. Jack knew him. He'd trusted Jack with everything.

"Did what?" The look was practiced, mask-like.

"Don't lie to me, man." He shook his head, pulling out the folder, the little printouts that proved what Bev had suspected and he knew, now. "Millions. You've taken millions. Why? I've never told you no. I got your back, for fuck's sake."

Jack snorted. "What are you doing, messing with the numbers, son? You're not smart enough to do that. Do you even know what you're looking at? You don't have a head for numbers; you never have. I've known you for damned near your whole life. You've never even balanced a checkbook."

Jack reached for his papers—like those would be the only copies. This stuff was electronic; it was everywhere. Still, Seb pulled back. He wasn't stupid. He knew when column A and column B didn't add up. Music was math.

"I've had three people look over the numbers, man. You're skimming, and it's not just a couple of bucks. It's millions. Why?" He needed a reason—someone was dying of cancer, someone was going to break Jack's legs, something.

"It's just accounting, shifting cash from one thing to another, to protect you." Jack's eyes narrowed. "Three people? Who? Who have you brought into this? Your fuck buddy? His bitch manager?"

"Watch your mouth." He wouldn't give Markus up. He couldn't.

"I don't have to." Jack shook his head. "Don't you get it, kid? I don't have to. I own you, and what I don't own, the label does."

No. No one owned him. Markus had made him repeat that over and over. Practice it. Markus'd said that was what Jack, and the label, would say. What they always said.

"Bullshit. Don't be like this, man. Are you in trouble or something?"

The mask seemed to flicker, and for a moment he thought it would break. Then Jack's mouth hardened into a thin line. "Are you trying to fuck me out of my retirement, kid? Is that what this is about? Get rid of the old man?"

"What?" Him? Fuck Jack over? How?

"I have pictures, kid. Of you and your fuckbuddy. I have the first ones, and I have new ones. You know what releasing them will do? To your career? The band's? Markus'? You think he won't drop you like a hot rock when he has to pay all the bills at his big place in Austin without a label? How long do you think he'll stay clean around you? Does he know about the hallucinations? The way you can't do without the drugs? This isn't a drinking problem, Sebastian, you're fucking crazy. Mental. Medicated, you at least function."

Sebastian stood there, feeling like he was getting beaten on by a million words like bees, the anger just crashing into him and he didn't know what to do. "I didn't do anything to you."

"Who's been hiding how crazy you are? Who? Me. Just me, going from doctor to doctor, paying them to keep quiet, paying them to make sure you get what you need, and this is how you repay me? You ungrateful little fuck."

Somehow everything was backward. Screwed up and his fault. Again.

Jack stood up, yanked the papers out of his hand. "You get your fucking ass downstairs, you get ready for your day of interviews, and then you get ready to go. I have a flight for you leaving at three, you bastard, for Japan. You have commercials to do and then a video to shoot. I'm traveling with you."

Wait. Wait, what? Japan?

"I'm not..."

Jack put both hands on him, shook him, hard. "Stop being a brat, take your goddamn meds and move. I will destroy him, you hear me? I will destroy him, that pregnant bitch manager, your sister, Bev. Everyone. I will put those perverted pictures of you on the Internet and you'll never be able to breathe without someone watching you, hating you, and you'll never play again."

So, that was it, then. Jack knew. Seb was right about the money, and no matter what Sebastian did, it didn't matter. He could survive it, the tidal wave of shit that would hit when he was outed, but could everyone else? Could Markus?

God, he was tired and he'd just had enough. "I'm not doing interviews today."

"You're doing what you're told and I'm going to crawl up your ass to make sure it's done. You're out of choices. Fucking little shit."

Sebastian couldn't breathe, couldn't see. He stumbled a little when Jack let go, and he reached for his phone. He needed to call someone—Bev, Markus, 911. Something.

"No." His phone was grabbed, shattered on the edge of Jack's desk. "Let's go. Quit being a child. Jesus, I should have known you weren't capable of touring without me there every fucking second. From now on, I'm your fucking shadow."

Sebastian thought, maybe, all the times Markus had said that the demons that he saw, that the people that were waiting to eat him were just in his head, maybe Markus was wrong.

The demons were real; they just hid, really well.

The phone rang, *Silent Love* playing as his ringtone. Markus snatched it up, hitting answer before he even looked to see who it was. It had to be Seb. Had to. "Hello?"

"Mr. Kane?" Bev sounded like she was a million miles away.

"Bev? What's going on? Are you okay? Seb? I haven't heard from him."

"I'm... I don't suppose. Do you happen to need a personal assistant?"

"What?" He blinked, not quite able to process what she'd just said. "Bev, honey, where are you? What's going on?"

"I'm in Nashville. Management fired me. Me, the band, everyone."

The air whooshed out of his lungs. "Everyone? Have you talked to Bruce?"

"You haven't?"

"No, honey. I've been calling and calling and no one is answering." He got off his ass, went to get a bag and start tossing shit in. "Where do I need to go? Where are you?"

"I'm in Nashville. I... I can come to you. I'm scared for him, Markus. Genuinely. He was there, on the other side of the glass when they called me in. He was...it was like someone had killed him or something."

Bile rose in Markus' throat. "Is he overseas? I'm not seeing any stuff about him on the E-news."

"He was in Japan for a couple weeks, here for two days, now they have him in Sao Paolo."

"Sao Paolo?" How did he find someone in Sao Paolo? "Okay. Okay, you come here. I'll get a hold of Bruce and find out what he knows."

"Okay. Okay, I'll be there in...twelve hours, hopefully less. I'm sorry for calling, but I'm scared for him."

He needed to call Tawny. Bruce.

"Don't apologize, honey. And don't worry about the job. I won't leave you out in the cold while we straighten this mess out."

"Okay. Your house?"

"Yeah. Yeah, let me know when you're coming in and I'll have Helen come get you."

"Thank you."

They said their goodbyes and then he called Kyle. That man knew fucking everything that happened to everybody.

"Hey, man, what the hell is up with Sebastian?" Kyle asked without even saying hello. "His camp is shut down tighter than Nazi Germany."

"I was hoping you knew, man."

"Shit, Bruce is out of the fucking country, like with his kids and everything. They fired everybody. All of them. I got hold of that little boy they replaced Kerry and Jonny with, and he says Longchamps wasn't even coherent, never said a word. They're taking him to do some promotional shit and then he's going to be sequestered to write a new album? Without his band?"

"Not without Bruce." No. No, this was officially a kidnapping. "Bev is coming here. I'll call Tawny. Can I--" Was it fair to ask Kyle to help? "Can I count on you to be here in the States and coordinate when I go get him?"

"Shit, man. I got your back, no matter what. This ain't right. They're eating him alive because he's queer."

Markus made a sound, half-laugh, half quacking duck. "Yeah. I mean, that has to be what they're holding over his head, but Jack—It's bad, Kyle."

"Good thing we're all old and ready to retire. You could buy me an island."

"I could buy me and Seb one and you could come visit. Bring doughnuts."

"Fucker. You know how many Weight Watchers points a doughnut is?"

"If you jog on the beach you can eat as many as you want."

"Maybe, if you chase me with a knife."

"Boo! Serial killer Markus." He sighed, rolled his head on his shoulders. "Tell me there's nothing I can do until Bev gets here."

"There's nothing you can do. Log onto Rock Band; we'll play."

He could do that. Distract himself while he waited.

Then he could go get Sebastian. And maybe buy that island.

He sat on the patio and stared out over the ocean, watching the moon float over the water. He'd been there since dawn without moving. There was a fence with a lock, a door with a lock. No television, no phone, no radio. He had his guitar in there by the bed. Paper. Pens. The things he needed. Too bad that Sebastian had lost his mind.

There was no writing. No playing. Just the silence in his head and the distant roar of the ocean. Every so often Jack came out with some little nurse, someone gave him a shot, took his blood pressure and left.

He looked over, saw Maman sitting here, looking at him. "Hey, lady. You coming for me?"

She smiled at him, her face the face of his twenties, lined, but not lost. "No, bebe. You not ready to go."

He wasn't sure about that. "I'm real tired."

He wasn't scared anymore. The hallucinations had stopped. Now all he could feel was this creeping numbness in his lower body. He figured by the time it reached his lungs he'd stop breathing.

She shook her head. "You done wore my baby boy out. You gon' go be with your man, love on him, make music."

"I was. He asked, and I said yes." That had to count for something, right? That they'd made promises to each other.

"Not was, bebe. Are. You are gon' be there." Her accent always got worse when she got aggravated with him.

"You think so?" He didn't, but that was okay. "Did you make it to Heaven okay? Did you find Daddy?"

"Ain't no sense worryin' about me. I'm dead, bebe. You still alive. Act like it. Ain't no way what they threatening to do to you can be worse than what they are."

He nodded. He knew. He wasn't sure he could do anything about it anymore. Everything was heavy, quiet. The music had left him. He wanted to hear Markus sing. More than anything. Right now.

Maman reached out, not touching him, because she wasn't real or she was a ghost or something, He could smell her vanilla and jasmine perfume, though. "He's coming for you, bebe. Your *coeur*. Be ready for him."

Now that thought, that made him smile. Markus, his avenging hero. He liked that.

"What are you smiling at, kid?" Jack stood there, the nurse beside him with an IV bag.

He looked at them, but he didn't have anything to say. Nothing.

Maman said Markus was coming; his job right now was to stay alive a little bit longer and see if she was right.

"They're not in Sao Paolo. They're in Santos, on the coast." Tawny had come in half an hour after Bev, and they were both in his kitchen, Tawny's sky high heels clicking on his terrazzo floor. The stilettos were completely at odds with her thickening waistline, which worried him.

"Can you sit?" he asked, trying to get her to take a stool.

"No! We have to mobilize here. Jack has gone

completely rogue. The label thinks Seb is taking a sabbatical to write the new album.

"What can we do? Can we call the police in Brazil? I mean, Jack can't kidnap him!" Bev had been tireless, calling and researching and crying. The woman was possibly as OCD as Seb in her own way.

"Can't y'all just go get him?" Helen set out a platter of veggies and cheese.

"That's my plan." Markus looked to Tawny, who was arrangement woman. They'd talked while she was on her layover in Dallas.

Tawny smiled, nodded. "I have a very good friend that's a local down there. He's a bullrider up here most of the year, but he happens to be home in Sao Paolo. We're all going to visit him, talking about possibly having him in a video."

Markus couldn't help but laugh. "How does Jim feel about this good friend?"

"He hates him, Scooter. Absolutely hates him." She tossed her long hair. "It gets me laid, every time. Jim is meeting us down there. I figure the more of us, the better. Eduardo has a huge place—a fucking compound."

"And he speaks the language." Bev gave Tawny a spontaneous and very grateful-looking hug. "Now we have to work on getting Markus down there without Jack knowing."

"I got that," Markus said. "Seb has a surfer friend who's a pilot. He loves the beaches in Brazil. He'll happily ferry us down."

Bev nodded. "Justin Clark. I've got his contract information."

"Okay, you deal with that. I'll have Eduardo meet us at the airport." Tawny met his eyes, winked. "What else, Scooter?"

"I just need to see him, Tawn." The sick feeling in his

gut wouldn't go away until he had Seb with him. "That and we need to be ready for the media shit storm."

"I'll deal with that." She met his eyes. "We just have to decide whether you're going to come out and proud or you're going to retire. If you come out, we'll break the news on our terms. If you retire, then people can say whatever."

"I'm ready to step down. I would come out just fine; you know that. I won't make that decision for Seb, though. If we retire on the QT, we can make good money writing." If Seb wanted to come out, fine, but Markus was content to live quietly.

"I have the lawyer ready to sue Jack's management company and the label. Seb just has to say the word."

"Good. He'll sign the papers. No doubt." That one he didn't care if Seb wanted to do it or not. This was not just a difference of management style. This was criminal.

"Justin says he'll be at the municipal airport tonight at nine p.m. He'll have to file flight plans and stuff, so we'll leave around five a.m. It will take us about sixteen hours, maybe eighteen, in his plane." Bev chewed on her thumbnail, her under eye bags multiplying by the second.

Tawny finally sat, grabbing cheese off the plate and munching. "Everyone have their passports? Their shots? We've all been overseas in the last six months." When they all nodded, she slapped her hand down on the table. "Then I say we all sleep while we can."

Bev opened her mouth to argue, and Tawny shook her head. "That means you too, lovely. You work for us now, and that means sleep and food and time off and no kidnapping."

Markus smothered a grin, thinking how good it felt to smile. Seb would be smiling soon, and that would make this whole mess if not worthwhile, then at least salvageable.

Tawny met his eyes, once everyone had wandered off. "You okay?"

"No." He grabbed some grapes. "I'm scared. This isn't just bad business, Tawn."

"No, it's not. Jack's a gambler. He was stealing from the label and, I don't know, Tad retired and it was like they sent leg breakers or something. Regardless, he's lost his shit. You better be prepared, huh? They had Seb pretty medicated before."

The heaviness in the pit of his belly got worse. "I—do we need to get a doctor? Can your friend do that?"

"Yeah. It couldn't hurt to get one on call, huh? Just in case?"

He hated this shit, but they had to be prepared for anything. Markus just kept making himself the promise that no one would ever medicate Seb again unless it was truly necessary, like penicillin or a tetanus shot.

"You know that he might be deeply fucked up, right? He lost his mom, his manager—this whole thing has been harsh."

"He's stronger than he thinks. Than anyone does." He had to believe that. Had to believe that the man who could write a song like *Silent Love* and sell it to him without ever letting him know... yeah. Seb was strong.

Seb loved harder than anyone he'd ever met, including himself. The man gave himself up, trusted. Fucking believed even after there wasn't any reason to.

"He's a lucky guy, to have you, Scooter."

Markus knew better. He was the lucky one. Sebastian Longchamps had loved him from afar for years, had been the one to call, the one to hold it together. If this had been left to him, he'd still be having silent blowjobs from people who couldn't even remember his name, quietly letting retirement have him and telling reporters about the good old days when he used to tie one on.

Now he had something to live for, and if he had to do it loud to get Seb back, so be it.

Chapter Twenty

The numbness was turning to pain.

It wigged him out a little bit, when he could think well enough to be scared. At some point, they'd stopped talking to him, Jack and Maman. The nurse came, changing tubes and bags, hitting play on the iPod.

Had it been just days?

The curtains were open, but he couldn't see the ocean, just the sky and the top of the fence. He thought he'd seen the moon.

Sebastian shifted, his legs feeling like they weighed a thousand pounds, maybe more. His belly felt like he'd swallowed a rock. This was what Markus had been talking about, about how the drugs could swallow you up like being inside a whale.

He chuckled, the idea of being the rock himself amusing. Weren't those Doc Holliday's last words? "Damn, this is funny."

He turned his head, which felt like a giant turtle's or the biggest baby ever, looking back out the window after peering at his toes.

Huh. Look at that. Someone was scaling the fence.

Someone tall and brown. Neat. Maybe they were going to steal a chair. Those chairs had been comfortable as all get out. He frowned. At least he thought he'd been in those chairs. Had it been a dream?

Another man popped over the fence. Did it take two to steal a chair? Maybe they were going to steal Jack. How hard would that rock?

Oh. Oh, that looked like his Markus. Maman had promised he'd see that face again and she'd managed it. For him.

God, she'd loved him so much.

The two dark forms came closer and closer to the house, looking like movie cat burglars or something, and he would have clapped his hands with delight if he'd had the strength. It was like his own personal movie reel. Markus the thief, coming to steal him away.

He kept his eyes open, refusing to hardly blink, because he didn't want to miss any of this mess. Was that his surfer friend Justin? Did Maman know Justin? Did Markus? Why would he be hallucinating Justin?

There was a flurry of doorbell ringing and shit from the front of the house, raised voices in Portuguese and English. What a racket.

About that time was when the big sliding glass door came right off its track. Cool. It was like a fire door emergency thing. He'd seen it happen once at a Macy's. His Markus charged into the room, looking like an avenging angel in a black gimme cap. It was the best fantasy ever.

Well, maybe not the best. The best involved that hand warming his ass right before the man fucked him into oblivion, but still, this so worked for him.

Then his favorite apparition opened his mouth and spoke. "Baby? Seb? Are you ready to go?"

Go. Go. God, yes. Anywhere with you. He couldn't remember how to make his mouth work, but he nodded. He'd go to hell itself to stay with Markus and their music.

"Good." That smile was like the sun breaking over the ocean. "Justin, help me. I don't know what to do about the drip."

"We'll take it with us. They've got him catheterized, too. We'll just... take it all and let Eduardo's doctor sort it."

Justin sounded so...Australian. Sebastian wasn't up to surfing, though. Not today. He wanted to sleep. He thought he ought to wave at Just, though, because it was nice to see him. He tried to lift his hand, but Markus was lifting him. It was just like flying.

He breathed in deep, the scent of Markus hitting his nose, and he blinked. It was almost like it was real. Warm lips grazed his cheek, and God, Candy needed to shave. The cheek whiskers were going to burn his skin right off.

"Come on, mate. Let's go. Let's get him out of here."

Justin had a wonderful idea, there.

Go. Just go.

Anywhere but here.

Markus fought the urge to go and kill something, anything, torn between tears and rage. He cradled Sebastian in his arms, and his lover seemed to weigh no more than a fucking child. They were starving Seb to death, slow but sure.

He glanced at Justin, who had the drip bag. "You ready?"

"You know it."

Eduardo was still talking, loud and cheery. The man was a fucking celebrity of mammoth proportion down here, and was more than willing to draw the attention away from them. One of his brothers—Markus had been introduced, but fuck, there were like thirty of them and they all looked damn near the same, hot, dark, sexual as hell—was driving their getaway car so that Eduardo could take the other car into the city, draw the media.

They just had to get Seb over the--

"Come fast!" Eduardo's brother stood at the back gate with a pair of bolt cutters. "Is easier now!"

Markus was beginning to think a villa in Brazil was better than an island. These guys cracked his shit up. "Good job, buddy. Run."

The man could flat out run in those cayman boots, and Markus and Justin got to the old truck, Markus sliding into the back of the king cab with his precious cargo. "Seb? Can you talk to me, baby?"

This was wrong. So fucking wrong. The man's lips were cracked, dry, and Seb's eyes moved so slow, like each blink was deliberate.

He thought about giving Seb some water, but it might make him sick. Better to let the doc have a look and decide what to do. He did use some of the bottled stuff to moisten Seb's lips. "I'm right here, baby. I'm so sorry it took so fucking long."

Seb just smiled at him, like he was a fucking hero or something, grinning like an idiot.

He stroked one sharp cheekbone, bracing himself as Eduardo's brother barreled out of Santo, toward the ranch.

Who the fuck could do this? What kind of fucking lunatic could take someone they'd worked with for years and... He was going to fucking lose his shit.

"Hold it together, mate." Justin peered at him over the back of the seat. "Half an hour."

"Okay. Sure." His own voice sounded so reasonable. Shaky, but reasonable.

"Sing to him, huh? He sings, yes? Eduardo tell me. You too. Singing."

He gave Eduardo's brother a grateful smile in the rearview, then started singing *Jolie Blonde*. He slid into *Fais Do-Do*. He knew Seb loved those old Cajun songs. Hell, he'd do *Jambalaya* if he needed to.

He could feel Seb, relaxing in his arms, breathing in time with him. At least he knew the man heard him. Those cracked lips moved along with the words when he started on one of his own songs, the slow, waltz-y *In My Arms*.

Oh, Jesus. Please. He wasn't a praying man, but he knew the good Lord had Seb's mamma there, talking hard, so he'd send one up. This was it for him and he couldn't let loose now.

The ride seemed to take hours, but they made it, and Seb was asleep by the time they did. Markus kept checking to make sure he was breathing. Compulsively checking.

Tawny and the doctor were there, along with about a thousand Brazilians, grabbing Seb from Markus' arms and hustling the man into the big house, into a bed. It was Bev, though, who took one look at Seb and just collapsed, crumpling to the floor in a snow white heap.

Markus stopped, lifting her to her feet and hugging her hard. "He's going to be all right, Bevvie. I promise."

"Markus. Markus, what... Look at him. Oh, my God. He's... That's *Sebastian*."

"I know. I know." He put his face in her hair for a moment and let the tears roll, let it all go. He had to before he went in there with Seb. Had to get it out.

They held each other like two little kids, lost in a fairy story, one where the witch was waiting at the end of the road. It wasn't going to fucking end that way, though. He had his lover back, damn it, and God help anyone that got in his fucking way.

He kissed Bev on the top of the head. "Okay. The doctor is going to need stuff, I bet. Eduardo will translate, but I need you on the finances end of it. Anything he needs. Okay?"

"You got it, boss. Anything. How about you? What do you need?"

"I'm fine." Then again, maybe he wasn't. "Ginger ale. If they can find me ginger ale, I'd appreciate it."

"I'm on it." And she was. Shit. Him and Seb, well, they were just going to have to keep her. She was like Santa Claus with a Blackberry.

He took a deep breath, then another, watching her walk away, already issuing orders. It was Tawny's turn, then.

Mrs. Hormonal though, she just stood there, staring at him, arms crossed. "Good job, Scooter. If you ever decide to go into, like, paramilitary hostage negotiation rescue-y shit, I'll back you. Only monetarily, though. A gun would break a nail."

A laugh burst out of him, his eyes drying up a little. "We skipped the first two phases of negotiation, though. Went right to the incident phase." The fact that he knew that meant he'd watched too many Russell Crowe movies.

"You always did like someone else to deal with the weird details." She winked. "Come on, let's have a sit. Someone will be out in a minute to tell us he's going to be fine, but it'll cost us a fortune."

"I need to see him, Tawn."

"Not while he's being poked and prodded. It's an indignity, and he doesn't need you to see it." She said it flatly, giving him the lizard eye.

"Tawny, I just carried a bag of his piss. Dignity is sort of a non-issue."

Her eyebrow lifted. "You realize that I could go somewhere truly nasty and make you squeal like a little girl right now, yeah?"

"Don't." He hadn't puked yet. He didn't want to.

"Then be good, Scooter. Sit. Drink your ginger ale." A housekeeper had appeared with a glass of the fizzy drink right as she said it. Like magic. There was some crazy ginger lime carrot juice that Tawny had been mainlining since she got there, too.

"Okay. Okay, yeah." He looked across the fancy, marble-covered everything room. "Tell me he's going to be okay."

"He's going to be fine. I'm going to play hardball with who motherfucker that hurt him, you're going to announce that you're going to work on a new album somewhere quiet, and then we're going to find you a place with a pool, a hot tub, and a private chef."

"I like that idea. I like it here." Brazil was crazy, loud, colorful, and somehow wonderful.

"Okay. I'll find somewhere here. As soon as I can. First, let's drink our juice and shit." Logical old bitch.

He sucked his drink down, watched Eduardo bounce into the ranch house. "We did it, my friends! I was safe, I promise. It took no minutes to lose everyone. I know my way here!"

He stood up, held out one hand. "Man, I owe you, big."

Eduardo came over, hugged him hard, slapping his back. "Non. Non. We are friends, the bonita Tawny, sim? Now we are all friends."

Justin came in and Eduardo's eyes left him, trailed over the surfer like the man was starving. The blond Aussie glanced at Eduardo, and man. Zap. There was some serious electricity there. Markus wondered if it was any easier for Brazilian bullriders to be queer than it was for American country singers.

He'd bet not.

"Christ, is there any straight man left alive in the world? Besides you, of course, love." Tawny grinned at her husband, who came in, the songwriter looking about as dazed and confused as he always did. Lost in Tawny and the songwriting, that one.

Everyone not Tawny and her man flushed, suddenly busy. Including Markus, because one of the nurses came out. "Senhor Kane? You come now?"

"Shit, yeah." He stood up, everything but Seb disappearing from his brain. "Is he going to be okay?"

She waved him into the back of the house, and he cursed the language barrier, hurrying to get to Seb's side. The doctor stopped him when he got to the suite they'd put Seb in, motioning for him to step to one side.

"Senhor Kane." The tired-looking man smiled, deep lines around his eyes and mouth. "He is lucky you found him. He is very weak. Dehydrated and deeply medicated. The worst, however, is his nutrient level. He has been starved badly."

"Fucker." He bit the word out, growling. "Sorry. He's going to be okay, right?"

"He is strong. I am doing proteins in the IV, electrolytes. We will watch for now. Pray. There is nothing else but to reduce the drugs slowly and see he rests."

"Thank you." Markus shook the man's hand hard, the tears right there again, a knot at the base of his throat, like he'd swallowed a rope.

"You go see him. The drugs—they were psychotropics, yes? He may not know you."

Seb would know him. No matter what, Sebastian always knew him. Markus walked into the room, closing the door behind him. He stopped, taking in every detail and getting his shit together before he sat down.

It was like looking at an old man, like someone had taken Seb and shrunk him, made him nothing but cheekbones and sunken eyes and long, long fingers.

The rage at Jack came back, burning bright. Jack had loved Sebastian once. How could the man do this? How?

Markus sat, clearing his throat and taking Seb's hand in his. "Hey, baby."

Seb's eyelids fluttered, and sure as shit, he got a slow smile. He'd known it. Seb knew.

He stroked the back of that thin, bruised hand. Clearly they'd been running out of places to put IV needles. "Missed you."

Seb's mouth was moving, the man just talking to him from somewhere deep inside. There wasn't a sound to it, not yet, but that was the core of who Sebastian Longchamps was. That voice was bigger than this shit, bigger than them.

It was when Seb stopped talking that he'd given up. Markus squeezed the hand he held. "That's it, baby. Just talk to me."

It would start with talking. Then they'd sing. The music always healed them. Always.

Chapter Twenty-One

Hank Williams was playing. Sebastian frowned, focusing on the song. He loved *Jambalaya*. Loved it. Then George Strait started singing about falling to pieces. That was Markus' playlist. He hummed along, so tired, too tired to lift his head.

The iPod usually didn't sound this good with the little speaker the nurse had. This sounded kinda huge, in fact, like one of those really good systems. He managed a few words, his lips feeling less dry today. Yay.

The song changed again, and this time it was Markus Kane singing one of the rare cover songs that had made it onto the big music sales websites, *Good Year for the Roses* ringing out. It sounded odd, though, almost like it had a weird echo. Like it was a live recording, He didn't have that in his collection, though.

Then the voice dipped into harmony and he smiled. Oh, be real. Please be real.

"Markus?" His Markus didn't like to sing harmony. That was his job.

"Hey, baby. Just practicing. I have lead singer disease." Markus' voice moved closer with every word until the man was there, leaning over him. "I was on my laptop over there."

"Markus." It was him. His lover looked tired, worried, but real. "You're here."

"So are you." Markus' smile widened, lighting up the room.

"Jack says... You have to go. He'll hurt you."

"Jack is on the run, baby. Tawny's friend, Eduardo? He's real influential here in Brazil. He spread the word that Jack is an embezzler and kidnapper."

He was sure, in some other life, all those words made sense together, right? "He says he'll destroy you. I think... I think he was trying to kill me." At least shut him up.

"I think he's lost his mind, baby." Markus touched his hand, so careful. "I'm not scared."

"You're real." The thought was overwhelming and he closed his eyes, squeezed them shut.

"Seb?" Markus petted him. "I'm so sorry."

He wasn't sure what for. Markus hadn't done this. Maybe Markus was leaving. Maybe... God, he was tired.

Markus touched his cheek, stroking gently. "Sleep, baby. I'll be right here when you wake up, okay?"

"Am I...okay?"

"You're gonna be fine. You were half-starved and heavily medicated."

"Oh." His heart started pounding hard, the world moving just a little too fast.

"Shh." It was like Markus knew, Hell, maybe there was a machine hooked up to him or something. "It's all right, Seb. I promise."

How could it be? How? He didn't even know where he was and... "Don't go."

"I won't. I'm here. Right here."

"'kay." He looked down, watched his fingers curl around Markus'. "Okay."

"Now you just need to sleep. Heal. I'll sing a spell."

Sebastian closed his eyes, tight. "Please."

At least that would make sense.

Markus had turned off the music, but that didn't matter. The man could flat out sing, even if that rich voice sounded rough, overused.

In his head, he sang harmony, and it sounded good.

"Hey, baby."

Seb had been sleeping the sleep of healing for days, according to the doctor. Markus was all about that, but for the last hour Seb had been dreaming, and it wasn't good. So Markus was ready to wake him up, chase the nightmares out of the man's mind.

Green eyes popped open, bloodshot and scared. "They're going to get you. Markus. Candy. You have to run."

"Shh. I'm okay, baby. No one is going to hurt us here. I promise."

"You don't know. You don't..." Seb sat up, grabbed him, and Markus was stunned. The man hadn't moved in days.

"Hey." He pulled Seb close, holding on. "I got you. I—you wanna go outside? Eduardo has this amazing courtyard."

"Uh-huh. What's outside? Are we in... Japan? I was in Japan."

"We're in Brazil, baby." He gathered up the blanket wrapping it around Seb before lifting the man. "Can you hold the bag, baby? You're on all sorts of vitamins and stuff now."

"Brazil? I love it there." Seb held the IV bag, looking like an owl. "Are we at a hospital?"

"No. We're at a friend of Tawny's. He's a bullrider."

"As in eight second ride, latigo, he's got a fever?"

That actually made Markus smile. If the man could pull three bullriding songs out of his ass, he was going to be okay.

"You know it. He's studly. I think he has designs on your pilot friend." There was a huge chaise lounge made out of old wood and cushy pillows, and he settled Seb there, the sound of fountains tinkling.

"It's sunny."

It was spring here, which seemed weird, given that autumn was coming at home. "So you need a hat or some sunglasses?" He'd been basking when he wasn't with Seb, so Markus was pretty brown.

Seb shook his head, face hidden in Markus' chest. "Is this okay? Will someone see?"

"No one will care if they do. Eduardo has this huge ranch. I can't wait to show you."

"I... I feel like I've missed everything." Seb's fingers slid over his arm, loving on him.

"You were a little out of it." God, it was good to hear Seb talk. Talk and make sense.

"Yeah. Maybe more than a little."

"Maybe." His mouth kicked into a smile. "You look better. Got some color."

"You're like a nut. I like it."

"Yeah?" He grinned. "It's weirdly easy here. To just be."

"Did I fuck up? Did I do something wrong?"

"What? No. No, baby. You tried to do what was right." Rage wanted to just bust out against Jack, against the assholes who were more worried about their money than their talent. He didn't want Seb to think it was aimed at him, though.

"Okay. Okay. I... I don't remember a lot. It's all weird."

"The drugs they had you on did that. Well, that and the starvation." He breathed deep, relaxing each muscle in turn.

"I don't eat much."

No. No, but Seb was going to fucking learn how to. Breakfast, lunch, dinner. Food with chewing. No shakes. Damn it. Pineapple only if it came with upside down cake.

"Well, not recently, you haven't. They have amazing pastry here."

"You and your doughnuts." Seb actually smiled.

"Better than Kyle's potato chips and Twinkies." He needed to call Kyle, actually. Later.

"Twinkies are unnatural."

"They are." He held Seb close, listening to the man breathe. "We got your guitar. Jack left it when he cleared out."

Seb went still, so still he actually thought something had happened, that Seb had stroked out.

He pulled back, peering down at Sebastian's face. "Seb? Are you okay?"

"He... He took my guitar. That's my fucking guitar. I have had that acoustic for twenty five years!"

He stroked Seb's hair, which was odd, that he had hair. Markus stared at it, the pale stuff so soft. "We got it. It's okay. Not a scratch on it that you didn't make."

"He... He said... He..." Seb stared at him, eyes like an unbroke horse or a dog that had been hurt bad, deep inside.

"You can tell me, baby. I'm right here." It had to be like infection. Better out than in.

"He said I deserved this shit, that you all knew I was crazy. That I needed to be kept in my place."

"It's not true, Seb. None of it. Jack is the crazy one."

"I'm not crazy. I got clean. I... Let me up. I have to get up."

There was no way Seb could walk. No way. He didn't want to hold the man down, though, make him feel unsafe. So he sat back, waiting to catch Seb when he fell.

"Fuck. I'm not crazy!" Seb stood up, swayed, taking a stumbling step before collapsing into his arms.

He heard footsteps in the house, and he shook his head. No. No, now Seb needed some privacy. Bev came charging out, but Markus held up a hand, shaking his head. She stared at Seb, tears rising, but she nodded and backed away, taking Tawny with her.

"I'm not crazy. I'm not. I just did my FUCKING JOB!" Seb's fists beat at his chest, so weak they were barely tapping at him.

"You did. You did." He let Seb whack at him, let the man get it out. Markus remembered how it felt, and he was glad he could be right here.

"He took and took and I didn't..." Seb sucked in a breath, panting. "I would have given it to him. I would have given him the money."

"You're the most generous person I know, Seb. Bev always says so, too."

"I would have just let him have it. I just want the music."

"The music I can do, baby." He smiled, letting Seb rest that sweaty forehead against his. "I love you."

Seb breathed with him, in and out, blinking slower and slower, letting him hold on. Those poor, torn-up hands were tangled in his shirt, and he eased Seb to the chaise again, checking the IV line.

Seb was dozing for him, trusting him, and he made sure all the man's dangly bits were covered before texting Bev, telling her to come say hi.

She came out of the house with a tray of juice and a plate of bizarre fruits and cheeses. And cheese breads. Uhn. He loved those strange round balls of dough.

Seb woke up for her, head lifting so he could see her where she stood across the way. "Bevvie."

"Boss, man, you scared me. I thought... I was worried."

"Me too."

"You ever fire me again, I won't come to your rescue." Bev was holding it together by the skin of her teeth. She pushed the tray of food at Markus, who took it. He let Seb ease up, and Bev sniffled, leaning down to hug Seb tight.

"Shh. We're okay."

"You look like a concentration camp victim. That's not okay."

Seb just snorted at her, which made Markus smile and pop a piece of bread into his mouth. Bev leveled a glare at him.

"Don't laugh at me," she said.

"Just feed Candy and let me laugh."

"Markus is snarfing away."

Snarfing? Markus chuckled. "It's good."

"The man loves Brazilian food." Bev gave them both a grin. "Can I get you anything, boss? Anything?"

Seb shook his head. "I'm okay. Tired."

"We'll get him tempted with something, Bevvy." He'd make Seb eat. First, though, he had to get the man strong enough to fight.

She didn't look convinced. "You're all fuzzy, Seb."

"Too tired to wax. Markus will just have to deal with it."

"I can handle it."

Look at Seb smile for her. It looked real. Bev was a good friend.

"I bet." Beverly winked at Seb, her pale skin actually starting to pick up a little gold. "You should have seen him, arranging this with Tawny."

"Tawny's here?"

"God, yes. Tawny. Justin. Me. Bruce calls every day."

"Kyle gets daily updates, too, Seb."

Sebastian chuckled, but the sound was bittersweet. "Y'all love me."

Seb had no idea. The man's band had held a coup of headliner proportions. There was legal shit flying around that was the stuff of legend. The label was taking a shot to the balls. If Markus had anything to say about it, they'd take more than one. Hell, the way Tawny was working this, she was going to castrate the bastards. It gave him glee. Downright unholy fucking glee.

"We do love you," Bev was saying. "Markus is crazy about you, huh? I mean, really." Bevvie smiled at him a moment, fond as anything.

He popped her nose, gently. Seb had always kept her busy. Together, they'd run her crazy. It would be fun as fuck.

Seb chuckled, the sound watery but so good it squeezed Markus' heart. "Thank you. Thank everyone for me?"

"Yeah. You look like shit, boss, and you need a bath."

Seb glanced up at him. "Do I stink?"

"Not to me. You might feel better, though. Let's see what the doc says about this drip, and we can maybe shower in a bit."

"Make everyone go away. Everyone but you."

"Okay, baby." Markus nodded at Bev, who grinned and nodded.

"I'll put this in your room," she said, grabbing the food. "I had them change the linens and all while you were out here."

"Thanks, honey."

She left them, and Markus hugged Seb close. "You want to go in?"

"I just want to sit here for a minute. I can't breathe."

"In and out." Markus stroked Seb's back, hoping to hell it helped.

Seb didn't say anything, and he started singing again. It was stupid, but he knew that it helped. It helped him; it was what they were, damn it.

Score and lyrics.

All he could do was hope it would be enough to get Seb back to the world of the living. Markus didn't really know how to make music without the man anymore.

Chapter Twenty-Two

The moon woke him up and Sebastian slipped out of bed, feet leading him to the pool. The IV was out, and the doctor was only coming in once a day to check on him.

Bev had found him clothes—soft and loose. He was always cold now, even if it was sunny. Markus just wrapped him in blankets and rubbed his hands. Sebastian wasn't even sure where Markus was, not really. Sleeping somewhere, he guessed. Or having supper. Or watching TV.

It all seemed like those things—those normal, simple things—couldn't even be real anymore.

He sat at the edge of the water, watching the moon dance in the tiny waves. The sounds of night birds and small animals came to him, the whole world alive. That was so weird. Hotel rooms and rented condos always seemed so dead.

Part of him wanted to slide into the water, just float, but he wasn't sure if he could get out and getting wet was so weird and the water might be too cold.

The scrape of a soft shoes on flagstones reached him,

and he grinned, thinking how strange it was to see and hear Candy wearing flip-flops.

"Hey, baby. It's pretty out here, huh?"

"It is. It's a little like magic." A little like Heaven, although he wasn't ready to be so close to there again.

"I was thinking of buying a place down here. Of course, Kyle wants an island."

"Kyle loves Austin. He'll never leave."

"I think he wants to vacation there. Maybe I'll get him a condo in Galveston." Markus sat next to him, close enough to feel the heat from that big body.

"The moon is big here. Can I ask you something? Am...do they have me on stuff or not? I feel... different."

"The drip was antibiotics and proteins and stuff. Fluids. Now you're just getting some vitamins in your smoothies." Markus nudged him gently. "We'll wean you off those, too. The smoothies."

"I hate smoothies." He'd heard the doctor, when he'd been dozing. No scales, no weighing, no more marathon exercise sessions.

"Oh, me too." Markus chuckled, the sound low, intimate. "I like cheese bread."

"I'm worried. I don't know what's going to happen next and I don't know what I'm supposed to do. I don't... I don't want to do a show right now." Or ever, he thought.

"So, we don't. You're on sabbatical. Writing." That big body moved closer when he shivered. "We could just write for other folks."

"We?" He let himself lean. "I could be we. Us. I mean, yes, huh?" How could someone who wrote so many lyrics not have the right words?

"I think we're definitely a we." Markus kissed the tip of his nose. "You gonna get mad at me if I drag you inside and hand you a guitar?"

"Why would I get mad at you?" Writing music was

bigger than breathing, in his soul if not his body.

"Because the last time I mentioned your guitar you got upset." Markus was carefully not looking at him, not pressuring.

"No. I got... Pissed. Man, I was so fucking pissed off. He tried to steal that, fucking steal my music from me, like it was a goddamn commodity." He knew, practically, that it was. It was his livelihood, but... Shit. It was more than that.

"Good thing that's sunk too deep in you to get gone." Now Markus was looking at him again, then leaning in for a kiss, almost chaste, but not quite.

That little kiss let him breathe, let him pull in Markus and moonlight flavored air. "Do we have score paper?"

Markus led the way to the big family dining room in Eduardo's house.

One by one, then in twos and threes, everyone had been visiting Seb, either in the suite they had, or out in the courtyard. Bev was back to spending an hour a day with him, planning all the paperwork Seb had to file, feeding it to him in sips. Tawny had come, not mentioning work, just talking about the baby and her plan to go home before she got too big to travel.

Justin, the surfer pilot had stayed on, and played checkers with Seb at lunchtime every day. Hell, even Eduardo's numerous sisters had come and gone, every one of them delivering plates of nibbles. When Tawny had taught one of them to make biscuits and gravy, though, Seb had actually eaten. Everyone had cheered back in the kitchen.

Now it was time for Seb to meet their host. Eduardo had cleared out most of his truly exuberant family, and supper would be a small affair of about seven people.

Seb still felt damn near like a bird in his hand, the skin right next to the bone. The shaking had gone away, though, and the constant panic had eased. They'd spent hours together floating in the bathtub, entire days writing, him playing his acoustic when Seb's hands wouldn't work.

He thought it was time, though. Time to get Seb back into the world and know other people could be kind.

"Hey, boss." Bev waved when they walked in. She looked relaxed, in a little sundress, her hair down. "I like the pants."

Seb flipped her off, lazily. He was wearing a soft pair of sweats, a T-shirt, the man's skin still sensitive.

Markus fought his grin. "Hey, y'all. Eduardo, this is Sebastian."

"Sebastian." The name came out with like, four more syllables than it would in English. "I saw you once, at the running of the snowboards in Chamonix. In France, sim?"

"I was there. You rode Destiny's Child for ninety point three in Baton Rouge and he damn near took your riding hand off."

"Yes!" Eduardo hooted, this totally crazy tropical bird sound, and slapped the table. "Welcome, Sebastian Longchamps!"

"Thanks for the help, man." Seb went over and gave the man a hug, and it felt good—damn good—for Seb to reach out to someone, touch them. "I appreciate it."

Justin didn't look thrilled about it, though. Man, that whole thing with him and Eduardo was going to go nuclear. It was going to be fun as fuck to watch.

They were going to watch it, too. They'd found a huge plot of land with a lake, a pool, a beautiful house with a room for a studio, plus a little two bedroom house separate for Bev, when she was in country. He'd gone to see it and had fallen in love. It was only about thirty minutes from Eduardo's place, so Markus knew they'd always have a friend.

"I'd like to propose a toast," Tawny said, raising a glass of some kind of guava and grapefruit juice. "To me going back to the States where there are toilet seat covers and Pop-Tarts."

Sebastian snorted. "We'll send you baby Wranglers for a shower gift."

Her husband, Jim, chuckled. "You mean Scooter isn't coming to help at the delivery?"

"No fucking way. She's going to castrate any nearby male." Markus grabbed his glass. "A toast to good friends."

"To a new home." Bev lifted her glass.

Seb just clinked glasses.

"To new friends, too! When you are well, Sebastian, I will let you ride my bulls, huh?" Eduardo was just grinning ear to ear.

"Hell, yeah. I'm so there."

Bev looked at Markus, purely horrified. He winked at her, knowing he'd never let that happen. Now, he might get on one, just to see...

They all sat together, the huge bowl of black beans and white rice and cheese breads sitting next to slabs of meat.

"Wow, that's a lot of food." Seb looked like he was going to barf, which might fuck supper up a little bit.

"There's hearts of palm salad and fruit, too, baby." He knew Seb would need lighter choices. "Lots of juice."

"Sim. Sim. The pao—the bread—is tapioca. So good. You try, Justin?" Those dark eyes fastened on Justin and Markus would be damned if the man didn't blush dark.

"Sure. I like cheese." Justin popped a piece of bread in his mouth and dished up a bowl of rice and beans, which seemed to break the ice. Everyone else dug in.

Seb looked fucking panicked, and Markus kept one hand on the man's back. Seb had to do this. He had to. It took a minute, but Seb got some salad, some rice, some beans, and one of the cheese breads. Markus murmured praise as he filled his own plate, and he went light so Seb wouldn't be overwhelmed with all the food. When Seb made a happy noise at the taste of the hearts of palm salad, he could have cried with relief.

There was something fucked up about the fact that Seb's issue wasn't having too much of something, but not having enough. Hell, he wasn't sure what it was about, but he knew how to help. He knew how to help with almost everything now. They were working on it together.

The conversation was light, playful, Tawny teasing them about whether to write under their names or a pseudonym, Eduardo flirting wickedly with Justin, and Bev gently changing the subject whenever Seb seemed uncomfortable.

She was stunningly good at that. He hoped she stayed at least part of the year in Brazil. She was just so good with Seb, and they needed all the friends they could find.

Seb actually relaxed enough to joke back, to tease Tawny. "You sure you want to manage me, lady? I'm tough."

"Shit." She tossed a cheese roll at Seb. "I just brokered a huge settlement with your old management. You could buy your own fucking recording studio, thanks to me."

Laughing, Markus caught the bread mid-air. "No abusing the tapioca. And settlements are good, but a certain old manager had better not show his face in the States again. They're waiting to arrest his ass."

"If he is found here, my brothers will deal with him." The words were spoken with the confidence of a man who handled his own business. Eduardo didn't mess around. He was like a minor deity in this part of Brazil.

"I just hope he gets what he deserves." Seb munched a little more, eating all the rice.

Markus nodded. He just wanted the man never to show up at their door to bother his Seb, ever again. Then they'd need their friends to help hide the body.

"You two focus on getting tanned and healthy and writing music. I'll focus on the rest." Tawny sounded so sure. He'd see how business-like she was when that baby showed up.

"We're writing. No worries there." They had to finish the house, too. It was partly furnished, but Markus was looking forward to doing the work and making it comfortable. He wanted to give Seb a home. A real home. Maybe for the first time since the man had left his momma's house. It worked for Markus that it was with him. In Brazil of all places.

Seb's fingers twined with his, squeezed. "I think I'm done, Candy."

"Sure. Will y'all excuse us?" Someone would bring him dessert later. He was damned glad he'd taken up swimming again during the last few months.

Good nights were said, everyone waved, and they headed down the hallway.

"Three days before we're at the new place, huh? Helen's flying in?"

"She is. She's tickled. Had to get a visa and all." They wandered a little, meandering through the center courtyard instead of taking the inside route.

"Bev is flying back to the states to pack the bus, send guitars and clothes and stuff."

"She's coming back, right?" He wasn't sure he'd known that. Damn. They got to their room, Markus stripping down right away. He was so going native. Of course, he got to wear his Wranglers and play cowboy with Eduardo's many male relatives, too, so it was the best of both worlds.

"She says she'll be back in three weeks at the most. She has things in her apartment she wants to bring down." Seb stepped out of his shoes, out of the sweats.

"Oh, good." Bevvie seemed like an important part of Seb's recovery somehow. As soon as Seb was naked, Markus moved in, looping his arms around that lean body.

"Hey." Seb curled into him, snuggled close.

"Hey." He hummed, his cock taking an interest, and for the first time since the rescue, he didn't feel guilty about it. Markus didn't try to think about baseball. He just let it rise. He also thought he ought to warn Seb it was happening. "Oh, baby. I want you."

Oh. Sebastian had been worried that Markus wasn't wanting him anymore. He knew the man loved him, knew it. It was in the music, in the long hours in the pool, in the quiet hours when he slept for what seemed like days.

That hard cock, though, lifting and filling, against his belly? That meant that it wasn't gone, that hunger. He wanted to be hungry for something. Sebastian reached down, letting his fingers trail over the head of Markus' cock, and the man moaned.

"Mmm. Love that sound." His eyes closed, and he focused on the scent, the warmth, the pounding of Marcus' heart.

"You make me hot as hell, baby. Always have." Markus kissed the spot just under his ear, working down to his neck.

"Still, huh?" He liked that and he tilted his head, letting Markus have more.

"Always. I just wanted to make sure you were up to

it, Seb." Those lips moved against his skin, making him shiver.

"I want to be. I'm ready to feel things. Good things." Starting with Markus' fingers.

"Good." Markus must have read his mind, because those big hands started moving, fingers touching him. Gentle. Markus was so careful with him, like he might break.

"Take me to bed, Candy. I need you." He twisted a little bit, turning under the touches, giving Markus more skin.

"Come on, then." Markus lifted him, so damned strong, those arms roped with muscle. Swimming agreed with the man.

They settled into the big bed, pushing together under the light blankets. He fit against all those muscles, settling in close. The hair on Markus' chest rasped against his nipples, making him gasp. He'd finally gotten that wax.

It had hurt like a bitch, more than he'd expected, but he felt like him again, and once Markus had shaved his head, he'd been solid. Well, maybe not as solid as he felt now. He almost looked down at his prick in amazement, but Markus slid one hand behind his head, kissing him deep, tongue pushing all the other thoughts out of his head. He opened, one hand curled around Markus' arm, the other flat on Markus' back.

The kiss went long, slow, Markus tasting him, letting him get used to the touch. Those hands never stopped, though, not even when his skin was tingling madly, so sensitive he cried out.

"Jesus, baby, you're like a live wire."

He nodded, his heart beating hard. "God, yes. Don't stop."

"Not unless you need me to. I promise." Markus licked a path down his body, stopping to suck up the skin around his left nipple.

That mouth. That mouth, he was dying. Living. Flying.

Markus stroked his ass, his upper thigh, and that crazy feeling of Markus pulling up a bruise never stopped. It just got bigger and bigger.

His head fell back, his throat working as Markus loved on him. He could feel every thread on the sheets, every hair on his lover's body. Each time those lips pulled at his nipple, his heartbeat tripled, pounding in his chest, then easing off.

He reached out, fingers tangling in Markus' hair. "Love you." Sebastian knew Markus knew, but sometimes it was good to say it.

"Oh, God, baby. I love you, too." Markus nipped at his skin before slipping down across his belly, breath hot, lips like fire.

He watched Markus stop at the tattoo, trace the ink with his fingertips. That would always be right there for his lover, that song that said every damned thing. Markus just loved on it, slowly, almost meditatively.

The touches relaxed him—everywhere but his aching, heavy cock that proved that he was getting better, stronger. Strong enough to need. He arched up, trying to get Markus to give that some attention, too. His cock bumped Markus' chin, and his lover chuckled, bending farther to suck at the tip of his prick.

"Oh, sweet fuck. Markus. Your mouth." The pressure was steady, the heat perfect and he spread, begging for more.

Markus' answer was the best kind of noise, around his cock, vibrating his flesh. One big hand slid under his ass, lifting him. Markus loved on him, throat swallowing around his cock, then backing off, slowly building his need. The man was a machine, just giving and giving. He could feel how much Markus needed him, too, that cock hard against his lower leg.

"Want you, Candy. In me. Deep." He wanted Markus everywhere.

"Now? I want that, baby. I got lube. For when I—when you weren't able."

"Now, Markus. Please. Fill me up." He just wanted to feel. Everything.

"I'm on it." He knew that voice. That was Markus back in charge, confident now that they had a plan. It made him grin, and he admired the long line of body as Markus reached, grabbing a bottle from the nightstand.

Okay, that was the giant economy size bottle of lube. "Miss me, did you?"

Markus blinked, then laughed long and loud. "Oh, yeah, baby. I would listen to some Longchamps music and jack off for a fucking hour."

Oh, now, that was the most romantic thing anyone had ever said to him. He pulled Markus down for a kiss as a reward, tasting himself on those swollen lips.

Markus moaned against his mouth. "Can't wait to tear your ass up again like I did back on the tour, baby. I'll fuck you now, but soon I'll do so much more. Jesus, I can't wait."

"Soon." He met those near-black eyes. "Soon I'll need you to make me burn."

He knew that, knew he needed what Markus wanted to give him. "You know it." Markus popped the top on the lube, getting his fingers slick. "Right now I'm gonna love you so good."

Markus turned him onto his side, his back against Markus' broad chest. Sebastian followed easily, humming when two broad fingers pushed into his ass, opening him up easily. He groaned, and Markus' free hand covered his belly, pushing him back, encouraging him to move, rock.

Everything came down to Markus' fingers, his ass, the

music that played in his head when they did this. Markus held him there, pushing him to take more, then more as a third finger slipped inside him.

"Yes. Markus. Yes." When those fingers brushed that gland inside him, he gasped, hips rolling.

"Like that, baby?" Markus was a lot less careful now, a lot less worried. He could tell just by how that body moved, how everything flowed now.

"More." Like was a stupid word.

Markus gave him more, fingers working him until he wanted to scream with it, his knees pulling up to his belly. He bit out curses and pleas, needing that fat cock to fill him, stretch him.

"Now, baby. Yeah?" Markus pulled free, then pushed up against his ass, cock pressing his hole.

Seb rolled back with a moan, and took Markus in all the way to the root. "Yes."

"Fuck. Oh, baby." Markus bit him, right where his neck met his shoulder.

The sting was perfect, and his fingers opened and closed. "Don't fucking stop."

"Not now. No way." That thick cock pushed in and in until Markus' hips rested against his ass. He wished for a moment that his ass was hot from Candy's hand, but he knew that would come again. Soon.

"That's right, baby. Soon this will be our bed and I'll put you over my knee, make you shine for me, make you ache and burn."

His glutes went tight in response to that promise, those words. His cock reached up, begging for that hand on his belly, and Markus knew; the man always knew. That hand slid down, grabbed his cock, fingers closing at the tip, pinching his slit shut.

"Markus." He came hard, entire body shaking with it, whole world tilting.

"Oh, God, baby. Dreamed about you." Markus shot for him, too, just slamming into his ass one last time.

They rested together, Markus' hand rubbing his own come into his belly, the touch slow, sure. Mesmerizing.

"Needed that, baby. So bad." Markus sounded so damned happy.

"God, yes." He nodded. "Was beginning to think we'd never get to do that again."

"Oh, I knew better. I was just worried that I would be too rough."

How dear was it that Markus was worried about that. The man who had tanned his ass until Sebastian couldn't sit for a week.

"I want to feel good enough that you can be rough." He was getting there. Slowly.

"You will. We'll be in our house, our place, with no one else to care what we do."

"You, me, music." He blinked slowly, surrounded in Markus' warmth. He felt good. Really good for the first time in ages. It made him smile.

"That's right, baby. You, me, music. I promise."

He nodded. "Sing to me?"

"Anytime, Seb. Anything you want to hear." Markus started singing *I'll Fly Away* for him, and he could swear he heard his maman singing along.

By the time his lover had headed into *Waltz Across Texas*, he was asleep.

Epilogue

I swear to God, Markus Kane, if your man doesn't eat his lunch, I am going to beat him with a hammer," Helen said, waving a stalk of celery under his nose.

Shame, too, because he'd been working on a nap and a half, just him, his two person chaise lounge, and their new Fila Brasiliero dog, Fido. Fido took up a person and a half's space. He also reached right out and grabbed that celery in his teeth. Go Fido.

"Well, if you were trying to feed him celery, I don't blame him."

"I was trying to feed him anything—peanut butter, apples, ice cream, hummus. He says he's not hungry."

"Okay." Markus rolled to his feet, wrapping a towel around his waist so as not to embarrass her. "Bev?"

"She tried Ensure. He told her nothing but pineapple."

Huh. That was a habit of a Seb who was about to hop on the treadmill and run for three hours. So not gonna happen.

Markus headed inside, Fido padding along next to him, celery dangling. "Find Seb, buddy."

A low, happy bark sounded, then the pup started

moving. That damn dog thought Seb was pure magic, the most amazing human on earth. It made it hard to leave him outside the bedroom at night, but it turned out that was a necessary thing, too. Silly dog thought they were fighting...

"There he is." Seb was pondering the treadmill, head tilted to one side, arms crossed. "We at the contemplative stage, baby?"

"Figurative." Those pretty green eyes looked back at him. "Helen or Bev send you?"

"Helen. She says pineapple? That's not enough to keep you going." He moved close, let his hand slide over Seb's ass.

"I'm not going to fit in my jeans, if I keep eating." Seb leaned into his touch, encouraging him.

"You fit in them just fine. Trust me. I would tell you if you didn't." He tugged Seb away from the exercise machines. "How about some mashed potatoes?" As much as Markus loved Brazilian food, Helen always had American staples on hand.

"Mashed potatoes?" Helen would put cheese on them, too, give Seb some protein.

"Uh-huh. I know there's some in the fridge." That was it. Seb followed him right to the kitchen, humming a little.

Fido was following along, tail wagging, and Seb found the pup a bone, even as Markus got two bowls of mashed potatoes, cheese, oh. Bacon. Everything was better with bacon. Helen's shih tzu, Leona, came trotting it, grabbing the piece of bacon he'd put down for Fido and running.

Lord.

He handed Seb a bowl and sat at the long counter. "So, you want to work on that bridge?"

"Oh, yeah. I had an idea about moving the second verse to the third and bringing the whole thing up a half step." Seb grabbed his fork and ate a bite.

Helen walked by the kitchen, looked in, then kept going without a word. Good woman. She'd learned.

Seb just needed to be distracted. If you let his obsession roll, he could be in real trouble. Markus had learned, too. "I like the idea, but we'll have to see what the modulation does to the chorus. "

Seb nodded. "I think it's worth a try. Even if it doesn't work, it'll shake out something. Did you hear that our *Home With You* just hit number one for Kelly Greene?"

Ah. So that was the stress. Seb stressed success as much as failure. Still, Markus was getting Seb to tell him faster every time. "Go her! Go us. That check will pay for Bev's hot tub."

"She'll love that. She was tickled shitless to not have to share with your hairy ass."

"I know. I don't like to think about girl cooties, either." Bev was seeing a hot young Brazilian singer, actually, and needed some privacy when he visited the ranch. It was the least they could do.

"Uh-huh. We'll see how you feel about girl cooties when Tawny brings your goddaughter to visit. Or are we going to them?"

"Tawny wants to come down. She wants to see the house now that it's done." They'd all had a pow-wow about whether Seb was up to the media frenzy that was bound to happen if they got caught by the press, and the decision was to stay in Brazil for now. Still, he'd give Seb the choice. "Unless you want me to call Just, see if he can fly us."

"He's with Eduardo in the jungle on some...safari, trek, thing." Seb rolled his eyes. "I have no doubt there's lots of mosquitoes and sex. I think Tawny should come here, see things. Relax. We can write with Jim."

"Cool. We could get Bruce down, too, maybe." Bruce would be great for the studio, getting more shit set up. They both needed a little more organization than they had, and Bev wasn't much of a mixer or sound tech.

Seb nodded. "Or Kyle. I know he misses you."

Markus hooted, feeding Seb a piece of bacon off his bowl. "He's in Aruba. Some all-inclusive place. His Tweets are hilarious."

"Aruba? Huh." Seb opened his mouth for another bite.

Markus got a bite filled with cheese and bacon goodness and popped it into Seb's mouth. "His wife insisted. It was that or a cruise."

The most amazing things about his life now were these little moments. He got to spend them with Sebastian; he didn't have to hide or rush or worry.

"Can we grill chicken tonight? After we work on the song?"

"Hell, yeah. With that blackening spice? I'm so there." Helen would be one hundred percent behind it, too.

"Cool." Seb looked confused for half a second. "Were we about to go make music?" Sometimes when he sidetracked his lover, things slowed down, derailed.

"We are. Soon as I finish my potatoes." He gave Seb one more bite, happy now that the man had consumed enough lunch.

"Good deal. They're good, the potatoes. Bacon is sort of magical."

"It is." He gave a piece to Fido, who had finally just sat on Leona's furry, evil little body.

Seb put things away, drank a huge glass of this weird guava sparkling juice stuff that Eduardo brought. All the while, the man chattered away at him about the song they were working on for their old buddy, Hank Bitters.

Markus watched, only listening with half an ear, focusing on the rise and fall, the rhythm of Sebastian Longchamps. This was his—he got to hear it, live in it, every day.

Grinning, Markus herded Seb toward the room they

used for writing and jamming; the studio was too much pressure for that. Sebastian was just laughing, the sound like music. There was no song he would rather hear. Hell, he might even have to say he was addicted to it.

Silent Love Song

Like a fire we were burning
Red dirt roads and
Sun soaked days
All the while things were turning
Moving like a
Record plays.

In the night, stars were blazing
Shot through the sky
Rocket fast
Knew life would make me crazy
Took a stumble
Couldn't last.

Chorus:
Lost my voice. Gave you my song.
All I got is whispers.
You're on the stage, singing strong
My mouth's covered, leather glove
My lips moving without
Giving breath to silent love.

Now you're soaring like a bird
Flying higher
Out of sight.
All that's left is love I heard
From your guitar
Taking flight

Chorus.

Bridge:
I knew I was your white knight
I knew I was your man
But we couldn't bear the spotlight
I had to let go of your hand.

Chorus.

CPSIA information can be obtained at www.ICGtesting.com
Printed in the USA
LVOW070601041012

301322LV00001B/42/P